A NOTE ON THE AUTHOR

ROBERT GLANCY was born in Zambia and raised in
Malawi. At fourteen he moved from Africa to Edinburgh
and then went on to study history at Cambridge.
His first novel, *Terms & Conditions*, was published by
Bloomsbury in 2014 to critical acclaim. He has recently
been awarded the Grimshaw Sargeson Fellowship in
New Zealand, where he currently lives with his wife and
children.

@RobertGlancy

BY THE SAME AUTHOR

Terms & Conditions

Please Do Not Disturb

ROBERT GLANCY

BLOOMSBURY

LONDON · OXFORD · NEW YORK · NEW DELHI · SYDNEY

Bloomsbury Paperbacks
An imprint of Bloomsbury Publishing Plc

50 Bedford Square   1385 Broadway
London   New York
WC1B 3DP   NY 10018
UK   USA

www.bloomsbury.com

BLOOMSBURY and the Diana logo are trademarks of Bloomsbury Publishing Plc

First published in Great Britain 2016
This paperback edition first published in 2017

British Library Cataloguing-in-Publication Data
A catalogue record for this book is available from the British Library.

ISBN: HB: 978-1-4088-6629-0
TPB: 978-1-4088-6630-6
PB: 978-1-4088-6632-0
ePub: 978-1-4088-6631-3

2 4 6 8 10 9 7 5 3 1

Typeset by Integra Software Services Pvt. Ltd.

To find out more about our authors and books visit www.bloomsbury.com.
Here you will find extracts, author interviews, details of forthcoming events
and the option to sign up for our newsletters.

For Mum and Dad

THE FOX

Bwalo Radio

WELCOME, BEAUTIFUL PEOPLE OF *Bwalo*. *Cocks crowing, sun shining, maize rising and* DJ *Cheeseandtoast here to start your day the Bwalo way. If you're listening to me, that makes you the luckiest man, woman or goat in the world, because you're living right here in the sweet soul of Africa. Ha! Our countdown continues to the Glorious Day of Our Splendid Independence, when King Tafumo, warrior of warriors, King of Kings, talks to his people and we, with one heart and one voice, shall rejoice, rejoice – rejoice! In honour of the auspicious occasion our gracious sponsor, Life cigarettes, is selling a limited-edition pack that comes with five free cigarettes. Yes yes! Life are grown and made in Bwalo. So buy Bwalo, smoke Life, and always remember: never marry a woman with bigger feet than you. Ha! Now here to pleasure your ears is the new song, 'Kwacha!', by Bwalo duo Lost & Found. The Ngwazi is glorious!*

Charlie

H<small>E</small> APPEARED THE DAY our hotel vanished. Adults always went on about how the hotel was *invisible*. Made no sense to me. Besides the King's palace, our hotel was the biggest building in town. But Dad said it was all about the way you looked at things. And when they finished painting the hotel again, I understood. Under the burst-yolk sun it shone brand new and when I squinted it evaporated into mist, the sign suspended in haze: *Hotel Mirage*.

She was repainted because the biggest day of the year was approaching, *the Glorious Day of Our Splendid Independence*. Which most of us just called *the Big Day*. A day when the King spoke to his nation, a day when everyone from across the country came to celebrate, a day when people sang, danced and polished their skin with Vaseline. A day, Dad said, when everyone made a big hoopla out of a wee fracas.

The day celebrated booting out the men who stole Bwalo. When I asked how you steal a whole country Dad said, there's nothing an Englishman can't steal. When I asked if we'd be kicked out, Dad said, they never kick out the Celts, but Mum said, yeah right, and when I asked what she meant they told me to stop asking so many bloody questions.

I stood with Dad and Ed at the front of the hotel and watched as the guest arrived. When the taxi pulled up, the passenger stumbled out, and Dad whispered through his smile, 'Steel yourselves, men, we got a live one here.'

Dipped head-to-toe in khaki, the man wore what Mum called the UWA, the Uniform of White Africa, which she always said as if smelling a fart, *Uwwwa*.

In the posh accent Dad put on for guests, he said, 'Welcome to the Mirage. We're honoured to have you stay and...' The man cut Dad short. 'I reserved a room, eh.'

People here put *eh* at the end of sentences. I used to do it but Mum made me stop, eh.

'Great stuff,' said Dad. 'I'm Stuart, hotel manager, our concierge, Ed, and my boy, Charlie, he's our hotel mascot.'

Dad always made that joke. It wasn't funny but Ed and Dad laughed every time. And the guests did too. This man didn't. He just stared, until Dad said, 'And you are?'

At first the man didn't reply. He just stood there like he'd forgotten his name, time stretching like chewing gum, until he finally said, 'Willem.'

Willem means William in Africa. Covered in copper freckles and with a big body but skinny legs, Willem was built like a badly baked gingerbread man. I followed him into the lobby, staring so hard at the sweat-lake on his back that I nearly bumped into him when he stopped, looked up as if checking the fans, then fell flat on his face.

'Don't just stand there,' Dad shouted. 'Help the man, call Dr Todd.' But from the floor, Willem moaned, 'No doctors,' then slowly got to his feet, wobbly as a calf.

Dad said, 'Let's get you to your room, shall we,' and helped Willem to the lift.

As Ed gathered the bags, I asked, 'Do you think he's a celebrity?'

'Maybe so,' said Ed. 'I am hearing celebrities are often drunk in the mornings.'

That's all the town talked about these days: *celebrities*. The adults used to talk about how Bwalo was a broken nation. When I asked how you break a whole nation, Dad said, it's complicated, which was what he said when he didn't know the answer to stuff.

When I said I'd put it into my school project so my teacher could explain, Dad said it was probably best to leave it out. But what else can I write about? Nothing happens here. Willem falling on his face is the only thing that's happened all boring summer long. And since the King announced celebrities were coming, no one even talks about the drought or the broken-nation stuff any more; all anybody ever talks about is celebrities.

So when Sean arrived and asked who the fainting giant was, I replied, 'Ed thinks he's a celebrity because he's drunk in the morning,' and Sean said, 'That'd make me more famous than Madonna,' and laughed a lot, because Sean loved his own jokes.

'I thought you could use this,' he said, and handed me an awesome Dictaphone. 'This is amazing, Sean! Can I honestly have this?'

'All yours, chief.' Then he walked off to his favourite place in the world: the bar.

When Dad crossed the lobby, I ran after him to show him my Dictaphone. But I stopped at the office door when I saw Dad and Mr Horst bent over, staring at the radio as if it were a television. TV was banned because, Dad said, the King was worried freedom of speech would spread like fire giving people the impression they had rights. Also the Internet was so blocked that most searches returned zero results. Dad called Google *Frugal* because it gave so little back. The King owned all media, bar the BBC, which, Dad said, snuck in like a subversive whisper. And Dad and Mr Horst were listening to the radio as if it were doing just that: whispering secret things to them. Mr Horst wore the UWA: wool socks pulled up, khaki shorts, and a gold Benson & Hedges pack winking from his top pocket. And in his charcoal suit, Dad looked like Mr Horst's skinny shadow. Dad scratched his beard, which he did when thinking, and Mr Horst scratched his balls, which he did all the time, as the BBC said: 'This is the BBC World Service ...'

That posh voice travelled thousands of miles from a place where Mum and Dad were born but rarely talked about beyond

7

how much it bloody rained. I'd never been but it sounded like a fairy-tale land – *The United Kingdom* – even though postcards from there were of punks in safety-pinned clothes. Normally the BBC reported British problems like strikes, taxes and bad weather. Things that meant little to a boy brought up in a country of black people, tea and sunshine. But today the radio said: '…the international community is imposing sanctions against the Eastern African nation of Bwalo in light of the suspicious disappearance of Finance Minister, Patrick Goya…'

I knew this was important by the way Mr Horst gave his balls a sharp yank. Bwalo is so small that we are almost impossible to find on a map. Yet here we were, on the BBC no less. It was exciting being on it but scary too, because the BBC only talked about bad things. I made a noise and, quick as a lizard, Dad flicked off the radio as Mr Horst turned and shouted, 'Charlie! It's just you. Howzit?' But before I could reply, he turned back to Dad, 'Right, Stu, time to put my hotel on the map, eh. Get her spick and span.' Then, touching the windowsill, Mr Horst looked at his finger and said, 'Dust. That's the problem here; dust everywhere. Worse than bloody Rhodesia.'

Mr Horst still called Zimbabwe Rhodesia, even though Rhodesia is its old name. Dad said that was because Mr Horst fought hard to keep it Rhodesia, therefore it was his right to keep calling it that but Mum said it was just because Mr Horst was an arsehole.

Soon as we heard the tick-tack of heels, Horst snapped up straight as a mongoose. Mum said Marlene would fall on her face if she didn't balance a fag in one hand with a whisky in the other. Luckily she had them both in hand today, leaning on the door, saying, 'Hiya, boys.'

Horst hissed, 'We've the Commissioner tonight and you're already half-cut.'

Half-cut means completely pissed. Marlene just shrugged, then opened her eyes crazy-wide, pointed at a new painting of Horst on the wall and squealed, 'Is that it! Is that what you paid a bloody fortune for? Sat all those dry-ball days for. Ha-Jesus Eugene.'

'What do you know about art, woman,' Mr Horst shouted. 'And how many times have I told you not to wear those heels, you'll pockmark the parquet. It cost me a bloody fortune.'

'Parquet, my arse,' Marlene sneered and tick-tacked away, as if really pushing her heels into the soft wood. Horst turned bright red then ran after her.

Dad just shook his head and I noticed that Mr Horst had hung his picture higher than the official portrait of King Tafumo: that was against the law. I was about to warn Dad that Mr Horst would get in big trouble when Mum arrived, carrying fresh sheets stacked like pancakes.

'Mum, look what Sean gave me. Cool, hey? Can I interview you guys?'

Before they could say no, I hit record – *Click!* – and asked, 'So Mum and Dad, when the BBC said Patrick someoneorother disappeared is that like our hotel vanishing?'

Dad mumbled, 'It's complicated,' but Mum said, 'Here's a nice story for you, sweetheart. First time Innocence bathed you, she slathered you in Vaseline so you were slippery as a wee seal. I told her white kids didn't need Vaseline. You were so adorable.'

'Mum!'

Hope

I WIPED HIS SEALED ANUS. Impotent hole hadn't shat in years but he gets his phony wipe. Keeping up appearances, I suppose. Who we're keeping them up for, I don't know. Can't even remember if he demanded the wipe or if it's something I fell into the habit of. Habit's all that holds us together. I disposed of the real waste, swapping his colostomy, draining his catheter, and all the while he admired himself in the mirror. Vanity dies last.

In the bedroom, I got him dressed to go nowhere. Helped him into a suit that fitted him back when he was a big man but now he swims in it. His wardrobes were packed with clothes that fitted him fine, lines of black and white suits hanging like ironed zebras, so I whispered, 'Why do you insist on wearing this big old thing?'

Eyes blank as buttons. Shouldn't talk to him like that but when he's off in his own world I do it to keep myself company. Helped him back into bed. Pushed a needle into an arm so deflated the plumb drip seemed to be sucking him dry. That, I know all about. I used to think about me. Now I'm the empty husk thinking only of others. Whittled away. Strange to think there was a time when I'd happily have hollowed out my heart for you.

From the window I spied on the Mirage and her pool stared back at me. With her fresh coat of paint she shone as brilliantly as she had on the original Big Day. On that first day, through the stirring dust of celebration, a name travelled on the tongues of a new nation: *Tafumo*. The hero who slayed our oppressors and granted us freedom. And on that day, with dancing and singing all around us, the air thick with the scent of cooked meats, my Josef got down on bended knee, a small ring in his shaking hand, and our love resonated with the joy of the nation.

Everything was ripening: our nation was born, portraits of Tafumo were hung in shops and houses, to watch over and watch his people; I became Tafumo's nurse and Josef was promoted to head of his department, the youngest man to hold the position.

We honeymooned at the Mirage. Unusual for locals to stay there, as it was mainly expats and tourists. Part country club, part hotel, it was a world inside our world, rich pulp within the coconut, with its idling fans and uniformed staff. We must have looked so out of place. Josef in his only suit, a slight flare to the leg; me in my best dress. We stayed in the presidential suite, formerly called *The Livingstone*, but renamed *The Tafumo*. Above the four-poster bed a mosquito net rippled in the breeze whispering in from the window that captured a view of the capital: from scruffy markets along Victoria Avenue weaving its way up to Tafumo's new palace on the hill. We rarely left the room, embarrassed, I suppose; scared we'd be mistaken for staff.

Catching my reflection – *Who's that old woman?* – shocked me into the present. Turning away from the fool in the window, I switched on the radio to hear the dim echo of a once bright day: '…and for the very first time, celebrities will be attending our Big Day. Superstar Truth is coming all the way from the US of America. Yes yes! He'll be right here in Bwalo, sweet soul of Africa, to celebrate our greatest day of independence. Glorious Ngwazi…'

The glorious Ngwazi was snoring. He was weak today but I was wise to his game. He didn't fool me. He wasn't done yet. African rulers are often likened to lions but Tafumo was a crocodile, lying static for weeks, a trap pulled taut, recharging his rage. I checked his pulse and made sure his drip was dripping. Then I sat, listening to crickets and air conditioners hum the tune of wasted time, until a nurse relieved me.

I walked carefully down the buckled corridor of the staff quarters. This once magnificent wing had been left to fall to ruin. Built too close to a baobab tree, its roots were warping the floors into gentle waves as its trunk tenderly nudged the walls towards collapse. When I got to my room, I swapped my nursing shoes for trainers and chose a diamond necklace, a gift from a time when Tafumo still rained favours on his staff.

My trainers squeaked as I made my way along the corridor into the bright gleam of the kitchen, where Chef had my breakfast in a bag. 'Fresh guava for you today, Hope.' He had to shout over the clatter of the kitchen, the relentless engine of the palace, this stainless-steel room with copper pots dangling like deformed fruit. In the centre of all the pale metal sat a scruffy wooden table, where Essop and Chef were drinking tea. They made an odd couple. Chef in his starched whites, hat rising like a puff of smoke; Essop in his crumpled suit, bald head garlanded by grey hair. All week the palace had echoed with whispers of Patrick's disappearance. I could see in Essop's eyes that he was thinking of him, however, with staff swirling around us, we shared a smile but held our tongues.

I thanked Chef and walked out the kitchen door, through the palace gates, then off the road, following the path that ran like a dirty ribbon to my tree. Sitting in its shade, I ate, watching the reflected dots from my necklace dance on the soil. I scrunched up the bag, used my knife to scratch a scar into the bark, shoved the bag into the hole in the tree and returned for my next shift.

Sean

THE PHONE WOKE ME, wailing bloody murder in a far-off room. Straining to recall the night before, I trawled my tender brain but snagged not a thing. The phone stopped. Praise be for small mercies. Before moving, I checked my condition: it wasn't good. Sprawled on the sitting-room floor, concrete cooled my face as rivers of ants dined on some sticky treat coating my hand. Summoning all my strength I stood up and prayed a shower would wash away the horror. With head hung low, the water working its mild miracle, I grabbed the soap. It felt odd, soft, and there, slopped on my palm, sat a toad. Disgruntled, as if woken from a sweet sleep. Well, I know the feeling, pal. A toad. Christ. First bad sign of the day.

I dropped the toad out the window, got dressed, and discovered the second bad sign in the cabinet where I was digging for Panadol. Stella's pills, with two days unpopped, staring at me like evil eyes. My heart did a jig. No kids, no way! Only good thing about not having sex was, bar an Immaculate Conception, Stella couldn't be pregnant. Not by me anyway. Cold comfort for my aching balls. Two bad signs and they travel in threes. Pocketing the pills as ammo for later, I then found real medicine: a spliff, the only cure for a hangover of this magnitude. As I closed the cabinet I flinched from my reflection of burst veins, putty cheeks and general disrepair and went in search of coffee.

The kitchen was a pure disgrace. Surfaces furry with dust, flies wallowing in rotten food. Stella had fired the cook; he was insolent apparently. She was the queen of insolence, so I suppose if anyone could spot it…I made a coffee, sat on the kitchen stoop, took a drag of spliff and, just as the sweet buzz settled in, the phone whipped it away.

Searching for it, I listed the possibilities: Stella arrested, again; Stella found in a ditch, again; Stella reminding me she hated me, again. So it was a surprise to hear, 'Sean? Gav here from the *Telegraph*. Remember me?'

'The man who hates semicolons.'

'That's me. Do you know Truth? Pop singer, performing at this Big Day thing.'

'No. But I already hate his name.'

'Could you do a piece? The hook is big stars taking big cheques from bad men. He's staying at some place called the Mirage.'

Years back I started saying no to guys like Gav, believing my grand self to be so much more than a mere hack. I was an author no less! And my next book was just around the corner; a corner, it transpired, that looped and met itself in an impotent circle. Over time the fog of my pride lifted enough that I could see these calls would soon dry up. Then where was I? Neither author, nor hack, just some soaked teacher in a country you couldn't even call *forgotten* for the fact no one had heard of it in the first place. So I said, 'Sure, Mr Semicolon, I'll do it,' jotted down the details and said goodbye.

When I returned to the stoop I was greeted by the rising sun. Magnificent. Scientists say one sun services the earth but the poet in me believes this is different to other suns. How could that pale blob smearing the Celtic sky be the same as this majestic African orb? The sun was low, rolling up the drive towards me, a wild eye glancing through the wire fence, firing up the bald lawn and free-range weeds. Stella sacked the gardener; lazy apparently. But when the jacaranda pods started rattling in the wind, I knew those black tongues were sounding the end of my peace. For the third and final malevolence was upon me.

Out of the sun she stumbled, first as a silhouette but as she closed in, blocking light, she took shape, fattening, hips swelling, hair spreading like a storm, here she came: my Stella, blasted from the core of the sun with the sole purpose of making my life a living hell. We started mean and loud, just where we left off.

'Where the hell have you been?' I said and she sneered, 'Out of my way, old man,' shoving past me like I was a mangy dog.

Holding up her pills, I yelled, 'And what's this?' resisting the impulse to tack *Ah-ha!* to the end.

When she screamed, 'None of your business!' I balked. 'It bloody is my business! We agreed we weren't throwing kids into this tidy mess we've made for ourselves.'

She stared at me as if concocting a curse. I braced myself for blood-curdling screams, ejaculations of bees from her gaping mouth – the crickets hit a dramatic pitch – but no bees came, no blood, no screams. She just looked right through me, like I wasn't even worth the curse, kissed her teeth – *tss!* – then stormed into the bedroom, cranking up the radio loud enough to wake the gods: 'Today the King honoured our football team, the Tafumo Tigers, with new Bata Bata boots...'

Stella didn't take long to sleep off whatever poison she'd punished herself with the night before. Then she'd be out polluting the house with her mood. So I went to my study and grabbed a new Dictaphone I'd bought with some daft notion of recording Bwalo's oral history for yet another book I'd never write. I'd forever been promising it to Charlie and right now, this very minute and not a moment later, was the time to fulfil that promise. And maybe, once I'd done that, and since I was there and all, I'd treat myself to a wee nip to fortify the day.

Escaping Stella was, as always, grand. Riding through the fresh morning, exploding bugs punctuating my visor, the brightly painted Mirage rising up before me like the sweet hope of a bad day about to turn good.

When I entered the lobby a real scene was playing out: a fella sprawled across the zebra skin, like he'd squashed the animal flat, and people prancing all around him. Goodness, someone in a worse state than me. He got up, dazed, hitched his arm over Stu and off they staggered like drunks. When I gave Charlie the Dictaphone, I enquired about the fainting man and Charlie assured me that the man was a celebrity. And sure enough, there was something faintly familiar about the fella.

Josef

SOMEONE HAD TOUCHED MY desk. I felt it before I saw it, before I sat, before I checked. No fingerprints on the polished surface but, like the first wince of indigestion, I knew something was wrong. Patrick said his office had been tampered with. My diary still sat in the centre; three pens beside it like bright excla- mations – black, red, blue – and my lamp bent low to the page as if reading with its dusty glass eye. I opened the drawer, pushed the false bottom and there – in the drawer within the drawer – was my folder.

I turned to Levi's page, bible-thin from a time of carbon copies – *everything in duplicate* – those oily pages, black as the back of a mirror, upon which our pens impressed grey words. Levi's original page was burned but I had kept the shadow page. A staple, rusted red as an ant's pincer, clipped Levi's photograph to the delicate paper. Looking like a boy, gone so young and so long ago, my memory forever tried to file him under ancient his- tory. I returned my folder to the drawer.

We all assumed Tafumo's promise of democracy was genuine. Even Tafumo – before the heady whiff of adulation, before step- ping off the plane to be greeted like a god – believed his promise. Levi tried to hold him to it. It was the first time we saw Tafumo's rage, not loud or obvious but condescending, like a disappointed father: 'My people aren't ready for democracy. Too naive. Until they're ready, everything I say is law.'

Vanishing is harder now. Digital spirits are more indelible than paper ghosts. There was a time when they could wipe a man clean out of existence, everything burned, exported, expunged, friends, family, property, even his spirit. The *sing'anga* say spirits can't survive unless someone remembers you. I remember you, Levi.

Jack

WITH THE BLADE TOO wide to penetrate the crooked smile of the keyhole, I jemmied it, slipped, and sliced open a tidy flap on my thumb. Sally always said that after each mess-up I returned, shaking my head in disbelief, saying the same thing. How did this happen? Said she'd write it on my gravestone: *How did this happen?* And if she knew where I was right now, she'd put me straight in the grave herself. So why? Why, even as my guts churned like a sack of snakes, had I said, 'Sure, I'm in'? Everything was wrong about it. Even the amount of money was higher than normal, and though that should have scared me off instead it sucked me in. Everything about it stank to high heaven. He'd called out of the blue. And last night I'd gone to the bar. Couldn't miss him; only white guy in a black bar. I'd couriered for him before; small stuff, weed, documents, black-market money, back when I lived in Bwalo. He'd aged badly in the passing years, got pale, fat. Though it was almost dawn, the bar was still humming, guys with arses hanging out of their tatty trousers drinking cartons of the dark local brew.

A woman bothered us and he waved her away. 'Piss off, men at work.' Then he whispered, 'Steer clear of the pussy, Jack. Girls full up with the AIDS. Most expensive fuck you'll have. You'll pay with your life but, before you die, your dick'll drop off.' When he finished laughing, he asked, 'Now, Jack, what do you know about gold?'

'I know Sally can't get enough of the stuff.'

'Yah. Well I want to extract it. But in Bwalo they've bullshit regulations preventing me extracting it with a process involving potassium cyanide.'

'Cyanide? I thought I was moving documents.'

'Calm down. Not cyanide: *potassium* cyanide. Totally different. Don't worry, the stuff's inert, safe as houses. Worst that'll happen is they slap you with a fine, which I'll pay. All very low-grade illegal. And I've got the best guide, he'll be with you every step.'

'Why not get him to take the stuff?'

'Because you can't trust a kaffir to do a white man's job.'

Right then, that was the moment – to stand, to smile, to say goodbye – and I said, 'Sure, I'm in.' He handed me a case and an envelope and said, 'First payment and a map. Drop-off is at a safari lodge. Start back here at eight. Don't mess it up, eh. I trust you.'

When I returned my guide was there. The bar was closed and the area was littered with sodden cartons of Chibuku. My guide told me his name was 'Fantastic'. I smiled. He didn't smile back but looked me up and down, checking my fitness, reviewing if I was capable of keeping up, his eyes gliding over my backpack as he said, 'We go.'

As we walked through the bush, my brain kept wandering back to the bar and I realised the scale was wrong. What I was carrying was a few ounces at best. I knew guys involved with chemical extraction in the Copperbelt and it was industrial scale, barrels of the stuff coming in on the back of Bedford trucks.

So soon as Fantastic said he needed to scout up ahead, soon as the sound of his footsteps faded, I pulled it out and placed my nose against the briefcase. Cyanide would reek of almonds. But there was no smell, just the dry stink of dust: the smell of Africa.

That was when I dug my blade into the cheap fliplocks and sliced open my thumb. I began thumping the lock with the handle of my knife, cracking it again and again until the first latch popped. The second gave easily. When I heard the crunch of footsteps getting louder and closer, I yanked open the case and peeked inside: it was empty.

Charlie

*C*LICK!
   'Mrs Horst, did you know when a hippo poos it spins its tail like a propeller so the poo flies all over the place in a poo circle? Isn't that amazing?'

'What do you want, Charlie?'

'Mum said I should interview you because you'd be fascinating.'

'Fiona said that? Really? OK. Just make it snappy.'

'What do you do for a living, Mrs Horst?'

'I major in drinking, minor in smoking.'

'And what were you like as a child?'

'I was a princess. Generations back we were royalty, blue bloods. My father, God rest his soul, was filthy rich, worked in diamonds in South Africa. We had servants galore, my chariot was a Mercedes, my house was a castle that kept the riff-raff out.'

'And what do you think of the Big Day?'

'The Big Day is just another stinking day in this burnt-out excuse for a country…Bambo! Alias! Hey, whisky! No ice! Quicksharp!'

Click!

Hope

HAVING CHECKED HIS PULSE and temperature, I sat and waited. Waiting is what we do. We've not left the palace for nearly a year. Watching him sleep I saw that I needed to shave his head again: a week's growth, a grey patina, rested like a dusting of icing sugar. We've grown old together. Seemed to happen in an instant. Years leapfrogging days, time crowding in with invisible fury, memory slippery as mud. Though, like the deepest carving, some memories remain clear as the day they were cut.

After independence, as the palace was being built, men crawling like ants over scaffolding, Josef and I got married. We had just moved into our first house, on the university campus. I spent hours in the market fussing over rugs that had to have the green and gold of our new flag. That mattered: my national pride revealed even in the weave of my rugs. It normally took years to be granted a campus house but we had been blessed. I believed Jesus had bestowed this gift upon us. We were good people, faithful people, and God was pleased with us. I see now that innocence is a form of blindness.

I suppose, even then, I knew that part of our luck was due to Josef. He'd played a small role in our independence, a junior member of the uMunthu Party. Together with his university colleagues, Essop, Boma, Patrick and Levi, he'd campaigned, demonstrated, and brought Tafumo to power.

But before the wedding, Josef was on edge. Had he already fallen out of love with me? He became flustered when I'd asked if he'd like the missionary who educated him, a man he spoke about with great reverence, to marry us. Josef and I had met at church, I thought it would be good to include his teacher and mentor, but Josef said sharply, 'No.'

The joy of the day was a delicate thing I couldn't quite reach, forever a fingertip away. Something about Josef's manner, his strained smile. All morning I'd struggled against a curious detachment, so much the centre of attention that I felt I was outside looking in. So the moment it happened, I was just as much relieved as excited. The reason Josef had been on edge was nothing to do with our love; it was because he'd arranged a surprise. The arrival of the bride was not the main event at my wedding.

Spilling from the cool church into the heat of the day, we chatted excitedly, released from the formality of the service, shining with sweat and happiness, when everyone suddenly stopped talking. For a Rolls-Royce was gliding down the silvery road. And next to me my Josef was smiling that knowing smile of his. His little secret was out. The source of his unease revealed. The King attended our wedding. Surely such fairy tales can't be true I thought, as Tafumo kissed me and presented me with a gift: an ebony carving, black as smoke, of mother, father and child delicately intertwined. After Tafumo was swamped by guests, I went and kissed Josef. 'So that's why you've been acting strangely, Mr Songa,' and he grinned, 'I'm full of little secrets, Mrs Songa.'

After our marriage fell apart, my mind travelled back to that day, to the start, the wedding. The bad seed planted so long before, maybe further back than I'll ever know. My mind ceaselessly digging at that day, sifting through to that one image, a split-second moment that returned again and again and never came right. Naturally, on the day itself, this unease was muffled below a sort of manic happiness. A blur of small talk and big speeches washed down with a glut of food and

23

wine. I was so proud of our new home that I'd insisted on holding the reception there even though I knew it was far too small. As with most Bwalo weddings more people turned up than were invited.

Josef's guests, and this should have concerned me more than it did, were few. As an orphan, he had no family. He had colleagues, fellow uMunthu members, but not a soul came from whatever life he'd had before he arrived at the capital. The bulk of the guests were my large, loud family, my snob of a mother fawning over the King. And Tafumo himself – had he noticed my rugs shining with the trim of our new flag? – sitting in my own house, looking bemused. Not a bright or brazen King but a muted presence swarmed by wild-coloured *chitenges*, a green-gold storm engulfing the dark-suited epicentre. Having just started at the palace, and being just one of many nurses, I hadn't yet met him. He was forty, a fit man with little need for nurses. So I, like all around me, pretended not to stare at the god at my table. He behaved like any man; politely talking to those that dared talk to him, expertly brushing off my mortifying mother. And I truly felt as if I was at the centre of the world, working in the palace, married to one of the brave men who risked his life to free our nation. There I sat, at the head table, a stretch away from the King, sitting at the very heart of history. Pride before the fall.

Though at the time we believed we were at the forefront of life and society, looking back at the one remaining photograph that Essop took, I cringe at how childish, how backward and somehow homemade we seemed, acting the adults we had not yet become. My outfit was an unflattering nightmare of eighties puffery, an enormous creamy scone of a dress, my face and hands peeking from the layers like raisins. And even though it was the early eighties, Josef and his friends were stuck very much in fashion of the seventies; a decade Africa remains reluctant to abandon. Josef's neck is lassoed by a thick pink tie that hangs like a tongue down his custard-yellow shirt. Essop is in a flared checked suit and young Boma appears to be wearing a straw cowboy hat.

But at the time we all believed we were at the very cutting edge of fashion, society, politics and history itself. And in all the excitement of the day, it wasn't until we were seated at our reception dinner that I realised Levi was absent. Petulant bride that I was, I grabbed Josef, demanding, 'Where is Levi?'

I had hosted many dinners with Levi, cooked for innumerable meetings of the uMunthu at the house, while they prepared for the return of Tafumo. Even the King himself was here. I insisted that Josef call Levi and ask him to explain himself. The dining room was so noisy and smoky, Boma sweating through his shirt, singing some silly song, Essop chuckling, but through all the noise and smoke and space, Josef's face floated towards me, his eyes cast down, staring at the phone. When he returned I said, 'Well? What's the story?' and Josef muttered, 'He's not answering.' I remained annoyed, put out that Levi hadn't shown up, hadn't even had the decency to call.

Very late that night, long after the King had left and most of the guests were gone, we drank with Josef's close friends. As we sipped our wine, I realised that this was the first time that all of us, except Levi, had sat together since independence. For months before Tafumo's return, they had met, most nights, at this wicker table, planning protests and preparing to overthrow the British. Yet since Tafumo had come to power, these men hadn't yet gathered to celebrate the role they played in freeing our country. So, in a brief moment of silence, when Boma had stopped singing, I raised my glass and looked closely at each of them – Essop, Boma, Patrick and Josef – and said, 'A toast. To my brave uMunthu men.' Glancing at one another slouched in their chairs, they briefly emerged from their stupor.

Essop jumped up and forced everyone to sit in the order we had once sat for a photograph he'd taken at the last uMunthu meeting before independence. Shuffling us, 'Come, come, this is a historic reunion,' he balanced his camera on a chair, fiddling with the timer, running back into shot. Josef grabbed my waist, something desperate in the clinch, as Boma raised his bottle and we all sang, '*Kwacha!*'

And it was not long after that I noticed Josef and Essop together. Even now I see the image so clearly: the two of them under the jacaranda tree, Josef so tall next to Essop, touching Essop's back as one might comfort a child.

Charlie

C^{LICK}*...*
 'Mr Horst, did you know marabou storks pee on their own legs to cool off?'

'Charlie, I'm busy as a bugger so...'

'Mum said you would be really interesting to talk to.'

'She said that? Really? OK, well, if Fiona said so.'

'Mr Horst, what was your dad like?'

'Mean. He raised us boys like livestock. If I was slow, I got a boot up the arse. If I cried, he'd boot me in the arse again for being sissy.'

'He sounds horrid.'

'No, no. He made me what I am today.'

'What are you today?'

'I'm a success, Charlie, a bloody great success.'

'And what do you think of the Big Day?'

'I think it's going to make me a very rich man.'

Click...

Josef

I OPENED MY FILE TO Patrick's page. It was thick stock. His photo not stapled like Levi's, but printed on the page. When he vanished last week we were ordered to destroy Patrick's paperwork but, as always, I held on to a page. One page per man. Patrick knew. Again and again he asked, *Am I blacklisted?* Ministers believed in a blacklist of those fallen from favour. A childish notion. The problem wasn't being on a list; the problem was no longer being on any list.

Leaning low I returned the folder to the bottom drawer, slid the false bottom over, and when I sat back up I felt blood rinse my gums and I winced. For days a vibration had been building, humming an insistent note, my sweet tooth playing a childish tune. And before I was fully conscious of it, my tongue plucked the raw nerve and I grimaced, waiting for the shrill pain to fade.

I left my office and asked my secretary, 'Beatrice, has anyone been to see me?' She replied, 'Mr Jeko,' and I snapped, 'Well why didn't you tell me!'

The fear on her face was all the reply I required; Jeko had instructed her not to. When I asked if he had left a note, she shrugged helplessly. Jeko didn't leave notes. I suspected he was illiterate. Dressed like an accountant, he ran Tafumo's secret police, the Young Pioneers, with disquieting efficiency. He was lighter skinned than me, his bald head the pale brown of an avocado stone. His almost featureless face personified the system he ran. He wasn't just bald but without eyebrows or eyelashes, as if even they were surplus to requirement. I was momentarily overpowered by an image of Jeko's gloved hand wiping the surface of my desk, the slits of his nostrils flaring.

Walking the short distance to the Ministry of Communication, Broadcast and Tourism, planes pass overhead; the world was arriving. The passengers would barely register this grey cube. Five levels up and – like a dark reflection – five sunk below. Entering it was like being beamed from a dusty African university to a shiny Zurich corporation. With leather chairs and acres of silver servers, it was strikingly modern. It wasn't always like this. It began as an amateurish affair. A few women plunging wires in and out of a giant wooden operator station. They didn't record back then. Just listened. And if negative words crossed the wire, they pulled the plug. In those early days, those simpler times, I didn't know when I informed on Levi that he'd vanish. I was naive.

What, I wonder, was my excuse now? After Levi, I took over his position as University Dean and, to begin with at least, I fought hard for funding, which I rarely received. Of course, by the late eighties, when I was appointed Minister of Communication, no financial request was ever denied. Tafumo had no interest in the education of his people, only in their surveillance: he wanted always to be the sophisticated father of simple children. This building was empty when I became minister; we had no opposition, no enemy. I never thought we'd fill it. Not in my lifetime anyway. Yet now as I walked its corridors, lined with miles of manila folders full of secrets and lies, I listened to the hypnotic rhythm of my footsteps and someone called out, '*Sefu?*'

I pitched forward, hands hitting the wall to break my fall, as I tried to steal breath back into my lungs. *Sefu.* An old name. *Little sword.* Like pulling a tiny weed only to yank a large tangle of roots, the name dragged many memories in its wake. Long ago I secreted *Sefu* inside the sheath of Josef. Now, it seemed, time was turning me inside out.

29

I shouted, 'Hello?' and jumped when the word returned, 'Hello?' Scared of my own echo. I scuffed my shoe, making a *schu* sound: *Sefu*? I tried to smile, to shrug it off, but wasn't convinced by my own nonchalance. Diagnosing them as panic attacks, my GP prescribed useless pills. But this wasn't panic. I was being overwhelmed by weakness, emerging from these episodes as if from brutal exertion. Thankfully, my *sing'anga* gave me real *muti*. And when I sipped from the bottle the dark drops revived me. I slowly made my way to the Listening Room. The ancient operator station had long ago been replaced with cubicles manned by men in headphones. It looked dull as any call centre. Only no one was talking here. They were listening and transcribing our unofficial history.

I sat in the meeting room and looked down the line of identical cubicles, giant cells multiplying across the floor. Closing my eyes, I listened to the light splashing of people typing. So much of what we heard was useless, gossip and lies; endless currents of chatter through which we had to sift. What we heard was rarely significant, it was the whispers we missed that mattered most. By the nineties, my job title had expanded to Minister of Communication, Broadcast, Education and Tourism. African governments specialise in long job titles and in Bwalo people joked that the longer your job title the bigger your Mercedes. I imagined my title to be a snake gobbling up departments. A title so long it barely fitted on my business card. Behind my back, other ministers called me the Minister of Everything, but in truth, I always felt more like the Minister of Nothing. The real work of Tourism, Education and Broadcast was delegated to my deputy ministers, and in fact all I did was listen. I was the Minister of Whispers and Lies, listening to the nation's secrets; listening to what Tafumo's simple citizens were saying about him.

I remembered my first British High Commissioner. They came and went, these bored men posted like unwanted letters around the empire. They had their differences – some were fatter than others; some couldn't hold their gin – but each, to a man, failed to grasp how Bwalo really worked. My first Commissioner was as ugly as he was dull. And when the gin loosened his tongue, he said, 'I know who you *really* are, Josef. They call you *Minister of Everything*, or *God*. All-seeing, all-hearing and all of that. Second oldest profession, the oldest being whores. Spies and sluts make the world go around. But I was briefed by our MI5 bods who said your service sorely lacks technology and sophistication. That it is a far cry from our own impressive British secret service.'

What the fool failed to realise was that our service was a human one, of flesh and souls not wires and microchips, and that even as he sat condescending me, the servant filling his glass was one of mine, the maids searching through his things were mine, and they all formed a fraction of a devoted army spread across Bwalo and beyond. Not that they ever heard an interesting thing he said. He was a consummate ambassador in that sense: he never said anything worth repeating.

His MI5 briefing also omitted a key point: our service was a facsimile of his. For a simple reason: the British actually created the Bwalo service. After we gained independence, the British were paranoid about communist infestation. We were wedged – crushed – between communist states. With Zambia to the west and Mozambique to the east, we were the final domino – the last stronghold – to be toppled. And so MI5 actually came and taught us. They gave us training, shared intelligence and equipment. MI5 was the midwife of the Bwalo secret service. Like some zealous nanny unable to accept her charges were grown, the British simply couldn't leave their lost empire alone.

At the end he winked, sealing a gentleman's agreement, 'We'll work well together. We want the same thing, old boy.' This man actually believed we were the same: that we thought, felt and desired the same. He supposed his empire hadn't just spread syphilis but also its psyche. Yet the distance between us – a metre of mahogany desk – may as well have been miles. For any man who believes all men are alike has never spent time in Bwalo. His crumbling empire mind, soaked in gin, couldn't

31

grasp how raw a nation we were. How many would die for Tafumo, believed him to be God, how we cherished principles about which he had long ago grown complacent.

My reminiscence was broken by a knock on the door. And, as if my thoughts on fanaticism had manifested into a man, David limped into the room. He worked hard to mask the twist in his spine – a remnant of the deforming hand of polio – stretching the kink to excruciating straightness, the pain of which left his young face lined with agony. Today he wore his black suit; he seemed to own only two, which I assumed was due to some sort of self-imposed austerity.

As my right-hand man, David also had a rather cumbersome job title as Deputy Minister of Communication, Data and Information. He handed me a folder and I flicked through the banned websites and transcripts. The Commissioner had been right in one sense: back then our technology was limited. But since then, the global defence market has let us purchase whatever we need to listen to whomever we want, creeping like rising damp into homes, businesses, even to the edge of people's minds. But technology's advance assists subversion as much as surveillance. If we have it, they have it. When the world was paper we held it back. But the relentless proliferation of the digital world means the termites are chewing the dam closer to collapse.

When I started here everything was physical. Newpapers, magazines and books were either banned outright or incriminating articles and salacious images were blacked out with marker pens or cut out; long tables of men with pens and scissors blacking out articles and slicing out flesh. When we banned a song, we would physically scratch it off the vinyl, scarring the soft wax, so that one song on the album would never play. But the tangible world is now long deceased, haunting the ether, streaming in, weightless and dangerous as an idea. Utterly impossible to stop. You might as well try to catch the wind. My eager young deputy, David, loves the new world, this coded realm, where every action leaves a stain, where we can trace every conversation, text, purchase and search. He's too young to appreciate one day that same slime will be traced back to the soles of our shoes.

Pulling out a transcript, David explained, 'I've an account from a Watcher near the border in the north, a bar owner, said he saw a man who fits the description of Horst – the owner of the Mirage – swapping goods with another man. In itself it's minor but this morning the Listeners got this from the new bug on Horst's portrait in the hotel office. One of the men is Horst himself. We're checking with Ed now, trying to get verification on the second man. He's a recent arrival into the country, a man called Willem. Something about the conversation is not quite right.'

Eugene Horst: Cost a bomb but I'm happy with the painting…

Willem: Sure captures all of you. You got a little excess baggage since…

Eugene Horst: Bullshit. Marlene has me on this prehistoric diet.

Willem: You chewing through a dinosaur a day?

Eugene Horst: Still a bloody joker. So, how's Scotland?

Willem: Miserable. Left our big house in Zim to live in some semi-detached shithole with shared walls. I'm in Scotland sharing my walls and here, even in mud huts, even the poorest *bambo* in Bwalo has his own walls.

Eugene Horst: You're starting to whine like a pom. So you play golf? First tee is tough, eh?

Willem: Not too bad.

Eugene Horst: Sure?

Willem: Sure.

Closing the file, I said, 'Don't waste time on this, David. It's nothing. White men talk golf until boredom himself begs for a change of subject.'

With undisguised contempt, David stood up and limped out, and as he swept past, I caught a whiff of bad meat.

33

Charlie

*E*VERYONE AT THE BAR was dressed in their best clothes because of the rumours that celebrities had arrived. I knew they hadn't but Dad told me not to tell anyone because he said the rumours were good for business. In fact, Dad was the one spreading the rumours.

Solomon, Aaron and I sat in the frangipani tree at the end of the pool where the hotel stopped and the golf course started.

Aaron looked at my new Dictaphone and said, 'But this machine is magic, Charlie.'

Aaron was my nanny's son. He lived in the *kaya*, the servants' compound at the foot of the golf course. His toys were made of wood and wire, so he never got to see cool stuff like this. It was probably one of the coolest toys I'd ever seen too.

Solomon just shrugged and said, 'My dad has one just like this, but better.'

Solomon said that about everything. His dad worked for the government and drove a Mercedes like Tafumo. Dad told me to always be nice to Solomon. And when Mum said, you always be nice to everyone, Dad explained, that's what I meant, dear. But then Dad whispered to me, just be *extra* nice to Solomon.

Earlier in the afternoon, I'd snuck up behind Mrs Horst and her best friend Debs. Their backs were squeezed through the deckchair slats like sausage fat. It was so gross. Every single day

Mrs Horst and Debs lay by the pool, sizzling in the sun, yacking away. Mum called them the Ministry of Information, because they knew everything about everyone. So I'd crept up and left my Dictaphone recording under them.

Before I hit play, I said, 'Listen, guys, there are so many cool new words.'

Click!

'Bastard crickets, what's to be so fucking chirpy about?'

'You got a bout of Bwalo fever, girl? Need a shopping trip to the Cape, only cure for the fever. Is that that girl from that film about the crash where they ate each other?'

'Jesus, check Eugene flirting with them. Pathetic. I'd that dream again...'

'Oh yah, the hunky gardener riding you like black tar...'

'Not that one! The one where I kill Eugene.'

'To hell with the shopping trip, Marl, you need a divorce.'

'Who wants a dried old prune like me?'

'You're in good shape...for your age. Talk to me, Marl, I'm listening.'

'Why, so you can tell my business to everyone in this tiny fucking town.'

'I never, Marl!'

'All right relax. Look at Sean there, pissed as a newt before lunchtime.'

'Man's got a face like a punched testicle. Shame, yah. That's what you get for going native. I hear his fiancée was a lady of the night before he made an honest woman of her.'

'Nothing honest about that woman. Fuck this, eh. I'm off. There's no famous people here except that creepy hobbit guy.'

'I'll call you if Clooney comes.'

'Yah, yah, pigs will fly. See you for sundowners.'

'Ebony or ivory today?'

'Cheeky bitch.'

Click!

For a moment, we all just stared at each other.

Then Aaron said, 'I think we should definitely not be listening to this. This is bad trouble, Charlie.'

'Rubbish,' Solomon shouted. 'What do you know, Aaron, you know nothing.'

I took a bottle top from my pocket. Then, on the tree branch, near the old words – BUGGER, CRAP, SHITSILU – I scraped the new word: TESTACULS.

Solomon smiled and said, 'We need a whole forest to carve out all their curses.'

'This is bad,' muttered Aaron and Solomon snapped, 'You don't know anything about anything, you are just ignorant.'

'Well, I know a new word too,' Aaron said defensively, and Solomon and I looked at him suspiciously. Solomon didn't like other people knowing anything he didn't and he whispered to me, 'He doesn't know anything, he's just stupid.'

'I do know a word,' Aaron said. 'About what they were saying about Sean's wife. My mum spelt it out to Ed, so I wouldn't be understanding it.'

I said, 'They're always spelling things, it's so annoying!'

Aaron nodded. 'Yes. It's a strange word, not a Chichewa word. Mum uses English words if she really does not want me to be understanding her.'

I offered Aaron the bottle top and said, 'Well if they spelt it out then can you remember how to spell it?' Aaron hesitated, as if he was scared of the word, and Solomon taunted, 'Yah, they don't teach you to spell at your rubbish falling-down school.'

Aaron snatched the top and carved: W O R.

White sap bled into the letters and I said, 'What's a wor?'

When no one replied, I jumped off the tree and said, 'I'm going to ask.'

Aaron shouted, 'No, Charlie,' and Solomon said, 'Just shut up, ignorant Aaron.'

I walked up to Stella and shouted over the noise, 'Hey, Stella. Are you a wor?'

Lots of people, who'd been chatting, suddenly stopped talking, turned, and stared.

Mrs Horst leant down and whispered into my ear, 'Say it with an H, sweetie.'

I said, 'Whore?'

Dad said time never stops but sometimes it pauses. That's what happened. Everything paused. Then, as if time was trying to catch up with itself, everything moved really fast. Stella looked like a dog had farted in her mouth; people were laughing behind their hands; Mum was dragging me into the lobby where, with arms folded, she shouted, 'Who told you that word?'

'I'll never reveal my sources, Mum.'

'What? Look, right, Charlie, you can't say these things.'

'Why?'

'Because.'

'Because she's a wor?'

'It's *whore*.'

'Whore.'

'Stop saying it, Charlie!'

'Not even correctly?'

'Especially not correctly. Not till you're old enough.'

'But you told me to always ask questions.'

'That's true...just come to me first. Ask your dad or...no, ask me first. Got it? Don't just blurt it out. Now it's way too late for you to be up, so go to bed!'

After a sharp kiss, Mum turned me towards home, and gave me a gentle push. She rushed back to the bar and I started to walk home. But as I passed Dad's office, I heard shouting. So I went inside and tiptoed over to the window, where I spied out to the car park. From my low position, Stella's legs vanished in pillars up the darkness of her dress, as Sean's feet shuffled about like a boxer. I placed the Dictaphone on the windowsill and lay low, so they wouldn't see me. I was trying to listen when I heard the slip-slap of flip-flops and when I looked up my nanny, Innocence, stood over me, hands on her hips. Avoiding her eyes, I looked down at her toes, hoping she didn't know what Aaron had told me about Stella. But I bet she did. Innocence knew everything, even more than Mum. When she said, 'Master, bed now!' I left the Dictaphone running on the windowsill, and weaved past Innocence, who flip-flopped me all the way to bed.

Click!

'Your friends have no respect for me, Sean.'

'Come on, Stell, it's not like that. They were just embarrassed…'

'These men have all looked at me differently in the past, now they're hypocrites.'

'Let's not get into that right now, Stell.'

'You don't defend me. I need respecting. I'm a member of this club too.'

'Well, technically, you're not actually a member.'

'What did you say to me?'

'Nothing, dear. Just calm down. Christ's sake, Stell. Don't do that, don't hurt me.'

'I was happier as a whore. You're nothing but a bitch! A misery! You're the only whore here today!'

Click!

Hope

*B*EFORE THE PALACE WAS finished, the Mirage was the most extravagant building in Bwalo. Though it wasn't long before even Tafumo's palace was put in its place. A year into the job, I accompanied Tafumo to a Commonwealth dinner in London. Josef was so proud. He carved me a good-luck charm: a London bus painted ochre. He kissed me and I told him off for his itchy moustache. Tafumo had grown one so all the men had followed suit.

We flew in Tafumo's Jumbo with his *mbumba*, his one hundred dancing girls. I'd never been on a plane. The girls were used to it, these village girls, plucked from fields, wrapped in *chitenges*, dancing around the world in his honour. As the engines roared I searched the girls' faces for fear. Was it supposed to sound like it was exploding? They looked bored as the earth released us, the plane pulled up, and Bwalo shrank below.

We stayed at the Ritz, where a tailor came to measure Tafumo for a suit. The same suit he insisted on wearing today, his body lost inside it like a buckled coat hanger. Back then, he was an ebony giant: hard, powerful, stretching the suit to perfect tautness. But the trip soon soured. Tafumo was denied a private meeting with the Queen. He sulked; I administered Valium. Then Tafumo's lady-in-waiting, Mama Angelina, fell sick and was unable to attend the state dinner. No one knew who I was, so I was the natural replacement. I remember being so thrilled and anxious as I put on my best dress.

When the limousine sliced through the wet night, I was overpowered by déjà vu. Though I'd never seen Buckingham Palace, I simultaneously knew I recognised it. Stepping out, I realised where I'd seen it: Tafumo had modelled his palace on the Queen's, erecting a quarter-sized Buckingham Palace in the middle of Bwalo.

The inside of the Queen's palace was magnificent. Everything and everyone shone with splendour. And my own dress, the most expensive I owned – which moments before had seemed so extravagant – was magically transformed into a bright embarrassment of cheap, homemade rags. Chandeliers lent the guests a rich glow and it was there, sitting in that majestic hall, that Tafumo's palace was reduced to a glorified doll's house, a failed imitation of grandeur. Until my teens I'd never left my village and when I did my nursing degree in the capital, I believed it was the greatest city in the world. Yet here I sat in a city many times bigger than my whole country.

I heard dignitaries from across the world speak in the same accent as the Queen. I remained mute, not wanting my African accent to escape my mouth, to embarrass me, to shame Tafumo. But I had my first seditious thought that night: that even Tafumo's power paled when held up against the might of this woman who once ruled the world. But where I was awestruck, Tafumo was agitated; he drank heavily, sulked, and eventually fell into conversation with an aide to the Sultan of Brunei.

The aide was a confident, boastful man, who said, 'Goodness, these things are so dull. The Queen waffling on about the importance of the Commonwealth in modern times. Rada-rada-rada, blah-blah-blah.'

Tafumo nodded, happy to have found another man disgruntled with the Queen.

And seeing he had Tafumo's support, the aide continued, 'When actually, as I'm sure you are more than aware, ruling an empire really isn't so hard. One need only look at this German lady, bewigged and bejowled, to see that it is all about the power of pomp. It's so simple really. Sustain the traditions of your people to sustain the support of them.'

I never thought it possible but Tafumo was actually intimidated. He clearly wanted to impress the aide, when he replied, 'Couldn't agree more. In Bwalo, no man is allowed to grow his hair. Hippies come and we shave their heads at the airport.'

'Splendid,' said the aide, smiling. 'In Brunei it's forbidden for a layperson to wear yellow, for this is the colour of our royal family and is their exclusive entitlement.'

'I banned miniskirts,' Tafumo said, 'to retain the chastity of women,' and the aide volleyed back, 'We banned alcohol and karaoke. Keeps the Chinese in their place.'

Watching these powerful men acting like schoolboys, reducing the rights of their people to pawns in a game of one-upmanship, sickened me. It was the first time I'd considered Tafumo's laws. He always spun the line about retaining the chastity of African women but now I saw what a fool I'd been to believe it. Around us hung portraits of mustachioed men in long sleeves and trousers, women trussed up like peacocks. My ancestors were barebreasted and naked to man and God. Tafumo wasn't upholding his African code, it came from his other side: it was the code of the colonists.

I was so happy to return to Bwalo. To be free of that strange and cold kingdom. When the aeroplane door breathed open, I was wrapped in a gentle hug of heat. Home again. I had bought Josef a toy black cab and when he opened it, he smiled and then parked both the cab and the ochre bus together on our bookshelf. And that night, for the first time, I didn't have to cook. Josef had hired a lady called Ruby. We were doing well in the world. After all the limp British vegetables and soggy grey fish, Ruby cooked a chambo and its fresh pearly eyes filled me with such happiness. As we ate, I told Josef all about the palace dinner and he joked, 'Well from now on I shall have to call you the Queen of Bwalo.'

I giggled and then tried to explain the conversation between the Sultan's aide and Tafumo. But in my tipsy state I failed to articulate what I found annoying and I stopped when I sensed Josef's mood had fallen out of harmony with mine. He spoke to me with an authoritative voice, one I imagined he used in lectures, telling me never to spread silly stories about our great King. When I smiled and told him to calm down, he told me to shut up. Like that: *Shut up!* Then he stood, towering over me, and like heat off a fire I felt his violence. When I asked, 'What's wrong, Josef?' he didn't reply but slumped back down beside me. When he eventually cooled, we worked our way back to a good mood, but in time I saw this moment was just the surface of something deeper.

Our fragile love was further tested by our failure to have a child. I secretly checked myself with a specialist and there were no obvious problems. When I begged Josef to get himself checked he screamed that I was a *chimbwira*, barren, scolding me for daring to question his mighty virility. Few monuments are as unmovable as the ego of a Bwalo man. I shouted back at him, I wanted a reaction and I got one. This time he punched me and through my throbbing lips I screamed, 'How dare you, how dare you.' But worse than the punch was the fact he showed no remorse, acting as if I deserved it.

I prayed to God to bless us with a child, greedily demanding more than I'd already received. No child came. Eventually Josef forced me to see a *sing'anga*, who offered vile potions, which I fed to the sink, and mumbo-jumbo about a man with many faces. Besides his faith in Jesus and his education, Josef still believed in magic, spirits and *mfiti*. For all his shiny English shoes he never quite scrubbed off the village dust. Hindsight makes a fool of us. Josef's promotions, our new house, our new wealth: it wasn't luck, it wasn't God, we weren't blessed: it was Tafumo. It was always Tafumo.

Jack

TRYING TO KEEP UP with Fantastic, I felt my backpack grow heavier with every step. My shoulders ached under the weight of it, even though it was no more than a few pounds. Worse than the sensation of weight was the feeling of loneliness gnawing at my guts. Every time I made a bad call I felt like this. Like I was the only person left in the world, like my wife Sally was a million miles away and I would never, no matter how much I tried, make it back to her. The feeling started the night before I left to come here. The moment I lied to Sally about taking a trip to Bwalo to see an old friend, an Irish guy I used to know. I don't think she believed me even for a second. And after the lie, Sal and I had dinner, the two of us sitting in front of the screaming television, eating in silence like a couple of strangers. I jumped slightly when Fantastic hissed at me and raised his hand. We crouched low and Fantastic's eyes flared as he pointed his finger out across the land. I saw nothing but scrubland with a few baobab trees squatting like lumps of badly poured concrete. I was prepared to see a line of heavily armed soldiers marching towards us. Instead I saw eddies twisting in the distance, the wind's hot breath blurring and rubbing out reality, and then my heart jumped. Off to the right, emerging from a dense patch of tall grass, marched a parade of elephants, a baby wedged protectively between a bull and his mother. Fantastic looked back at me and smiled. We stayed low, watching the beasts plod gently past. Once they were gone, Fantastic lost his smile, and said, 'We go.' As we walked on, the day started to fade, dusk dimmed to something blacker, and I felt a slight panic that we were lost. I grabbed my torch but it gave only a few feet of illumination before the blackness gobbled up the weak beam of light.

Josef

My DESK WAS SMEARED. I brought my eye level with the desktop, so I could stare across the polished surface: smeared. I was safe for now. When they got sloppy – when they no longer cared that I knew they were after me – that was when I would have to act. For now I assumed it was just David being over-zealous. I took out my folder and put it on the desk. It had grown fat over the years, with men I knew and some I didn't. I waited, I thought a long time before I did what I did next. I turned to Levi's page and on it wrote: 'Levi Manda, University Dean, execution by Jeko, under executive order of Tafumo.'

Each word was like a pinprick through which a mighty pressure escaped. But the relief didn't last. A swoon of fatigue turned my pen to lead and it fell from my fingers. Someone knocked on my door. I watched the weary motion of my hands, moving as if through molasses, dropping my folder into the drawer. The knocking grew more insistent. My hands acted like anchors, dragging me off my chair. I slid to the floor where, with immense effort, I pushed the drawer shut by butting my head against it, before collapsing.

Hands scooped me up by the armpits. I couldn't see him but knew from his muttering that it was Essop. Thank God it wasn't David or one of my staff who'd found me like this.

'Gently, gently,' he said, and when he lowered me into my chair, the room fell back into focus and there was Essop saying, 'Drink some water. Should I call an ambulance?'

'No, no,' I said, sipping the water. 'I'm fine, fine.'

He sat across from me, his face pinched with concern. 'Josef. You're pale as a ghost.'

Essop was framed by the office window, light blurring the edges of him, producing a hazy, dreamy quality. He looked, for a moment, demonic; his glasses like blank eye sockets in a dark skull. But as my vision focused my old friend formed, as if by magic, before my eyes: there he sat, smiling, concerned and slightly flustered. He was an odd-looking man. As Tafumo's translator, Essop was well paid yet he looked and lived like a poor man, like an impoverished teacher who'd stumbled out of a lecture, in his embarrassing tweed suit and silly kipper tie. Though bald, he let his side hair grow long and messy, so his scalp shone like an egg in a wool nest. And long after the fashion had passed and most of us had shaved off our moustaches, Essop's grew grey as soot. Long after we'd moved to the best areas in town, Essop remained in his small house in a bad area. Long after we'd replaced our old cars, Essop still drove around in his wobbly Peugeot which, when parked at the palace, looked like a joke car next to all of our gleaming Mercedes. Essop was infuriatingly naive. Of course, we all started naive, us country boys born in villages so far from the capital. But while the rest of us worked tirelessly to replace naivety with education, Essop never quite washed it off. It clung to him like a stink.

When I asked how the palace was, he said, 'Humming with excitement,' in a genuine voice, but I caught a sceptical smile flicker below his moustache.

Pulling something from his jacket, he looked fondly at it, before handing it over. 'This'll make you feel old. A photograph of young men from ancient times. I'd completely forgotten that your hair used to shoot up like a black wave. You look like a young Kaunda.'

'At least I still have hair.'

Essop touched his baldness as tenderly as one would touch a wound. I stared at a photograph of five people sitting at a

46

wicker table heavy with ashtrays and beers. The only woman in the photograph was Hope, my Hope, with eyes so wide some nights I felt I was falling into them, an expression so innocent it made me want to shape the world to resemble what she dreamed it should be. Next to her sat Boma in a ridiculous gingham jumpsuit, swigging beer, that dense skull of his never penetrated by a complicated thought. Essop was half out of the frame but even a fraction gave him away: his face fixed in the repose of a man flinching at a world he expected would hurt him. Among the faces was a smiling ghost: Levi. Normally I glanced at photographs but this one stole my attention so entirely, tore me so deeply into the past, that I was shocked when Essop said, 'Keep it.'

Staring at the other ghost, the slim face of Patrick Goya, I whispered, 'Any word on Patrick?'

Essop looked flustered and said, 'I was going to ask you the same thing.'

A wave of fatigue washed over me, sapping me so thoroughly that I wanted to lay my head on the desk and sleep. The world slipped out of focus but I didn't want to take my *sing'anga* drops in front of Essop; it was bad enough he had found me on the floor like a sick dog, weak and pathetic. Instead I allowed my tongue to fish in the crevice of my rotten tooth, probing the nerve to give me a refreshing shot of pain and energy.

When I winced, Essop asked, 'What's wrong?' and, touching my cheek, I admitted, 'One of my teeth is causing me problems.'

Ever the good friend, he wrote down a name and number, 'You must get that seen to, here's my dentist, he's good. Dear Josef, you are falling apart.'

Then Essop fell silent, he looked nervous, embarrassed, until he finally said, 'My friend. I don't wish to place more pressure on you but listen. There has been...talk.'

'About Patrick?'

'No. About you, Josef. I don't normally listen to gossip, bored palace staff and jealous ministers, but people are questioning your…authority…your…judgement. From within your own Ministry.'

'Thanks, Essop, but I'm aware of my staff testing my authority. The young are programmed to overthrow the old.'

'*Mututomera iphere, kusal' injumbura*,' Essop said.

'Kill the old, let the young remain.'

'You remember your Ngoni,' he said, smiling. 'Your tribe always had the best sayings. My favourite remains: we always look for the devil in the wrong place.'

'Spoken like a sad academic,' I quipped and saw that I'd upset Essop just a little. He was a sensitive soul and to cheer him up I continued our game, saying, 'The child is father of the man,' to which he immediately replied, 'Too easy. The child is a man wrapped in his mother's womb.'

'No point crying over spilt milk?'

'Don't waste my time. *Madzi akatayika sawoleka*. Don't fret the loss of waters.'

'A stitch in time?'

'*Pang'onopang'ono ndi mtolo*. Little by little you make a bundle. You are never going to beat me at this game, Josef. I am the greatest at this and always will be. How about the Cameroonian one I heard the other day. She's like a road: pretty but crooked?'

I held up my hands in surrender. 'You win. I can't imagine an English version for that one.'

We both laughed together for a moment and it reminded me of how close we had once been and how, of late, we had been drifting apart.

So I said, 'Look, Essop, come to my place on Friday for sundowners. It's been too long between drinks.'

He grinned as if a great burden had been lifted from him: he had said what he had come to say. Then he shook my hand and made his way to the door, blinking like a mole behind his huge glasses. 'Lovely. Lovely. Yes, that will be lovely. Until then, my friend.'

Sean

MY DAY STARTED BADLY but it got worse. Though I did have a laugh when I popped my head into Stu's office, and there on the wall, huge in size, grotesque in taste, was a painting of Horst. To prove he was the great hunter, he'd clearly briefed the artist to include many a mounted head. So, like a bizarre family reunion, grumpy Uncle Buffalo, elegant Aunt Kudu and the excitable springbok cousins all jostled to get into the frame. Eugene sat in the foreground with a face so simple a kid could capture it with a crayon. The only risk was avoiding caricature, for Horst resembled a Hogarth slob and the artist had dodged this issue by scaffolding Horst's face on a fictional jawline. He stared out of the frame, disappointed at a world that failed to take him as seriously as he took himself.

Having lifted my spirits on Horst's bad taste, and seeing that Stu was nowhere to be found, I settled myself at the bar where, without a word, ancient Alias bent down to the fridge and placed a cold beaded beer in front of me. Alias kept my whistle wet, day slurred into night, and Stella, nocturnal by nature, arrived in this absurdly virginal dress, white, sweet and frilly as cream. But the dress wasn't fooling me. She could wear a habit as black as coal, topped with a wimple pure as snow, I'd still see through her skanky soul. So I took a breath, arming myself for Round Two, but trust Stella, she hit me with a kiss.

'You're in a good mood, sweetheart.'

'This is because the great Daniel Craig is arriving here tonight,' she replied, looking around as if he might actually be hiding behind a pot plant. I resisted saying, 'The odds of Bond turning up are on a par with you becoming Pope, my dear.' Instead I said, 'Well best make it a martini then.'

While ordering, we were joined by the fainting giant, so I said, 'I'm part way through a round, what'll it be, what's your poison? I'm Sean by the way, and this is my fiancée, Stella.'

The giant smiled. 'Carlsberg, thanks. Name's Willem.'

When he shook hands with her, Stella said, 'What a lovely name is Willem,' and I realised Stella, who was generally not nice to anyone, was flirting because she assumed he was famous. And he did look like one of those guys who turn up when they need a baddie with a vaguely South African accent. I asked him what I asked everyone who washed up at this bar, 'What brings you here, Willem?'

'Golf,' he said. 'My wife's a Scot and she dragged me off to live in freezing Edinburgh so I'm here to thaw out. I'm from Zimbabwe originally, so hate the cold.'

'Well, that's your fault for marrying a Scot,' I quipped. 'Celtic roots are long and unforgetting, they always drag you back in the end.'

Willem winked at Stella and joked, 'Careful, lady, this old paddy will drag you back to freezing Dublin in no time.'

Stella's shrieks of false laughter drowned out my reply, 'I'm from Cork actually.' And as Stella was still cackling away, I grabbed Stu who was wandering past and said, 'Hey, Stu, there you are. I've only one thing to say to you. Bond,' cocking my eyebrow, '*James* Bond. Spreading rumours again, Stu. Tut, tut. Stell will be devastated when Daniel Craig doesn't turn up.'

'Just tell her Peter O'Toole and Clooney are coming.'

'Fairly phenomenal considering Peter O'Toole's dead.'

'Is he?' said Stu vaguely then, looking around, he asked, 'Seen Horst anywhere?'

'Thankfully not,' I replied and, noticing Willem was now listening to me, said, 'Let me warn you, Will. Horst is the fool who owns this place. Steer clear of the old bugger if you know what's good for you. He's an enormous prick and...'

Stu developed a facial tic, Willem laughed, and when I said, 'What?' Stu explained, 'Sean: meet Willem. Horst's brother.'

Ah, right you are! That's where I knew the fella from. He wasn't an actor. He was a better-looking version of Horst.

When I protested, 'What about the code, man?' Stu said, 'I was winking like a bastard.' And I replied, 'Well, I just thought you were having a stroke or something.'

Our code was simple: if something bad was coming, or if Stella was on the warpath, Stu would whisper, *Praying mantis*, or he'd clasp his hands in prayer, giving me time to hike it down the golf course.

So when Stu began his dance again, I assumed he was just demonstrating it to Willem, as I was in the middle of explaining, 'Look, no offence, Will, but your brother's a dick,' when – what do you know – Horst crept right up behind me and shouted, 'Howzit everyone. Have you all met my little brother Willem?' Clearly not my night, I thought.

Now there are few things more awkward than Horst entertaining, possessing as he does the social grace of Nixon. And with his brother around, Horst was really playing up the great-host bit. So when Stu's lovely wife Fiona turned up for a drink, Horst made an almighty fuss, shouting, 'This one's on me, everyone!'

This was Horst's favourite line. He thought it showed his terrific sense of humour, when all it did was remind everyone that Horst owned the hotel, the drink you were sucking back and the seat your arse was spread over.

As Fiona told Horst she was too busy, I stared at her balsamic hair and sweet smile and thought what a lucky prick Stu was. We all had a soft spot for Fiona, even Horst who now insisted, 'Hey, I'm your boss, Fiona. Yah? So I'm ordering you to take a break, have a drink, meet my no-good brother Willem.'

Happily, Horst's performance fell apart when his own wife, Marlene, stumbled in. What a sight: a sloppy brunette with a belly swollen over her belt, sad drunken eyes, and the leathery channel between her far-flung breasts so mottled it made me dizzy. When she spotted Willem, she wrapped herself around him, squealing, 'The brother I should've married!' adding a disturbing humping motion to the hug.

Horst's discomfort was sublime. Twitching like a dog with an unreachable itch, he snapped at Alias to sort out Marlene's usual: whisky unlubricated by mixers or ice. Marlene dispatched the drink, tapping Morse code on her empty glass – SOS for a top-up – and things were settling into the dull rhythm of another humid night at the bar, when somewhere along the line I offended Horst. Though it looked tough as an elephant's scrotum, Horst's skin was actually remarkably thin. And midway through one of his African lectures, he was patronising me mercilessly. 'Sean, the real problem is we've all made a monster. A monster called Africa. I'm no racist; I'm just a realist. Do you know much about corn?'

'I know I hate it.'

'Corn's man-made, Sean. We created it from grasses centuries ago. If man doesn't break the husk and replant the seeds, it'll stop growing. It can't harvest itself. It's completely reliant on us to survive. That's what Africa is. Africa is a white creation and blacks can't sustain it without our continued support.'

My reply, 'Without continued *exploitation*,' got a laugh from Marlene, always one to side against her own husband. But then I noticed Horst's fat head turning crimson – and I caught Stu flashing me a don't-annoy-my-boss look – as Horst yelled, 'How often do I need to explain this, you dumb paddy? Corruption isn't a part of the economy: corruption *is* the economy. In the same way oil is the economy of Saudi Arabia, corruption is the Bwalo economy.'

At which point I served Horst my favourite line, 'You white Africans are all alike. You think just because you're born here you own it.' To which Horst returned his favourite riposte, 'Well you expats are worse. Running away from dirty secrets back home. God only knows what shit you are running from, Sean. Terrifies me to think.'

'The problem isn't corn,' I yelled, conscious that everyone was silently watching Horst and me, 'the issue is that Africa is the most over-owned continent in the world. The Dutch, Portuguese, Italian, French, Brits have all used her up like an old whore.'

'Well you know more about old whores than I do,' barked Horst and everyone took in a sharp breath. Christ. I'd walked right into that one. Stella pretended not to hear. I wanted to slap the smile off Horst's face but knew he wouldn't hesitate to hit me back. Eventually, Willem broke the strained silence, 'So the political situation is volatile, this finance chap vanishing...'

'Shhhhh,' I hissed, putting my finger to my lips. 'Don't talk politics, Willem. Learn from the monkeys,' and I covered my mouth, ears, eyes and, finally, my balls. 'Politics is officially off the conversational menu. It's actually illegal to talk politics. Bwalo may look like roses, with its safaris and smiling natives, but it takes a lot of terror to achieve this much peace.'

'Bullshit, Sean,' Horst shouted. 'The Big Man's lost it, he's just another dumb kaffir...' and Fiona spat out the word, 'Eugene!' with such scolding force that Horst spluttered, 'Sorry, Fiona, that slipped out, I meant to say...he's just a dumb *coloured*,' checking if the term was more acceptable but getting an equally appalled look from Fiona. Alias moved down the bar, out of range, Stella stared deep into her drink. Even through his dense lack of awareness, Horst knew he wasn't winning friends. And seeing him up against the ropes, I added a little upper cut. 'This isn't a Klan meeting, you prick. You have to watch yourself, Horst, your Kurtz complex is getting out of control.'

That's when Horst came at me with his fat fists. Willem actually held Horst back as I wobbled on my stool. Then Charlie skipped by – I heard the word *Whore* sliced clean through the hubbub – and in the confusion, I dodged a punch from Horst only to be dragged off, slapped by Stella, and left in the car park staring up at the confusion of stars.

When I finally returned to the bar, Horst thumped my back, giving me the fake crap, 'Don't worry about Stella, she always comes back, eh...like a fucking stray dog...'

'I've no fight left in me, Horst,' I admitted, plonking myself on a stool, raising my hands in surrender.

Horst thought a moment, then said, 'Fair enough, Sean, fair enough.' He snapped his fingers. 'Alias, get the paddy a cold one, he needs it. This one's on me, everyone!'

I sulked and by the time I'd finished that beer I realised it was getting really late. People were peeling off the bar, Marlene was slurring into her whisky, Willem made a shaky exit. But I waited a while longer, dousing my bruised pride in another beer, before bringing out something I'd stored for just such an occasion. 'Hey, Horst, your new portrait is great, by the way. It's really very impressive. I mean it. Beautifully done.'

Assuming our truce still held, Horst quickly checked my face, before saying, 'Thanks, Sean. Yah, cost me a fortune but worth it. That is art, my friend.'

'I don't know much about art,' I replied humbly, waiting a beat, before shouting, 'But I know that ain't it!'

This time Horst raised his hands in surrender, gathered Marlene up like sackcloth, and said, 'Fuck you too, Sean.'

Two beers later and Stu returned, sitting next to me, looking like a beaten dog. 'I'm so sorry about what Charlie said to Stella. No idea where he got that word from.'

'Boy's got a brain like his old man. Relax. *Hakuna matata* and that shite.'

'First thing tomorrow, I'll make Charlie apologise to you.'

'You get a kid to apologise for telling the truth it will mess him up. Forget it.'

We tapped bottles and I was mildly surprised by how maudlin I sounded as I said, 'We started happy, Stell and I. You know? I loved her fire, her pout, her arse, juicy and round as a mango. God really put the time into that one, I tell you. But now everything's crap. And did I tell you I got mugged on

Victoria Ave last week? Boys high on *gak* looked keen to slash my throat.'

'You can only rob a dead man once,' Stu said sagely and, when I didn't say anything, he asked, 'Hey, come on? Are you all right, Sean?'

I didn't reply, I was close to tears and I knew talking was a sure way to open the waterworks. The events of the day suddenly caught up with me and I laid my head delicately into my hands as if holding together a split coconut. Still feeling the threat of tears, I confessed, 'Shit, Stu, I'm being unrealistic trying to do anything here.'

Panicking slightly that I might actually cry, Stu said gruffly, 'Buck up, old boy.'

But I couldn't buck up and my voice thickened as I explained, 'We don't even have working toilets at the university. Place stinks of shit and I'm teaching classes of fifty with two books between all of us. And did I tell you about this bookcase?' Stu tried to get a word in, 'Yes, it's all you talk about...' but I ploughed on, 'Well it's still fucking there! So rotten it can't hold a piece of paper, never mind a book. Falling to bits and each time I scream at the Nazi librarian to throw it out he gives me this doe-eyed look and tells me it's government property, he's waiting for the paperwork to *allow* him to toss it out!' Stu tried to shush me but I wasn't to be stopped. 'That fucking bookcase is the bane of my life. My job's a joke, Stella's a liability, I can't write, I'm making a mess of everything, there's no hope here, Stu, no hope.'

He laid a hand on my back and whispered soothingly, 'Hey, hey, listen, come on, old man, you're doing the best you can. Remember: even a single act has an impact.'

'Scots saying?' I asked and Stu replied, 'Ashanti actually.'

'Ash-a-te,' I muttered, struggling to wrap my drunken tongue around it. 'Ass-tea.'

'Here's another goodie: the salvation of a nation begins in the mind of one man.'

'How about: every man, woman and child shall have my name on their lips?'

'That has to be Hitler,' guessed Stu.

'Nope.'

'Tafumo?'

'Charlie Chaplin.'

'Not far wrong then. Fiona's at me to leave too. Back to Britain, back to the *real world* as she calls it, to run some B&B, hating every cold, wet minute.' Stu stared up at the velvet sky speckled with stars. 'This place spoils you for everywhere else.'

'It's not looking good,' I admitted. 'No sir. But I tell you what'll happen next. Sure as my name's Sean, I'll be back on my kitchen stoop in a few hours, thinking I have to get out of here, how my African adventure is over, and right then, like clockwork, at the darkest hour before the dawn, when my head's filled with badness, my arse frozen to the stoop, that sun will rise and seduce me all over again, pulling up her dark nightie, flashing her mango-yellows and pawpaw-pinks, and I'll think, Ah sure, I'll stay another day.' A mosquito fizzed in my ear. I batted it away. 'Jesus, I'm getting poetic, that's a sure sign I'm pissed. Isn't that right, Stu?'

When no reply came, I turned to see Stu was now face down asleep on the bar. Alias was packing up, midges crowned the lights, and it was that late even the crickets were quiet. Sitting there, I made a small, fundamental, decision, nodding as the idea solidified. Tomorrow, first thing, soon as the sun cracked over the earth, I was going to go to the university and toss that bookcase away. Granted, it wasn't much. But it was something and I smiled, in control again, as I pointed at Tafumo's portrait behind the bar. 'Don't mess this up for me, Big Man. Believe it or not, this is the best gig I've ever had.' Tafumo glared back like a disapproving barman.

Josef

I SAT IN A LISTENING cubicle with my earphones on, eaves-dropping on Horst's office. When I was younger, I'd walk into the Mirage having heard what the members were gossiping about that week and I'd feel like God, like I had access to people's minds. Now that memory brings nothing but shame. Snooping around people's lives for what? To hear that someone slept with someone else's wife, that someone fired their lazy cook, that some minister was taking backhanders.

David hadn't let go of his Horst theory. Twice today he'd brought new transcripts, conversations with words, suspicious words – *codes* – highlighted in yellow. He'd run his highlighter so many times over certain words that parts of the page were wet with ink, dotted with sodden yellow suns.

I was reluctant to give credence to his theory. Horst was cast from an old mould: yet another white man who thought he owned Africa. But this wasn't Zimbabwe; Tafumo wasn't taking Horst's hotel or land. Horst thrived under Tafumo. He wasn't political, he was a racist but not a supremacist, he was no Terre Blanche, he didn't care who was in government as long as he kept making money. Having said all that, I've learned that men rarely do things for rational reasons. The tropics warp white men in strange ways.

Someone entered Horst's office. The door slammed like a starter pistol and a woman shouted, 'You're screwing a kaffir!

Don't deny it, Eugene!' I heard Horst try to deny it with an indignant snort but the woman yelled, 'Don't insult my intelligence, bastard. That tiny dingle-dangle of yours is the only indiscriminate piece of flesh on your bastard body!'

Horst interrupted, 'Just a fucking minute, Marlene!' but she railroaded him. 'Tell me you used a rubber! If you think you're coming near me with that diseased cock you've another thing coming! I'll chop it off, Eugene! When you sleep I'll fucking get the panga and chop your bastard cock right off…' There was another bang, which I assumed was the sound of the office door slamming, then the tick-tack of heels followed by Horst's stomping feet. There was some comedy to it, I suppose, but in the main it was depressing, people's secret lives, the time they wasted, betrayals and anger. I leaned back and waited, letting the static calm me. It was a pleasant noise and I pushed the earphones hard against my head, losing myself in the sound: a soft fizz, like waves against sand, the chatter of guests in the distant lobby, the purr of air conditioners, swish of fans, and someone, as if their lips were pressed against the microphone, whispering into my ears, 'Sefu.'

With my heart beating and beating, I stood and jogged the short distance back to my office, where I unlocked the bottom drawer, extracted my folder, stuffed it under my shirt and told Beatrice to cancel all my meetings. I drove to Patrick's house. The guard, who was one of mine, opened the gates. The house was similar to mine, not as big maybe. Red brick with a green tin roof and white bars bent over its windows.

A week ago Patrick came to me. Told me Jeko had called him into his office and said the World Bank wanted to see the national accounts. As Finance Minister Patrick was responsible for issuing a budget for the World Bank. Diligent as always, Patrick assured Jeko that it had already been submitted to Tafumo for approval. But Jeko shook his head. 'I know you're educated and I'm ignorant but your maths is wrong, minister. You see, the problem we are having is that we can't show deficit. The World

Bank must know we are doing well so we can borrow more money.'

Insulted and angry, Patrick had shouted, 'I'll not have a little man like you tell me how to do my job. I'll talk to Tafumo directly.' Never one to raise his voice, Jeko had apparently whispered back, 'When you talk to me, you talk to Tafumo. Now please, calm yourself down, my friend, and come and look here. I am not the enemy of you, minister. I am here to help. And I've just the thing to assist you with your little problem.' Jeko then opened the drawer of his desk. Patrick leaned over to look. He said at first he was expecting to see a set of fiddled accounts. Inside the drawer was a gun that lay on top of a photograph of Patrick, his wife and children. The photograph was strange, like a holiday snap but taken from a distance. Jeko said nothing more as he slid the drawer shut.

Patrick begged me to talk to Tafumo, to plead his case, ask Tafumo to spare him. I didn't admit that these days I had no more access to Tafumo than the man on the street. Instead I told Patrick he was being irrational, paranoid. I assured him that Jeko was just intimidating him to fiddle the books. And in part, I believed what I said. The truth was that for a long time very few people had actually vanished. After Levi, the country settled into decades of economic prosperity and, for a period, Tafumo became that very African oxymoron: a benevolent dictator.

However, more recently, since the financial crash, when charity and loans dried up, the rumours began again. Two ministers, who had been suspected of subversive activity, had vanished a few months ago. But most of us suspected they had fled to Zambia or Mozambique. I had intercepted calls from them, calls from outside the country, so I knew they had run away. And I said all this to Patrick but he didn't respond, he simply stood in front of me, with his head cast down. Then, before he turned to leave, he looked up just long enough for me to see his dark eyes filling with tears.

I walked down to the end of the garden and saw some of Patrick's servants were still living there, waiting for him to return, eating dinner on the hard mud compound just outside the *kaya*. Dusk had set in and the only illumination was from a fire and an outside light above the *kaya* door that splattered weak yellow light around the figure of a woman and a child. Flying ants bashed against the bulb and fell dazed to the floor. The woman picked them up, plucked their wings, and threw their bodies into the frying pan where they sizzled and popped into blackened mince. The boy was expertly rolling *nsima* into a ball, punching a hole into it with his thumb, filling the hole with the mince, tipping his head back to drop the dirty blob into his mouth. Then the woman sat, methodically dragging a metal comb through her hair in slow sensual motions, placing it back in the coals before repeating the movement. When I got closer, she sprang to her feet, ironing her *chitenge* with her hands. She made the slightest gesture and the boy scampered, leaving his metal bowl of food, which was quickly clouded with flies.

'You know me,' I said. She nodded and I caught a whiff of burnt hair.

'Where has Patrick gone? Did they leave in someone's car? With a friend?'

She looked puzzled, as if it were a trick question. Then she turned, her bare feet slapping the soil as she ran into the *kaya*. I went after her and when I got to the door I looked in and she was crouched in the gloom, her boy tucked up in the corner, watching. A uniform hung on a nail; the only other clothes she had was a threadbare *chitenge* draped over a mattress on the floor. Her sink was a plastic bowl. Neatly arranged on a piece of folded newspaper was a bar of Lifebuoy soap, a comb with many missing teeth, a tub of Vaseline and a Bic pen. A life's worth of possessions.

I shouted, 'Don't you run from me,' but she turned and handed me some paper. 'This is the place for Patrick's mother.'

As I returned to my car, I considered heading straight to the address. But it was a few hours' drive away and I was exhausted, the ceaseless pain from my tooth acting like a hole through which all my energy drained. So instead I drove the short distance home.

Ezekiel, my guard, waved and opened the gates. I glanced at the blinking light of the security camera as I drove in. 'Everything ok, Ezekiel?' He came to attention, an old man's best impression of a soldier. 'Yes, sah, all safe and all sound.' I'd bought him a new uniform, but he insisted on wearing his old one. He'd wear it until it disintegrated, shredded off him like old skin. His cheap polyester dungarees, an insignia of a lion on the chest, had been repatched so many times it was hard to discern their original colour. And instead of the army boots I'd got him he had on his dirty wellingtons.

When I got into the house Ruby was washing dishes. 'Evening, master, would you like some dinner?' She wiped her hands on a tea towel and awaited my reply. Just to the left of her I saw my reflection in the kitchen window and was struck by how we now seemed the same age. When I first hired Ruby she'd seemed ancient, a grandmother, a woman old before her time, worn out by a hard life. Now I'd caught up and we looked like contemporaries, me and my old maid. 'No, I'm not hungry, thank you.'

She turned back to the sink but I stayed, studying her. This old servant, in her blue headscarf – I'd never once seen her hair – with her cracked mud-brown heels: she was the thread that weaved through everything. I'd hired Ruby when Hope and I first married and she had cared for me, cooked for me, and then accepted Rebecca as my new wife. And when Rebecca died Ruby had cared for Solomon.

I left her to clean up and went to check on Solomon. I sat on his bed, watching him sleep a while before I went to my bedroom, opening the door to my walk-in wardrobe where I kneeled down. Sweeping aside my shoes, I used my fingernails to pull up the floorboard, and into the space below I secreted my folder. Having replaced the board, I realised I was too tired to even make it to bed. So I lay on the floor, allowing exhaustion to smother me.

Hope

LOVE HAS A LIFE of its own. After he beat me, our love lived on. After I left him and went to live in the palace, it lived on. When he tried to reconcile he ruined it by boasting about a new promotion. Even as I sat hating him – hating all foolish men and their silly pride – our love lived on. When he became a minister and attended palace meetings, when we saw one another but no longer talked. When he remarried so quickly and finally had a son. Even when his second wife died recently, my love still believed he might try me again. I was disappointed and relieved when he didn't. Yet still, our love lived on.

When I left him, friends told me to leave Bwalo. But why should I leave a country I loved? So instead I packed up my life and went to live in the baobab wing of the palace. I knew the day I moved in that the palace had become more than just my livelihood. It became my shelter and my cage, my home and my life. And I realised how important it was to keep my position there. But I understood something about Tafumo that would ensure I kept my job. It was a simple thing but it didn't flow with logic. It moved against the current. People assume tyrants desire capitulation. But if you submitted to Tafumo, he disposed of you. So as staff came and went, only Essop and I remained. I stayed because I never completely submitted. Essop joked that he stayed because Tafumo hadn't noticed he was still there.

Did it flatter me that I was never fired? Did I believe unseen emotions tied us? I suppose such foolish notions may have filled my head from time to time. Nursing a powerful, charming man, it's hard for emotions not to creep in. And I wasn't always an old woman, you know; I still carry the young woman I was inside me.

Sometimes when Tafumo took residency at his lake house – away from the ludicrous palace and inhuman scale of everything – more human-sized thoughts settled in. He took a skeletal staff: Jeko, Chef, and he never went anywhere without Essop, who he called Lin, his tongue. One summer he had ministers up to the lake house and they drank and basked on the rocks like sea lions. That night Tafumo suffered a migraine.

When Essop came to get me, he caught my arm and said, 'Take care, Hope.' In my rush, I assured Essop I always took care of him but when I got to the room, I saw Essop wasn't asking that I be good to Tafumo. He'd been warning me to watch myself. Tafumo smiled like a drunken monkey. He was naked. This was long before his body became a part of my ordinary every day – before I helped him dress and swapped his colostomy bags – so I was shocked. Below his leathery belly his cock swung like the thick rope off a buoy. He demanded a vitamin injection. A concoction created by his doctor, which had no vitamins in it but was a brew of amphetamines and testosterone. I was preparing the injection, expelling bubbles, when I felt a claw bite my thigh. I turned, thinking he was falling, grabbing hold for support, but the hand was shooting up my skirt and I slapped him, swiping the needle across his hand. We stopped, watched blood rise in a thin smile, I felt heat pour off him, that same rage that Josef released upon me so many times. But Tafumo cooled. He slumped back, hung his head and, like a wounded animal, raised his paw for me to mend.

When I returned to my room, Essop was there asking if I was OK. I told him I was fine but the moment he touched my shoulder, tears came, and I pressed my body into his, the first contact in

63

years that wasn't violent but tender, like a brother protecting me against the world.

Life went on, the incident was never mentioned, and it sunk into the vague sediment below memory. But that faint scar, like a pencil line a child tried so hard to rub out, reminded me it was true. It happened. The line drawn across a time when I'd been a foolish girl and Tafumo the great King had proven himself to be just another man. A time when I'd still believed the world was good, that truth and faith were all I needed and that Levi really had died in an accident. I looked at that line now as I pushed Tafumo around his palace to look at all his paintings, to remind himself of his own importance.

Tafumo gazed at one of his favourite landscapes and I stood patiently waiting, tuning in to the sound of the sprinklers outside, imagining the twisted hoses to be a feast of snakes tittering as they wasted water, jeering at the parched land that lay beyond the palace. I hated this musty old museum room. Like many others, it was modelled on some room in Buckingham Palace: gloomy, dark, oppressive. And many of these paintings were counterfeits of those that hung in the Queen's own residence, this replica room full of fake Masters. Even the palace air conditioning was kept low, a brittle chill pervading the rooms. So utterly British was the atmosphere that at times I was surprised to see Africa outside. As if the windows were paintings and the paintings were windows. The dark bulletproof glass enhanced the illusion that the windows framed exotic African art, while the paintings captured real views of the glum English countryside.

On the way back to Tafumo's bedroom we stopped short. Down the corridor came another fake, another counterfeit. This one a copy of Tafumo himself; a young and powerful doppel-ganger. Young Tafumo bowed, 'Excellency.' And Old Tafumo nodded. Then Young Tafumo walked on, off to warm up the nation, to drive down streets lined by people waving flags and chanting, 'Ta-fu-mo!' Sham double of a sham leader.

After my shift, I walked down the warped corridor to my room. I remembered Tafumo giving me a string of pearls not long after the lake incident. I got them and went to the kitchen where Essop was sipping tea and I joked, 'Are you the cook these days?'

'Might be a good move,' Essop replied. 'I could impress you with my cooking instead of boring you with my folk stories.'

'You're in the right job. You bore me well.'

Essop wore the same clothes he always had, frozen in the eighties with his bad suits, and something about this made me happy. He handed me a bag. 'Chef said it's beef with horseradish, as you like. Maybe I could make you lunch one day. We've not sat for a long time.'

'That'd be nice. Have you found yourself a good wife yet?'

With a cheeky smile, Essop joked, 'I'm married to Tafumo.'

'That's a shame because I'm married to Tafumo too.'

When Essop whispered, 'So many wives so little love,' I quipped, 'So many servants so few friends,' and we shared a secret smile.

I sat and Essop poured me some tea. I added milk. He watched me closely and when I looked up his eyes shot down as I said, 'What story will you bore me with today?'

'The biggest story of all. The story of a nation. Our history is not the one in textbooks,' he paused, 'no offence to the great history Josef wrote...' I waved my hand to show no offence was taken, and Essop continued, 'Like all nations, ours was built on the backs of slaves. When the Ngoni came they made the Tumbuka their slaves. The Ngoni sliced the tongues and lips off the Tumbuka. Some Ngoni women grew their thumbnails especially for the purpose of gouging eyeballs out of Tumbuka rebels.'

'That's disgusting, Essop.'

'History is disgusting, Hope. When missionaries came they asked the Ngoni if they could educate their children. But the Ngoni were too smart for this trick. Ngoni didn't want Christians softening their violent hearts. So instead of sending their own children, they sent the children of their Tumbuka slaves. So you see. The Ngoni sowed the seeds of their own demise by permitting their slave children the power of education. Only a generation later, those children of slaves were equipped to thrive in the new world, leaving the Ngoni for dust. It was these educated Tumbuka children that grew up and took on important administrative and colonial positions. It was these slave children that grew up and rewrote their own Tumbuka history and even convinced the white man they were the more powerful tribe and, according to their history, they had the rights to large tracts of Ngoni land. One of the rare times history has been written by the losers. The Tumbuka out-foxed their oppressors. Over time, Tumbuka became the official language, metaphorically slicing Ngoni tongues. Tumbuka used words as spears and because of their education they continued to be chosen for important bureaucratic jobs, as Ngoni grew weak and incapable of adapting. So you see, Hope, ultimately victory will go to the slaves, to servants, teachers, nurses, translators, who each day rise quietly to the top. The seeds of the future live in the children of slaves.'

I sipped my tea and said, 'I know, Essop. I'm a child of slave children. I am Tumbuka.'

Essop smiled gently and replied, 'Yes, Hope. I too am Tumbuka.'

Josef

WHEN I WOKE ON my wardrobe floor I was too tired to move. My tongue strummed the raw nerve of my tooth and the pain jolted me to my feet. I went to Solomon's room and listened to the rhythm of his breathing. His desk was piled with books. I flicked through *Bwalo History*, a book I'd written. Every Bwalo child knew the first sentence by heart: *A barefooted boy left his village to begin a journey that ended in him becoming King*.

According to the book, Tafumo was descended from the great Chewa tribe, 'splintering off the tail of the *mfecani*, settling on the spine of the lake, to build the bones of our glorious nation'. Textbook-Tafumo was a boy whose village was razed by colonial police, whose father was murdered, who walked miles to find a man who educated him and sent him to the UK to train as a doctor, to learn the ways and weaknesses of the British so he could return to Bwalo to defeat them.

All lies. Tafumo was distinguished only by greed. His mother died in childbirth; he fattened himself on her, emerging a brilliant sword drawn from a weary sheath. He was born in a nameless village, son of unknown parents from a small, unremarkable tribe. Most men accept their insignificance but into hollow obscurity Tafumo poured legend.

The greatest lie was that Tafumo was Bwalo born. In fact, his village was on the wrong side of the border. But as many hands wear a rough oar smooth, so a story many times told will start to ring true. Now even I struggled to feel false splinters. But I knew that first sentence, the most apocryphal-sounding, was true. Only a detail was missing: *A barefooted boy left his village to begin a journey that ended in him becoming King, and by his side walked his friend*, Sefu.

Tafumo didn't walk alone. I walked with him. I have always walked with him. Our true story lacked the drama that seasoned the textbook. Our village wasn't burned, our fathers weren't slaughtered. It was a more basic story that began the day a man drove to our village and showed us there was more to the world than mud, maize and chickens. A man with a car and a suit: unimaginable things for boys born in dirt. And while the rest of us wanted to talk to the man and touch him, Tafumo wanted to become him. The man had a car radio that we listened to for so long the battery ran flat and we had to jumpstart his car. And while the village talked about the magic music box, Tafumo remembered something else: a news report of the Queen saying her Commonwealth covered a third of the earth. It sparked a hunger in Tafumo for more than just food.

That night Tafumo told me we were going to become great men. We were to run away, educate ourselves like the man with the car. Tafumo knew of a missionary school across the border. My parents were dead and I lived with my aunt and, though I knew I would miss her, I trusted Tafumo. He had always protected me and I trusted him with my life. Due to lack of records, our age remains a mystery but I suspect we were barely teenagers when we ran away.

Following only vague direction we trekked through bush, terrified of animals. That area now has no animals, the wild has been driven north in search of moisture, but back then it was overrun by lions. We barely slept. Waking each morning more tired than the last, until Tafumo fell ill and for days I carried him on my back. And while I carried him, he told me what our story was. Speaking in a daze, like a witch doctor in a trance, he said

68

we were born in Bwalo, from a powerful Chewa village that had stood against colonial tax, fought to the death, and we were all that remained.

Words poured from his lips like sustenance for our starving bodies. Nodding and walking, I digested my new life as delirium dissolved my past. I couldn't know it then but his story would one day elevate us from dirt to power, mud to mansions. I carried him for days until finally we came to a courtyard where children sat in the shade of the kachere tree, writing with chalk on slate as nuns sang the ABC.

A priest ran over to us, 'Children, what's happened?' I was about to tell him we'd run away, that we needed to go back to our village. But before I spoke, Tafumo whispered from my back, like a voice in my head, 'We are Chewa. Our village was burned by colonial police. We need help, Father, we have nowhere to go.'

I noticed one of the priest's ears was odd; he had no right ear, no flesh around it, no lobe, just a hole. Seeing I'd noticed, he explained in his funny singing voice, 'It looks odd but still works fine. My full ear hears everything in this world but this special ear, it hears all the lies and fallacies. So here's the deal, my sons. I'll take you on, educate and introduce you to the one true God, but only if you promise that's the last time you lie to me. Understand?' I felt Tafumo's head nod against my shoulder, before I collapsed.

The first thing Father Lane did was rechristen us. Tafumo became Philip, a name he dropped when he left the missionary. I became Josef, the secret disciple. I wonder if Father Lane knew how accurate his name for me was. Was it so clear, even then, that Tafumo shone with a light of leadership while I was marked with the zeal of a disciple? Father Lane taught us everything. Prepared us for life. Though he could never entirely rub out our boyhood traditions, he added to them, teaching us what he called the True Trinity: God, the Father; the wise son, Shakespeare; and the Holy Genius, Einstein.

God, literature and science, he told us, were all the tools a man needed to see and fix the world. Father Lane taught us God's laws – Do not kill. Do unto others as you would have done unto yourself – lessons so childishly simple I foolishly outgrew them. But the main lesson he imparted was a story old as man, of good and evil, devil and God. He taught us that we – Tafumo and I, and all Bwalo people – were the victims of evil. And that his own people, his white brothers and sisters, were the perpetrators of that evil. Father Lane showed us the devil: and the devil was him. It was the warped irony of the empire that their own missionaries taught us that what they were doing to us was wrong, unchristian, unforgivable. Tafumo and I took different paths of the Trinity – I took to Shakespeare; he to Einstein – but we both spoke from a young age of freeing Bwalo. From dust, Father Lane created two great idealists and Tafumo and I left that school filled with the word of God and a desire to change our world. It's taken me becoming an old man to realise just how much Father Lane taught me. And how completely I've failed to live up to his lessons.

After missionary school, I did an English degree at Bwalo University, where I stayed on to become a lecturer. Tafumo's insatiable intelligence took him further; he won a Commonwealth scholarship to the University of London to train as a doctor. The day Tafumo left for London, we drank together. Using my old name, only done on the rarest of occasions, he said, '*Sefu*. No one knows us here in the city, us country boys from far away. You must keep our secret. When I'm away you'll tell me when the time's ripe to return. Great changes are sweeping Africa and you and I will bring freedom to Bwalo.' The idealistic words of a young man? Maybe, but so far everything he'd told me had come true. So I clinked my glass with his, and said, 'Yes, brother.'

Bwalo was a late bloomer, the last nation to break free, well into the eighties. In their last years, the British clung on with the desperate grip of a master who knew his power was coming to an end. By the time I'd become a junior lecturer, we were ghosts of our own nation. We couldn't vote. Only whites could shop in supermarkets. We had to buy goods through a letterbox. *No*

Natives No Dogs! We sat at the back of buses even when no white sat up front. We weren't allowed to own more than a measly strip of land. We were a people primed for revolution and it was then that Tafumo told me to start a party and I formed uMunthu with my academic contemporaries Levi, Essop, Patrick and Boma. The name uMunthu was Essop's idea. It meant: I am because we are. I am human because of others. Vague enough not to raise suspicion with the authorities, it was an inspired choice.

Tafumo told me to form, but not lead, uMunthu. Said I was more effective moving people from below. So Levi, the dean of the university, became uMunthu's secretary. Like all of us, Levi was an academic, not a politician or a man of the world. He was a man of theory who knew we needed a powerful figurehead to overthrow the British. So slowly, gently, I convinced these men that Tafumo was the man for the job. Being a tiny nation, we were not rich in options; not many Bwalo men had made their mark on the world in the way Tafumo had. Tafumo had done much of the hard work; already a famous orator on the international stage, adding his voice to the rallying cry of Kaunda, Banda and the independence movement. He'd become rich and powerful, a doctor treating white people no less, with his own London practice. He'd written anti-federation manifestos, travelling the world demanding Bwalo independence. This Chewa son was the perfect candidate, I told them. It wasn't hard to persuade them and once uMunthu agreed Levi called and invited Tafumo to lead us.

Days later Tafumo called me. We'd not seen each other since the sixties and our twenty years of correspondence had been by letter only. He sounded strange, posh, with barely an echo of his warm African vowels, as he said, 'Well done, *Sefu*. Everything is ready. We'll rise up together, we shall free our people. I'm returning to set all of Bwalo on fire.'

Before Tafumo's return, we promoted him as our great hope, printing a manifesto detailing how Tafumo and uMunthu would break the colonial monopoly on land and end the suppression of our language. We entitled the pamphlet: *Kwacha*. Meaning *dawn*, the word had grown beyond its roots to signify the movement, a new birth, freedom. The word acquired such power it became illegal. Our nervous masters beating and imprisoning us just for saying it. Days before his return, Tafumo told me to organise a protest. Forever the invisible hand conducting us.

On a drowsy afternoon, hundreds of us led by Levi marched to Colonial House. It was a peaceful protest and we were turning to leave when I heard the dull thump and mean hiss of tear-gas canisters. The students were brave, chanting *kwacha* as they marched towards armed police. Three men, students whom I taught, were shot dead that day. Tafumo told me to hold a joint funeral. This time thousands came and as the bodies were lowered we sang the word *kwacha*, our voices rising with the dust. But before the ceremony ended, the police arrived and beat us. They beat our people at a funeral for three innocent men. It sparked chaos and indignation. Essop and I were badly beaten. We preached peaceful resistance but that night, as Hope dressed my wounds, my Christian heart was tested. I wanted to kill every white man I saw. And I knew my feelings resounded in the hearts of every Bwalo man. It was time for Tafumo's return.

But beyond the photograph of him on the pamphlet, few knew who Tafumo was. He'd been away for twenty years and when he returned, even I barely recognised him. Tafumo was transformed. He wore a suit, an odd hat called a Homburg; even his tongue had forgotten its Chichewa, hence the need to hire Essop as translator. Tafumo had travelled so far to the other side he could no longer see where he began.

So when he emerged from the plane looking like an English doctor, we were shocked. Was *this* our saviour? The vast crowd, spreading out towards the horizon, clapped but it was far from hysterical. Even Hope said to me, 'Is that him?'

He squinted as he descended. Then, stepping on to the tarmac, he got on his knees and kissed the earth causing the crowd to scream and sing. He remained prostrate, a servant come to assist his many masters, and we roared until he walked to the podium, where his foreign accent shocked us back into a silence that held us in its spell.

'Bwalo, tonight you go to bed prisoners. And your jail is your own country.'

We shouted, an ambiguous sound, as if turning against him.

Then he yelled, 'But tomorrow – *tomorrow!* – you will wake up – *yes!* – you will wake up – *yes!* – and you will be free!' and we cried, 'Free!' and he screamed, 'Free!'

The ring of police, their dogs on taut leashes, tightened around us. Deliberately, Tafumo pointed to each of the policemen, one by one, turning in a slow circle, and each time he pointed we sang, 'Free!' There was a slight echo as Essop translated Tafumo's words into Chichewa but the crowd sang back in English, the oppressor's tongue.

Tafumo stared at one of the police officers, didn't take his eyes off him, as he leaned into the microphone and said three names, the names of the dead students, 'William Kilembe, Chimango Waya, Alfred Sibale.'

Before he had even spoken the third name, the crowd was already screaming, a confused, angry noise. Police tightened their circle, the crowd pushed back, skirmishes broke out, but before violence erupted, Tafumo held his fist to the sky and we fell silent.

Slowly, raising a finger to denote each demand, his fist flowered as he declared, 'My food! My tongue! My soul!' Provoking a deafening howl that forced the police back.

Then Tafumo whispered something. At first so quiet few could hear. Gradually he increased his volume and Essop didn't need to translate. For Tafumo spoke just one word, our word – the one they stole from us – louder and louder from deep within him, rising up his throat, until his face was tilted so the sun shone against his screaming lips delivering the word over and over: '*Kwa-cha! Kwa-cha! Kwa-cha!*'

73

And we echoed his chant, so that long after he'd stepped off the podium into the crowd, the word pulsed through the air as we reached to touch him, grab him, to lay pelts over his shoulders, so that by the time he emerged from within us, his suit was hidden below layers of animal skins and he was African again. He was us. And when I turned to kiss her, Hope was crying uncontrollably.

He stepped off the plane a man but left the airport a god. In the car park we met. He pushed through the people and greeted me politely, as one might address a stranger. Hope shook his hand but before we could say anything more, Tafumo was spun away. So careful and cold was his handshake that I wondered if I'd changed as much as he had, if he'd forgotten it was me, not heard my name as I shouted it over the noise of the crowd. But before stepping into the car, he turned, staring down the tunnel of people between us, and he didn't nod and he didn't smile, but he was telling me he knew it was me and that everything was about to change for ever.

It was then that I grabbed Hope, got down on one knee, she cried and nodded, and the people around us cheered. We kissed and though I couldn't tell Hope why, as we walked home hand-in-hand, I knew our life was going to be good. It was in the afterglow of that time that I believed what I did I did for the cause, for freedom, *kwacha*.

Tafumo rewarded my silence and loyalty. And I'll admit it was fun. For a village boy to walk in expensive shoes down the marble corridor of his friend's palace. My secret friend. In the early days Tafumo and I played formal if we were in company but as soon as everyone left, we relaxed and backstabbed the ministers. The time between those informal moments soon stretched. But Tafumo wasn't always sanctimonious. Back then his charm was so potent that when he was happy all around him were happy, his mood so expansive it flooded the nation. He loved to start silly rumours. He once told the British High Commissioner that he had kissed the Queen on the lips. The Commissioner spared no time in spreading the story. Days later a spy relayed the rumour which – filtered through black and white tongues – returned with embroidery: not only had Tafumo stolen a kiss, but the Queen now sent him a rose on the same day each year. Tafumo loved this.

All was not perfect, of course. Cracks in uMunthu were already starting to show. I wasn't yet a minister; Tafumo had told me that I was better placed at ground level, where people would still talk to me openly and tell the truth. So I was at none of the cabinet meetings with Levi and Tafumo. I'd only heard through Essop of Tafumo's quiet rage when pushed by Levi to agree to democratic elections. *Everything I say is law, everything.* I assumed Tafumo was merely disagreeing on the timing, rather than the principle.

So I thought little of it when I went early to pick up Hope from the palace one day and had my regular meeting with Tafumo, where I told him that the rumours around the university were that Levi was furious about being scolded in the meeting. That he was threatening to form a new political party to contest Tafumo, to force his hand, to bring about democratic elections. Tafumo's reaction was mild. He just laughed and said, 'Levi is a clever man but his skin is thin. Josef, you're a good man, thank you, old friend. And do not fret, good things are coming your way.' Then I told Tafumo of my wedding to Hope and I asked if he would attend. He smiled that vast charming smile of his. 'For you, *Sefu*, of course, it would be an honour.'

Our wedding day was bright with joy until Hope pulled me aside and said, 'Where's Levi?' I made a phone call but Levi didn't answer. It was his brother. And when I joked, 'Moses, we're waiting for your brother to come and eat, the dinner is being eaten by Boma, there'll be nothing left,' there was a long silence, until Moses finally replied, 'Levi is gone, Josef. Something has happened.'

I went straight to Tafumo. I didn't care that he was drunk and holding a captive audience of admirers. We walked through the house, smiling at guests, Tafumo nodding at the women who tried to stop him as he passed. Tafumo and I sat in the back of his Rolls-Royce and I said, 'What's happened?' Tafumo looked forward, let out a tired sigh, and said, 'I sent one of my men, Jeko, to talk to Levi, calm him down, tell him not to fight me politically, assure him I was as open to democracy as he was but not yet and…'

When he stopped talking I wasn't sure if Tafumo would explain anything more. He eventually finished his sentence, but he did so without saying the actual words, 'Levi fought back, things got out of control.'

That was the first time I'd heard Jeko's name. Tafumo didn't speak for a while, he read me well, he didn't fill the silence with explanation or justification. He was smarter than that: he let me do that. Then he turned, looked hard into my eyes, and said, '*Sefu*, it's sad, I didn't want it to happen. You must know that?'

I nodded before I really considered the question fully. I looked at Tafumo closely, as if seeing him properly for the first time. I wondered if this could really be the same boy who I'd once carried on my back through the bush. He seemed so alien in his fine suit, sitting in his immaculate car. And I realised that Tafumo had become that man; that man who all those years ago had driven to our village wearing a suit, impressing us all with his car radio. That one image had stayed with Tafumo. He had held on to it, imagining it for so long that it had come to life. There sat a man who had literally carved himself from nothing, from an image, from the air itself. And I wondered just how much a man would do to keep that image alive.

'Everything I do, I do for the nation,' Tafumo explained. 'We've come a long way and we've longer to go. But it's time to grow up, *Sefu*, life isn't so clear as we thought. Now you must take the next step, take Levi's position as dean of the university and lead the next generation. Democracy will come, uMunthu lives on, but it will take time and care.'

This was Tafumo's power. It mattered not if he was sitting on a tree stump in our village, telling me we would run away to be educated, or if he sat, as he did that day, cocooned in the soft leather of his Rolls-Royce; he somehow made me feel like I was king. And I fell under his spell: Tafumo the witch doctor, who didn't use roots and blood to mix his magic but potions of people's hopes, ambitions and dreams.

How many times have I thought of that moment? Have I remembered the day that I saw the world as it really was? I wish in some way Tafumo had been more of a monster. More of an Amin, a Mugabe. If he'd slaughtered thousands, kept the severed heads of enemies in his fridge, amputated the hands of children, sliced the tongues of dissenters, then – I tell myself – then, I would never have stayed. I'd never have stood and watched. But Tafumo was a subtle devil. His was a quiet terror that lived under the unspoiled surface. He worked with a doctor's methodical touch, bit by bit, *pang'onopang'ono*, so I and others could convince ourselves that each new violent act was unavoidable, inevitable.

That's what I've been telling myself for years. A man can justify anything. Sitting in that car, I reassured myself that I didn't kill Levi. I was merely a messenger. I told myself everything I did was a necessary evil. Now I know that's just the devil's excuse. With the country still fresh with freedom, I told myself I was fighting for principles greater than one man, greater than friendship. I was fighting for the cause, for *kwacha*, for uMunthu. The remainder of the wedding was an uneasy blur, smiling at everyone, working my way through as best I could. And long after Tafumo and most of the guests were gone, I sat on the *khondi* with the original uMunthu and, looking at my friends, I knew that this night was the last night of our innocence; nothing was ever to be the same.

The others were conscious of Levi's absence. Boma joked about the fact Levi was sulking about his cabinet quarrels with Tafumo. Essop was worried; either he had heard something or, like Hope, he was simply close enough a friend to know something wasn't right with me. Weeks later, the newspaper would finally announce that Levi had died in a car accident. The funeral was family-only and we didn't attend.

But that night, before they all knew what had happened, our world was still intact. I remember that Boma was joking with Hope that witch doctors were preparing a curse for Tafumo. 'Better keep your eyes open, Hope,' he warned. 'Make sure there are no chicken bones or snakeheads under his bed.' Joining in on the joke, Essop said, 'Collect every strand of hair, each nail clipping. That's what the *mutimen* use. Did you know Shaka Zulu even had a man walk near him so when he spat he would spit on the man's back, rubbing it into the man's skin so no *mutimen* could steal it.' We all laughed loudly, all of us too sophisticated, too educated, to believe in such hokum any more.

And when Patrick had finally staggered home and Boma was splayed out snoring on the sofa, Essop walked me down to the garden and asked, 'Where's Levi?' When I didn't reply, Essop knew. He understood. I could see. In the way he reacted, in the way sorrow filled his eyes. Forever Tafumo's messenger, I heard myself parroting his words, 'Listen to me. This is not easy, a terrible thing. But it is time we grew up, Essop. Life isn't so clear as we thought. This is the way it has to be until we change things for the better.' Essop looked at me like a child, desperate for assurance that the world was not what it had just become. I gently placed my hand on his back, as Essop fought his tears.

If you dress up a lie enough it becomes a principle. But it wasn't long before Tafumo whittled my mighty principles down to banalities. Today I flick through his list of banned publications, spiralling out of control, trying to shut out the world. First came the silly prohibition of long hair, then the puritanical ban on short skirts, followed by the frigid censorship of kissing in movies. Father Lane scolded us if we argued over trivial things: *Pettiness works like the putsi fly, boys. Burrowing under the skin, multiplying inside your organs and consuming you from the inside out, until you're left hollow.*

Pettiness consumed Tafumo. He once went so far as to ban a song that mentioned a woman named Angelina. Which was the name of his lady-in-waiting, Mama Angelina. A silly pop song by Dylan? Was this really what struck fear into the heart of the lion? Was this why I'd turned on colleagues, betrayed friends?

I often wondered why Tafumo didn't kill me at the start. Didn't dispense of the one man who might reveal he wasn't Chewa, wasn't Bwalo, that his was merely a life of greed and lies, not destiny and fate. I was a living liability. If they discovered Tafumo's rise to power was predicated on little more than a boyhood lie, he'd have been dragged from the palace and beaten to death by a vengeful mob. Maybe in the intoxicating haze of adulation that heralded his return, he needed to hold on to a sliver of his past.

I closed the book. A stylised sunrise with cartoon rays splayed across the cover. This false history had once seemed harmless. No different from other nations that imagined themselves into existence. All countries contrive bloody fairy tales to lend credence to illusory borders scribbled by men. But now I know it's a disgrace. I began life as a teacher seeking truth; I'm ending it as an old liar. We say children are the only hope, for they have no memory of what came before. Yet here I was filling them with fresh lies, even my own son.

I returned to my wardrobe, took out my folder, and began to write on Levi's delicate page. Not scrimping, nor editing myself out, I unpicked my propaganda. Time is a powerful acid that dissolves the past. It has made me forget so many sins. Now it seems my body is falling asleep but my mind is waking up again, reminding me of all the terrible things I've done. Father Lane said we look for blame everywhere, always at other people, friends, neighbours, relatives, in the weather, the stars, moon, blaming the dead, spirits, ancestors, holding history itself accountable, when all we need do is look closer, not outside, nor beyond but right here, *Sefu*, close as can be, right here inside, at nothing and no one else but me.

79

Jack

FANTASTIC TOOK US TO a village with ten mud huts and a ring of people sitting around a fire. They seemed unsurprised to see us. Fantastic sat and talked to the men, while I was taken to a hut where a boy showed me a yoga mat on the hard floor and said, 'Bed.'

Soon as the kid left, I got my torch, pulled the case out and opened it. I tapped it: a false bottom. I waited before I acted. I knew if I tore the material that was harder to hide than some popped fliplocks. I could say I dropped the case and the fliplocks broke. But if I tore the material, this false top, sewn so delicately together, there was no way of putting that right. I lay low on the floor, eyes close to the case, and without tearing too much, I tugged at the material. As I aimed my torch through the dark slit something glinted – a row of teeth? Gold fangs? Possibly nails. Certainly not chemicals. And as I tugged a little more it made a sharp sound and I saw a thin slice of blue light shining down the barrel, the gleaming eyeball of a telescopic lens and, embedded in felt, a clutch of bullets.

THE HEN

Bwalo Radio

D J CHEESEANDTOAST HERE TO *start your day the Bwalo way. Two days until the Big Day! Remember what your mother told you: never send an elephant to do a cheetah's job. Ha! Newsflash, listeners: Truth arrives today. A soul singer visiting the sweet soul of Africa. And as if life couldn't get better, this week our national beer, Chibuku, will be half price. Shake shake Chibuku to go with the good time. Yes yes! Bwalo FM thanks Tafumo, for it's under the wise and foresighted leadership of His Excellency that we're broadcasting today. Now, beautiful people of Bwalo, it's time for some sweet ear candy: here's the new song, 'Doctor Love', by Bwalo's own soul sensation, Young Buck. Praise the Ngwazi.*

Charlie

*C*LICK!

'Dad, did you know an aardvark eats a hundred thousand termites a day?'

'I'm busy, buddy, what do you need?'

'I need to know why you came to Africa?'

'Um?'

'Well what did you want to be when you were young?'

'Fairly sure hotel manager wasn't high on the list. All I knew was I didn't want to be my dad. He never left our town. Ironic, really, as he was a cab driver. Dad was dour.'

'What's dour?'

'Everything in life was a vice. I went to university, Dad said, What's Edinburgh got that we havenae? I joined VSO, Dad said, Sounds like a VD.'

'Who's VD?'

'Nothing. Delete that. I came here because of a great Scot: David Livingstone. He said: If you have men who'll only come if they know there is a good road, I don't want them. I want men who'll come if there's no road at all. For those men shall see what others have never seen, such glories as only gazed upon by angels in flight.'

'Sounds pretty boring.'

Click!

Charlie

RUMOURS BECAME REAL TODAY: the celebrities arrived. It was the most incredible day of my whole entire life. Ed, Dad and I took the Mirage bus to the airport to pick up Truth, his dancers and the journalists. Usually there's one plane a week; today there was a traffic jam in the sky. Lear jets too! Which Dad said are planes for the disgustingly rich. Dad bought me a Fanta at the arrivals bar and we sat with Dr Koma, who told us he was 'Off to the UK to make some pounds'. When Dad said, 'Now tell me, Dr Koma, do you plan on returning in twenty years to take over the country?' Dr Koma looked very uncomfortable, like he had ants in his pants.

Another plane landed, dazzled passengers poured out, their pale skins silver in the sun, and Dad said, 'Check out the hairy backpackers.' They looked happy, two young men both with long streaming hair. Dr Koma, Dad and I shared a smile. Dad got another round in and, as I finished off my second Fanta, passengers began arriving through the gate, and we saw the now unhappy backpackers with long faces but very short hair.

Dad pointed at the plane and said, 'My metal bird eats all your talented sons and shits out bald backpackers.' Dr Koma thought this was so funny and they shook hands as Dad said, 'Best of luck, Doc, watch those British nurses, they'll be all over you.'

Handing me the cardboard *Mirage* sign, Dad said, 'Come on, champ, let's rustle up some Z-list celebs.' The first out of the gate were the dancers. Truth had more dancers than Tafumo. Truth's dancers were black as well but, as Mum had had to explain to me many times, not all black people are from Africa. Though originally, Mum said, everyone's from Africa, even – and here's where it gets really confusing – white people.

But although they were black, Truth's dancers were very different to Tafumo's dancers, who were quiet and shy. Truth's dancers walked around like white people do: like they own everything. They were also shaped differently. Tafumo's dancers were round and wide. Truth's dancers had long legs and flapped about like bright flamingos. But most shocking of all: they wore *miniskirts*. I'd never seen miniskirts. Tafumo banned them. All the hotel magazines in the lobby were slashed with black marks and pages torn out because, Dad said, the chief censor was a bloody priest. So I stared with googly eyes as I whispered to Ed, 'They're in miniskirts, Ed.'

'Yes, *bwana*,' said Ed, smiling wide as a crocodile.

'But won't they get arrested?'

Ed laughed. 'I think the police will be letting them off with a warning.'

Next came Truth. And I couldn't believe it. Truth had more security than Tafumo. With everyone orbiting around him like mosquitos, you could barely see. One of the spinning people was a skinny man with Quiksilver slashes like graffiti over his clothes.

Quiksilver-man jogged over holding a video camera. 'I'm Wayne? I'm crew? Doing a reality show with Truth?' Wayne spoke fast and said everything as if it were a question.

'Welcome, Wayne, I'm Stuart, the hotel manager, and we are honoured to…' Wayne cut in, 'Any other celebrities arrived? Sean Penn?' Dad said, 'We're not in the habit of giving guests' private details…' but Wayne cut in again, 'Yeah I get it, Stuey?' then he filmed me and shouted, 'Hey kid! What I miss?' Before I could reply, he was shouting, 'Awesome? Now, Stuey? Need to make a pit stop? Need shots of Truth with authentic Bwalo kids?'

Dad looked confused; Wayne leaned in close, 'I mean…poor kids?' to which Dad replied, 'No shortage of those, there's a village nearby…' and Wayne shouted, 'Great stuff?' and ran off filming the airport, filming the sky, filming people carrying wood on their heads and all the other nothingness stuff that was going on.

A tired woman came over next. She wore jeans – also illegal for women to wear but it seemed the laws didn't apply to these people – she had a mobile phone in each hand and spoke in a posh accent, like people from the BBC. 'I'm Bel, Truth's publicist. Sorry he didn't say hello. Thought it best to get him on the bus. Truth's really tired.'

'I hear integrity is fairly exhausted these days too,' Dad said quietly, then he started his formal introduction. 'Welcome to Bwalo. May we say we're honoured to…'

She interrupted, 'Why can't I get Internet?' and Dad shouted to everyone, 'Folks, listen up, bad news: your smart phones just became dumb phones. No Internet on phones, limited on computer too.' A groan rose out of the group of crumpled journalists.

'And where's the other bus for the dancers and the crew?' Bel asked.

Dad screwed up his face, 'Other bus?' And Bel explained, 'Well, yes, Truth can't be in the same bus as everyone. Is there another bus, or do you have a limousine?'

After Dad and I had stopped laughing, Dad said, 'There's no limousines in Bwalo. The King owns the only Rolls-Royce in the whole country. There are only ten Mercedes, all of which are owned by government ministers and the rest of us drive old Peugeots. We have three minibuses in this town and I own one of them, so unless you want Truth to wait here, while I drop every-one off and come back for him, then I suggest…'

Bel nodded, 'OK, OK, fine!' then walked away.

Truth had so many bags that we had to pile lots into the trailer attached to the back of the bus. The trailer usually carried dead animals back from safari and there were bloody rivers dried in the grooves along the bottom. As I helped Ed load the bags, a chongololo rolled along the side of the trailer and Wayne shoved his camera down at it, 'What the heck's that, kid?'

'The chongololo is an African centipede,' I explained. 'Only bigger and blacker, like lots of Lego helmets squashed on a frilly petticoat. Watch this.' I tapped it, causing it to roll into a protective curl, tight as a full stop. 'Did you know chongololos and centipedes only actually have three hundred legs?' Wayne shouted, 'Awesome?' and filmed it slowly unfurl then glide away.

Once the luggage was loaded, the dancers rushed to the back of the bus, and journalists sat up front interrogating Dad. 'How bad is the drought?' 'Any news of Patrick Goya?' to which Dad kept replying, 'Well it's all rather complicated stuff.'

When we drove, Wayne jumped around filming and the dancers kept shrieking, 'My God. It's so real, it's like so out of this world.' When I asked Dad what *Out of this world* meant he said it meant *Out of America*, because Americans struggled to grasp the concept that there was a world beyond the United States.

I got my Dictaphone out and listened to Sean and Stella's argument from last night. After their fight they left, and there was a long boring bit where my Dictaphone just recorded the song of the crickets, then Willem and Marlene came into the office, whispering, and spent the rest of the time shoving the desk back and forth like they were moving furniture.

I deleted all that dull stuff, crept up to the back of the bus, sat by Truth and asked, 'May I interview you?'

'Talk to my publicist,' he said but Bel shrugged, 'He's just a kid.'

I put the Dictaphone on the armrest. 'What do you think of Bwalo so far?'

He glanced out the window. 'Love this place. Full of my brothers and sisters.'

'Do you have relatives here?'

'Just an expression, kid.'

'Do you come from Africa?'

'Detroit.'

'Mum says everyone comes from Africa originally.'

'Moms is always right so I ain't arguing. But I'm from Detroit. And if you're from Africa then I'm Mickey Mouse.'

'I was born here. I am African.'

'I stand corrected.'

'Did you ever meet Nelson Mandela? He was always meeting famous people.'

'He was the president of Africa, right?'

'Africa's a continent not a country. Mandela was the president of *South* Africa.'

'Check out Mr National Geographic.'

'What's National Geographic?'

'A TV show.'

'We don't have TV. Tafumo doesn't like it and he hates the Internet too because Dad says the King doesn't like articles about himself and he also hates boobs.'

The bodyguards and dancers laughed as Truth said, 'You're smart as a tack, kid.'

'Do you like our great and glorious King Tafumo?'

'He's a righteous brother. One of me, all of me. Me to the power of we. Black power to a black people. Right power to the right people.'

'You talk funny.'

'It's what they pay me for. Look, here's the deal, bring your thing close: I love Tafumo.'

'I love Tafumo too, he is the great Ngwazi.'

'Well I love that your president has given me so many of my presidents – Benjamins, that is – to play for the good people of Bwalo.'

'Tafumo is king not president? And you're weird.'

'I'm pure sense, kid. Truth by name, truth by nature.'

Wayne shouted, 'This place looks good? I mean pretty good…
for Africa?'

And Wayne was right in a way. The town did look good but it
was mainly because the shops got their spruce-up for the King.
Whenever they paint the town Mum says, here we go again
painting the roses red and Dad says, whoever's selling paint is
making a killing, and Sean says, Tafumo must think the world
stinks of wet paint. This year Bwalo had a bout of celebrity fever
with shops sporting new signs: *Tom Cruise Tailor*, *Oprah's
Bakery*. Dad said some were more successful than others and
wasn't sure he'd buy meat from *Russell Crowes Sparticus Butch-
ery*. The roadmen were out too, slopping tar into the gaping
mouths of potholes. What Wayne didn't know was that in a few
months the mouths of the potholes would gape open again, the
bright paints would be leached by the thirsty sun. Wayne filmed
a queue of cars curving out of the Shell garage. A bus sat heavily
on its wheels, the inside boiling with people; a woman held a
child out the windows, pee shot in a gold arc and the child was
retracted back.

When Wayne asked about the queues, Dad explained, 'Petrol
sanctions. A wee warning from the world that no nation's an
island.'

'Is it even safe living here, Stuey?' asked Wayne.

'I think so, most of it's just rumours and hearsay. In Bwalo
they say, don't disturb a sleeping elephant. The place is generally
peaceful. We've lived safely for years.' But then Wayne filmed a
shop with smashed glass and graffiti and before he asked, Dad
put his hand over the camera lens and explained, 'Ah, yes, Indians: their shops are targeted because of their economic luck.
Unfortunately Indians are the Jews of Africa.'

When Ed parked the bus at the village, all the children ran out
singing. Fires burned, gravy smoke curled in the air, a dog and a
cock fought for airtime, yapping and squawking, as children

formed a ring around the bus, waiting to see who was visiting. When Truth and his dancers stepped out, they didn't just look like celebrities: with their long legs and bug-eyed shades, they looked like aliens from another planet. They looked so strange that the children stopped singing and stared, as a sweaty journalist moaned, 'Here comes the Bob Geldof shit,' and another muttered, 'I need a cold beer, I'm crisping up like a fucking oven chip.' Children jumped around Truth, grabbing his hands and touching his leather trousers. Bodyguards tried to push them away but like ants they poured through the gaps. The kids had never seen so much gold on a black person, fingers thick with rings, neck crisscrossed with chains, teeth gleaming gold. Bel pulled out bags and the children gathered under a tree where Truth handed out his new album, *Mirrors*, which had a cool shiny cardboard mirror for a cover. The kids spun the CDs on their fingers, frisbeed them around, tore the mirror off and shoved it in their mouths so their teeth shone like Truth's.

When Wayne said to Dad, 'Isn't this awesome?' Dad replied, 'If you could eat a CD, then, yes, it would be awesome.'

Truth pulled out weird white sticks and Wayne shouted, 'It gets better, dude! Check it out: iPods? Heaps of Nanos, loaded with Truth's album! Awesome?'

'Look around you, Wayne,' Dad said. 'There's no computers, no electricity.'

'Dude!' shouted Wayne. 'You're such a killjoy?' then ran off to film the kids.

Ed asked Dad, 'What's this Truth man doing, *bwana*?'

'He's exploiting your poverty to steal the credibility he so desperately lacks.'

Ed screwed up his face, 'I don't understand,' and Dad replied, 'Me neither, Ed. But you better lock up your kids because it'll be like Madonna in Malawi soon, celebrities flying in with sacks scooping up your beautiful babies and taking them away.'

Ed looked even more confused then Bel shouted, 'Everyone, Truth, guys, Wayne: back in the bus, we need to get to the hotel, we're on a super-tight schej, guys. Safari then soundcheck. Let's go, go, go!'

The children waved goodbye, singing as we left, and I overheard Truth say to Bel, 'It's so good doing something real, you know, really making a difference.'

Jack

*F*ANTASTIC WOKE ME UP and handed me coffee in a tin cup. It tasted of mud and metal. When we headed into the bush, I wanted to run, drop the rucksack, run and never return. But two things kept me walking. I needed the money. Also I knew that this continent worked with the swiftness and rage of a small village. He'd track me down soon enough and he'd hurt me, or worse. A man crazy enough to be smuggling a gun like this around meant business. Just one more night, I kept thinking, and I'd be shot of the whole thing. We walked until we arrived at a filthy spot called Port Tembo. The water was low; ghost-lines on the rocks described how high it had once been. There was a cracked dirt road, baked dry as elephant hide, with shoddy wooded shacks on one side and a bar full of drunks on the other. Fantastic told me we had to wait for a boat, so we sat in the street. As the day grew hotter, the men got drunker and became increasingly interested in my backpack, which I held in a tight vice between my knees. I heard fear in my voice when I asked, 'When can we go?' and Fantastic shrugged that African shrug that said, *The world will decide in its own sweet time*. But the bums at the bar had more immediate plans. As afternoon darkened to dusk, two men came. They didn't draw their knives but they made sure we could see them, stuck in their shorts. Pointing at my backpack, they shouted at Fantastic. The nasty scars on the face of one of the guys suggested he'd used his knife a few times before and weighing up the situation I realised it wasn't in our favour. Fantastic was wiry and I was strong but no match for knife-wielding drunks. With weary predictability one of them pulled his knife and I froze. Never taking his eyes off the man, Fantastic said to me, 'Mr Jack, give them money.'

It was right then – right *after* I'd handed him the cash – that I knew I'd made a bad move. The men in the bar had seen the transaction; now more men would follow and I'd be handing out cash until my pockets ran dry, then what? Pay with my blood? A sick joke occurred to me: as my slow brain caught up with what was happening, I remembered I was armed. I had a gun. A bloody big gun, wedged against my balls. Yet it was useless to me. I'd no idea how to put it together and not the time or nerve to take the risk of pulling it out, snapping it together and…then what would I do? Intimidate them? Shoot them? It seemed ludicrous to die here fully armed. And I was lost in this thought when the two men started to quarrel over the money, then they started to fight and a few sloppy punches were thrown. The men at the bar gathered around the fighting men, snatching at the cash spilling to the ground, and I was completely absorbed in this when Fantastic shouted, 'Mr Jack, the boat.' We skipped around the scrum, down to the water, jumped in and pushed off. Watching the squabbling drunks from the safe distance of the boat, they seemed unthreatening and daft. Fantastic smiled and I raised my hand and he slapped it. 'High five, Fantastic! Shit, that was close, man.' And something about the way he nodded made me realise just how close it had been.

Charlie

*C*LICK!

'Ed, did you know lions sleep twenty hours a day?'

'Well did you know ants never sleep and I'm the busy ant getting the bus ready for safari, so you must leave me to…'

'Yeah, yeah, I know but, Ed, so listen, if Tafumo dies…'

'Shhh, Charlie. You can't say this. Gods don't die.'

'Yah but Mum says if he does die we'll all be up poo creek without a paddle. Mum says he's the rust holding the wreck together.'

'Eh but, *bwana*, no. Tafumo has brought education and freedom to Bwalo, he is a lion, a warrior, the great Ngwazi.'

'Yah, OK, sure, but can you at least tell me what a whore is?'

'You're like a baby with a gun.'

'Stop teasing, Ed. What is it?'

'A woman who gives too much for too little.'

'Stop talking in riddles.'

'I'm busy.'

'Final question: what's a coop?'

'A house for the chickens.'

'Why's Mum scared of a chicken house?'

'Go and ask your mother.'

Click!

Josef

I WOKE UP ON THE floor of the wardrobe. With frozen blood and bones of stone, I couldn't summon the energy to stand. I let my tongue stab the raw nerve of my tooth, causing pain to flash through me and jerk me to my feet. I was out the door before anyone was awake, even before the sun was up. Ezekiel saluted and opened the gate. Driving the grey streets, my tooth humming like a tuning fork, it wasn't long before a car appeared. I turned to see what might have been the outline of Jeko's hat. He imitated his idol, wearing the Homburg hat long after Tafumo himself had abandoned the affectation. When a man makes himself look ridiculous and people are still too scared to ridicule him: that's a sign of a man's authority. I could read the faces of most men but not Jeko. His smooth face possessed an animal fixity, an unreadable blankness. Jeko was an outsider. Not one of us. Never an uMunthu member, or even a Bwalo man. Tafumo chose an outsider as his weapon. Wise move in a small nation of mixed blood.

I drove to my *sing'anga*. When Hope failed to give me a child we came here. But Hope didn't believe, she didn't let the *muti* work, and it tore us apart. Years later, when I'd made a wife of my mistress, Rebecca, I returned to the *sing'anga*. This time for Rebecca's cancer. We weren't ignorant; we'd consulted doctors. Even flown to Switzerland where a specialist, like all the doctors before him, shook his head. But Rebecca wasn't afflicted with

Hope's cynicism. She didn't care that the woman lived in the township, that her sign was childish: *Good-Cheap Muti*. The *sing'anga* granted Rebecca time to see Solomon grow; bought us time to prepare for her death. And when it came near, when her bones jutted like blades, the *sing'anga* brought relief from the pain.

The *sing'anga* didn't dress her home in the paraphernalia of her idiotic counterparts, witch doctors and *mutimen*. It was a whitewashed house with deep-red concrete floors. She wore green-gold *chitenges* that hid the bearing of her body, and her skin absorbed so little light it disguised most of her features in its darkness, with the exception of her smile, which shone out of her face. She gave me a fresh bottle of tonic and I left by the back door; wouldn't be right for a minister to be seen here. Though I knew many ministers consulted *sing'angas*.

I drove to work early, hoping to catch up with the latest reports before David hounded me. It was the principal reason I'd kept my university office long after I could have moved into the Ministry. It allowed me distance from the noise, and from David. No such luck today: he was waiting outside. I mumbled good morning as I unlocked my door. I was unsure if it was the sewage problem that plagued the university, or if it was David, but something stank, a disturbingly human smell.

He sat and came straight to the point. 'It's the Irishman.'

We were wary of our expat community, especially teachers and reporters, and this man was both. But in a place as small as Bwalo it took only weeks for either my men, or more often than not, the restless expats, to weed out spies. British agents usually drank at the Mirage for a month, had an affair with someone's wife, then their cover was blown. Secrets have short shelf lives in Bwalo. But this Irishman had lived here for decades. He was no spy. For a start he was Irish, not English, something David, who'd never been outside of Bwalo, couldn't grasp. He couldn't appreciate that the English had treated the Irish more maliciously than they'd ever treated us. It mattered not. As was so often the way, logic played no part in this witch hunt, this obsession of David's.

David was a devoted follower of Tafumo; he was a relentless and pious person but not a clever man. Weeks earlier, he had run into my office, placed a postcard on my desk and I'd joked, 'A card for me, you shouldn't have.' David didn't smile; the righteous are a humourless bunch and I pity the man who falls under David's cold focus.

I read the postcard:

Mad-hot here, Mum. Drought's in full swing but my tan's coming along. How's that new Pope? Seems a nice enough fella? Book's coming great, pouring out like water. Big Day's tearing round the corner and this year we've celebrities. None of the Irish crew, though Colin Farrell may come. He's your man with one eyebrow you liked in that movie about Bruges. Stella is well, her volunteer work with the orphans is eating into her PhD studies but it's all in a great cause. Love, Seanie

I'd said, 'Look, David. It's time you stopped with this man. There's nothing here.'

'But he's lying,' David replied. 'This Stella is no PhD but a common woman; this is a code. He is a spy!'

'You're losing it!' I shouted, my voice breaking as I scolded him. 'You're becoming paranoid! You need to get a grip!' I calmed my tone a little. 'David, look, you're right in one way. He is lying but he isn't lying to Tafumo. He's just lying to his mother. Which may be the worst sin of all. But that's not our department.'

'Nothing's worse than lying to His Excellency the Life King N Tafumo.'

He gave Tafumo his full title every time he mentioned his damn name. Fanatics make icons of mortals.

'David, do you think a spy would send codes on a postcard?'

Predicting my question, David replied quickly, 'But the wording is strange.'

'It's just the way the Irish talk. This man's an idiot but he's not a subversive. As far as I know we've yet to draft a law against idiots. Great shame though that is.'

But today it was clear that David had more than just a postcard; he had something worthy of my time.

He placed a book on my desk and I said, 'Where did you get this from? You shouldn't have it.'

'It's not mine,' replied David defensively. 'It belongs to *your* students, from *your* university. The Irishman is teaching it...And there have also been sightings of the Irishman in the university library during the holidays, acting suspiciously and...'

'And what do you advise we do, David?'

'Kick him out of the country immediately. But hold his woman for questioning. He's stirring up student insurrection and the woman is a vital source. She is weak and will crack. I will question her myself and...'

'No, no you won't. You will do no such thing; you need to calm down. It'll start an international incident if you interrogate expats; you leave him alone. He's not what you think. You are, as always, wrong about this, David; you need to stop this craziness, stop wasting my time. This is ridiculous paranoia.'

David didn't mask his disappointment. He glared at me. Another black mark in my file, I'm sure. Concerned that he wasn't going to let it go, fearful that he'd pursue it and blunder into some incident, I said, 'Get a grip, David. First you're telling me the Rhodesian hotel manager is plotting something, now you're on about a drunk Irishman.' I heard the anxiety in my voice, as if warning myself rather than David. 'So calm down and do your job, stop being paranoid and leave the Irishman to me. I'll deal with him.'

Sean

*I*AVOIDED STELLA LAST NIGHT. I was too tired to face her again. She owned the house, not me. So after a big argument, there was some unspoken rule that I should find somewhere else to sleep until things cooled off. Luckily Stu had once again let me crash on his sofa. But I barely slept, twisting the night away like a rotisserie chicken.

Slipping out of the house, I walked to the first tee to watch the sunrise. I came loaded with a spliff but my head was so full of the booze and fights of the night before that the weed failed to work its mellow magic. Weed hadn't been the same since Jack left. Nice guy, feckless as me, who brought in Malawi gold. Nothing major. Just enough to keep the country calm. Then, as is the nature of these things, one day I popped in for my usual sack of gold and Jack was gone.

Hearing footsteps, I crushed the spliff into the grass and lit a less illegal Life cigarette. Puffing it like a bugger, I turned and shouted with relief, 'Oh Christ, it's only you, Willem. Thank God. I thought Stu had caught me smoking green on the green again.'

'Hey, no problems, Sean, I won't tell a soul. What you doing here so early?'

'Insomnia. What's your excuse?'

'I like to walk the course before playing,' and he sat down and we watched the sun float up the blue-bowl sky.

'So tell me, Willem, what was Eugene like as a kid? Got any dirt for me?'

'He was skinny as a twig, eh. Took him years to get as fat as he is today. Dad used to call him skinnymalink and piccaninny, bullied him rotten for being weak.'

That cracked the first laugh of the day out of me and I asked, 'You going to the Big Day festivities?' pointing down at the stadium below us.

'Nah. I'll be playing golf. The course will be quiet.'

'Careful,' I warned. 'Tafumo banned all sport on the Big Day. It's in honour of the previous Bwalo leader. Tafumo's very sensitive about the last guy.'

'Yah, what happened to the last guy?'

'Tafumo shot him in the head.' Willem laughed but I warned him, 'Really, be careful, though. The sports ban is the Big Man's way of spring-cleaning dissidents. Even if you're caught playing tiddlywinks they use it as an excuse to boot you out.'

Staring down into the mouth of the stadium, Willem said, 'I'll be careful.'

'So you miss Africa?'

'Like crazy. This is home for me. You miss Ireland?'

'No, no. Been away too long. Home isn't home any more.'

Willem nodded, distractedly looking over the course, plotting his golfing strategy. I thought it best to leave the big man to his thoughts, so I said goodbye and walked up the fairway, the pool winking in the dawn light, calling me to the bar. I considered settling in but, with the sun not yet detached from the horizon, I realised it was a little early, even for me.

Instead, I went on my mission. My heroic – some might say idiotic – mission. Warm telephone lines hung in slack smiles between poles, grinning as I rode to work. When I parked up I saw people inside the Ministry of Communication, a grey block of a building, like a Rubik's Cube peeled of its colours. But the neighbouring university was empty, eerie without people, this concrete slab, run on a pittance and ruled by a tyrant.

We had fifteen librarians working in an almost empty library. More librarians than books, was the joke. They were comically useless and I was convinced they were illiterate but all were friends and family of ministers, so I was careful what I said. I unlocked the door and snuck in. The library was a pure tragedy, bookshelves full of blank spaces like so many missing teeth. Hundreds of books were banned and the few we had were in dreadful condition, ancient paperbacks with broken spines and faded pages. The sun sucked sentences clean off the paper. The Bwalo sun is a famished one; she'll eat everything in the end. I'll be next. Be nothing left but a hank of beard and nicotine teeth. If you want to see where the big-haired hope of Live Aid ended look no further than here. The saddest indictment of good intentions gone awry. Never have so many given so much for it to go to so few. Geldof did his best, a great Irishman and a hero who convinced me I could change the world. Won't hear a bad word said against Sir Bob. He filled their bellies – which was the only thing to do – but what of their minds? This library is the answer. Give a man a fish, he'll eat for a day; teach a man to think and he'll build a nation. But I suppose that lurid brand of 1980s hope was better than what followed. The worst thing to happen to Bwalo was the fall of the Berlin Wall in '89. Until then Bwalo was economically robust, as Tafumo cashed cheques from both sides: from capitalists pouring in cash to keep out reds; and from reds pouring in roubles to keep out capitalists. Robbing from Peter *and* Paul. But the fall of the Wall brought an end to such profitable duplicity. As the Cold War thawed, the rivers of cash dried up, leaving Bwalo with barely enough to keep ministers in Mercedes. And corrupt currents redirecting the meagre streams of charity that remain will ensure the next generation will be less educated than the last, as the cradle of man sinks back into the womb of abject poverty.

I realised the futility of what I was doing. I came to save the world, to educate a generation, and yet now here I was tiptoeing about trying to toss out a bookcase. However, the disorder of the place, its outrageous corruption, the frustration of teaching sixty students with one textbook, had all boiled down and distilled into this one object. A wonky bookcase: chest high with shelves so rotten they were no longer capable of holding books. The librarians had placed it by the door where, every time I walked into the library, my big toe would find its way to smashing into it, leaving me buckled over, howling, 'Toss it out! Just toss it out!' To which the doe-eyed librarian would tut, 'Eh but, *bwana*, this is government property, we cannot throw this away until the proper paperwork says we can throw this away.' As my toe throbbed, the Nazi and I would work our way through a Beckett-like dialogue, the pattern of which never varied, in this tragedy wrapped in farce. 'Christ almighty, man! Just toss it out!' The librarian would then stare at it, terrified, the bookcase having taken on a voodoo quality; it was government property, *untouchable*, possibly even fatal. It could take years of paperwork before we could toss it. And I was more than aware of the fact that I'd allowed it to expand into a disproportionate fixation. But in the humid nothingness of Bwalo, small things overpower reason and proportion. And anyway, it was more than a bookcase. Every time I saw it, each time I thumped my toe into it, the bookcase broke my heart because it stood for everything about this wonderful, beautiful country, bursting with so much potential and greatness that I knew would never be realised. So, with the calm precision of a man who had spent a restless night rehearsing the moment in his mind, I placed my shoulder under one of the shelves and awkwardly shuffled out.

Looking like a man attempting to wear a bookcase, I hobbled to the kitchens, where I lifted and tilted it into the skip. Only a tiny edge of it poked out the top, like it was drowning and waving for help. Drown away, I thought, smiling at my triumph, the satisfaction as huge as the achievement was small. I'd definitely earned an early drink. Buoyed by my victory, I returned to the Mirage, plonked myself at the bar and said, 'Alias, my good man, I require lubrication. My throat's as parched as a vulture's snatch.'

Alias bent slowly down and placed a beer before me. Taking a refreshing sip I realised there are few better places for a restless soul than a hotel bar, offering a rolling cast of characters telling their tales, confessing sins, feeding my insatiable social glands. The hotel was swollen with new arrivals and I was lucky enough to find a rather attractive drinking partner. Exhausted, her eyes sunk in ponds of purple skin, she babbled away as cocktails and jetlag took hold. She could certainly fill a pair of jeans and over her white top she wore a photographer's vest with multiple pockets from which she extracted many phones that she tapped furiously, grumbling about the Internet.

When she asked what I did, I told her I was a teacher. Then I asked her my standard question, 'And what brings you here?'

'I'm the publicist for Truth.'

'What an easy job that must be. Everyone wants to hear the truth.'

'No, the singer. I'm his publicist, his nurse, his bloody mother.'

'Loving your job then.'

'Just a little tired. The thing is when you have an album that's selling you travel a lot. When you have one that isn't selling you travel even more. We're international door-to-door salesmen.'

'What a glamour nightmare.'

'Yeah, you're right. Best job in the world really. I used to tour with the Stones.'

'Now you're talking my language, I love the Stones.'

'Yeah, I loved that time. Roaring around in private jets. Flying in dealers and groupies. Truth takes his Pilates instructor and a masseuse. God help me. I never got bored back then, even after a hundred nights; I'd stand in the wings watching the Stones and I could still imagine their teenage signatures scrawled on the devil's scroll. You know? They got a good deal, those boys. The devil held up his end of the bargain. Making music like that's well worth the price of a soul or two.'

'Is the devil still making deals?' I asked. 'If so, musicians are being ripped off, because music don't sound like it used to.'

She sang out, 'Hallelujah, man,' then laughed.

'Alias, get this woman a drink; she's laughing at my jokes.'

She nodded a thanks as I said, 'I'm old enough to own records. Before they shredded that gorgeous vinyl into nasty tape then crystallised it into soulless CDs.'

'Showing your age,' she said, smiling. 'It's not CDs now, it's just digital dust.'

Alias gave her a fresh drink and she raised her glass, 'To the Stones!' She took a long drink then sighed. 'It's not even about the music now, most of the time I'm just a babysitter. I recently spent three days taking Truth to every strip joint in LA.'

'Again, your job sounds really awful.'

'Well, you might have got a kick out of it, but not me.'

'So why the lap dancers?'

'Well,' she stopped, looked about, then whispered conspiratorially, 'as a fellow Stones fan I assume I can trust you.' I nodded and she continued. 'Well the thing is, Truth sings a lot about sleeping with Beyoncé but the fact is he prefers sleeping with Benjamin. It's one of those things the industry knows but we keep it quiet. So the day his album dropped there pops up a photo, the subject of which bears a striking resemblance to Truth, in a club with his hand close to the crotch of a man wearing – and here's the inconvenient detail – a dog collar.' As I laughed and pounded the bar, she added, 'Cursed camera phones, bane of a publicist's life. World sprouts a billion eyeballs a day, staring into the celebrity sun to catch a solar flare.'

'Well he better not flash his flare round here. It's illegal. No gays in Bwalo.'

'He's been warned. Don't want to end up in a Bwalo jail. Could happen, knowing my luck. I've had a bad run on talent recently; they call me the cursed publicist. My last act lost his mind on meth and tried to gouge out his own eyeball in a hotel lobby.'

'Yuck,' I said. Then, unable to hold it in any longer, I confessed. 'Look, as I said, I'm a teacher by trade but I also write a little on the side. I'm actually, funny thing this, doing a piece for the *Telegraph* about this singer called Integrity, no, was it Honesty? No, wait, now what was it, oh yes, that's it: Truth.'

She turned white as milk and I said, 'Cursed indeed.' But I quickly put her out of her misery, saying, 'Look, relax, I'm only joking with you.'

'Thank God,' she said, her body deflating with relief. 'So you're not Sean Kelly.'

'No, I'm him but I'm not one for ruining a man's career for a scoop, not my style. I've enough skeletons clattering about in my own closet. Not gay ones, mind,' and I raised my eyebrows to punctuate my point. 'I'm all about the ladies, as I'm sure you're aware.'

'I'm aware of your wedding ring,' she replied and I quickly clarified, 'Actually, it's just an engagement ring.'

I stared shamelessly into her amber eyes, as she said seriously, 'So, listen here, Sean, you definitely won't write about this, right? What I told you. The truth about Truth, I mean.'

'Great headline that.'

She squealed, 'Sean!'

'No, no, I'm kidding. No, fear not, your secret is safe with Sean.'

She drained her glass and relaxed just enough that I risked a little more ribbing. 'In fact you're actually in luck there because I've this very rare condition called sexnesia.'

'There's no such thing.'

'It's rare but it's real, believe me. If I have sex with a woman I instantly forget everything she ever told me.'

She arched an eyebrow. 'Well, I'm equally afflicted by an allergy to engaged men.'

Jesus-man! Not just pretty but full of sass: she was a woman after my own heart, this one.

I shrugged and said, 'Well that's a terrible shame now.'

'Isn't it?'

''Tis.'

I laid off the flirty stuff and changed tack. 'What's wrong with Truth being gay anyway, thought we'd rolled past that stuff?'

'Teenage girls need to think there's some hope of one day becoming Mrs Truth. The entire music industry rests on the unrequited dreams of teenage girls.'

'And why the hell is Truth playing for a dictator like Tafumo?'

'No money left in music. If it wasn't for dictators there'd be no industry.'

'Can I quote you on that?'

'No. Because I never said it. And because I'm just the help; I don't actually exist.'

'You're a gorgeous ghost,' I said but it came off a little leery and it was clear that she was a pretty woman who'd fended off more charming chaps than me. So accepting defeat, I sipped my beer, saying, 'Dictators and pop stars are all in the same business. The business of distraction. Show business. That's a good angle, don't you think?'

But she was face deep in one of her phones and didn't reply. Across the other side of the pool there was an almighty racket going on. A young man was squinting at a camera, a stack of lights and silver umbrellas looming over him, as he said, 'They call it the sweet soul of Africa. A success story, under the benevolent leadership of Tafumo, Bwalo has gone from strength to strength, this peaceful paradise with its...'

When I asked, 'Who's the clown?' she explained, 'He was on *Big Brother*. You know? The TV show? They imprison people in a paradise with a pool, film everything, then interrogate them about their innermost thoughts.'

'You've just described life in Bwalo,' I said. To which she replied, 'Well this young man is telling the world that Bwalo is one of Africa's great success stories.'

'What a crock,' I shouted. 'You of all people should know better than to believe that crap. It's all PR and propaganda. That phony speech he's giving is what Clooney said about South Sudan the week before it burst into civil war. All the bullshit people spout about Africa. Pure propaganda, sounds like the kid's reading a script written by Tafumo himself. Who believes these moronic celebrities any more?'

'You'd be surprised what you can convince people of.'

'I'm stealing that line for my next book.'

Stu was standing by watching the filming. I waved him over. He trotted around to the bar and, when he got to us, immediately started his hotel-manager bit. 'Morning morning, beautiful day. Hope your jetlag's wearing off a little, Bel. So you two have both met, that's great. Bel: Sean. Sean: Bel. Sean here's the guy I mentioned writing the article.' Bel grimaced. Stu looked confused and added, 'He's a talented author too, you know.'

'Well, no offence, but I've never heard of you,' said Bel, a little sharply.

'My writing's been consistently received with universal disinterest.'

She smiled at this, softening a little. 'Look, Sean, we're off on safari this afternoon. Why not come do the interview on the way there?'

I checked with Stu, who shrugged and said, 'Plenty of room on the bus.'

Charlie

*C*LICK!

'Mum, did you know desert spiders hold ants on the sand to burn them to death?'

'That's charming, dear, but I'm busy so...'

'Why do you call Britain *The Real World*?'

'Do I?'

'Yah, if you're arguing with Dad you say, It's time to return to the real world, darling.'

'Don't say *yah*. You're not a yarpie.'

'Are you going to answer my question?'

'No. Why don't you ask me something else?'

'Why are you and Dad arguing?'

'Ask me something else.'

'What's Stella's job?'

'Something else.'

'You said to ask when I'm older and that was a day ago so I'm a day older...'

'Next question.'

'Will you actually answer any of my questions?'

'Next question.'

'Are you trying to be funny?'

'Next question.'

'What did you want to be when you were a kid?'

'Oh. Um. Fairly sure accountant wasn't high on my list.'

'The Big Day is, like, the most exciting day of the year, eh?'

'Don't say *like* and don't say *eh*. But, yes, it's the most important day for the Mirage, for business, especially this one what with all the bloody celebs.'

'Why do you always say *bloody* celebs?'

'Well, I think it's just a sad world where talentless people are so over-valued. We have a little boy who sings, makes millions, and everyone knows his name. Then we have Sean who earns nothing, slogging his guts out teaching a generation desperate for education. Yet no one knows who Sean is.'

'I know who Sean is.'

'Next question.'

'Why are you scared of a chicken house?'

'Huh?'

'You told Dad you were nervous about a *coop*.'

'Go ask your father.'

'He told me to ask you.'

'Next question.'

'Mum!'

Click!

Josef

I WAS MISSING SO MANY meetings that my secretary had taken to telling people I wasn't in. But I was. I was hiding, utterly spent, the pain in my mouth throbbing like a living thing. Moses, my Deputy Minister for Tourism, had caught me in the car park when I had tried to sneak out for lunch. He was babbling about rocks on Victoria Avenue. I watched him as if in a dream, his aubergine lips pleading, 'Minister, I am so sorry to detain you, but I really just must have some time with you. I'm worried about the rocks on Vic Ave, the King will be displeased, they're looking very ugly.' I focused enough to say, 'Well move them,' causing him to cringe, 'But all the cranes are being used on the stadium and ...' Before I could stop myself, I was shouting, 'Just fucking paint the rocks or something,' flecks of spit hitting Moses's face as I screamed, 'I don't care, I don't care!'

I walked away fast, up to my university office, snapping at Beatrice as I passed, 'Hold my calls, don't let anyone in.' Then I got down on my knees and gently curled under my desk, avoiding the pain of bright daylight, which had started to sting my eyes. It wasn't long before I heard David outside, demanding that Beatrice let him in. She fought him off well and I was relieved to hear him stomping away, a heavy step followed by a light one, twisted feet beating an uneven rhythm.

I was dozing beneath my desk, when I heard Boma's voice. Beatrice tried her best but Boma wasn't a man to be denied and as quickly as my body would allow I uncurled, crawling out from underneath, blinking as I sat on my seat. Boma marched in, Beatrice's shrill protest cut short as he slammed the door on her. Swivelling in my chair, I said calmly, 'Oh, Boma, hello, it's been too long.'

Like everyone who hadn't seen me for some time, Boma failed to hide his shock. His eyes crawled over my sunken cheeks, scrawny neck, the white cliff of teeth protruding from lips too thin to cover them. Walking directly to the drinks cabinet, he poured two whiskies, placing one in front of me, 'Looks like you could use one of these.'

Where I looked sick, Boma was in the bloom of health. He was the youngest member of uMunthu, still a student when the rest of us were lecturers. Now in his fifties, he was a man who had reached his optimal age. The unkempt Afro of his youth had been shaved to reveal his blue-black skull below, which soaked rather than reflected light. He sat opposite looking resplendent in his military jacket, a constellation of medals twinkling across his chest. The effect was only slightly undone by a large ketchup stain on his belly. If I didn't know him, didn't know he was a drunk and a womaniser, that he had never served in any real army, I would have believed what I saw. 'And to what do I owe this pleasure, General?' Brushing off my obsequious tone, Boma said, 'Tafumo asked me to check everything was in order with the ministers. This Big Day has to go without a hitch, the world's watching, we have reporters and celebrities, the show must be perfect.'

There was a code in his reply, the real answer to my question: three key words hidden among the jumble of extraneous ones. *Tafumo asked me.* He'd come to rub my nose in the fact he still had access to Tafumo. Where the rest of us had sought ministerial roles, Boma, our young blood, had been appointed to head the army. Though *army* was a grand name for what it was. Tafumo kept it small and weak. He knew big armies had a tendency to overthrow leaders. So Boma headed a bunch of badly dressed, ill-disciplined men. But Boma loved Tafumo with a ferocity that bordered on insanity and over time he'd wedged himself into the gap that had yawned between Tafumo and me.

In a sort of reflex to our old friendship, I nearly asked about Patrick. But Boma's views were already on the record, quoted in the newspaper, saying Patrick was a coward who'd run away, an incompetent minister incapable of balancing our books. Boma's was a simple world. The day after my wedding, when I'd confided to Boma that Levi's death wasn't accidental, he had shrugged, 'Such a thing could only happen if it was necessary.' A man's life dispatched with a shrug and cliché. I was shocked by his callousness. He may not have been a real soldier but he was a natural born politician whose heart burned with the cold flame of ambition.

'Josef, look,' he said. 'I've heard disturbing things; talk of internal conflict, plotting, vested interests. Even of your own men whispering about you. Please believe me that I say this not as a colleague but as a friend.' He lied so well. We were no longer friends. Boma had snubbed me, grown away from me as he climbed every day further up Tafumo's arse. Answering fast and confidently, I said, 'That's the nature of the world. There are always younger men pushing up against their elders, ambition is not illegal.' I gave the insinuation time to sink in. 'But there's nothing to concern yourself with...'

Boma waved his glass at me. 'Has Jeko come yet? Is he asking to see any reports? Requesting any extended surveillance?' When I shook my head, Boma said, 'Well, old friend, I would ask that you call me, not Jeko, if you hear anything untoward.'

Reduced to choosing between devils – Boma or Jeko – I said, 'I assure you that we have all our best men in the field and...' Boma's nostrils twitched in disgust; my breath must have reached him. 'Phones are tapped and all offices are wired so...' Suddenly a gush of putrid fluid discharged into my mouth and I stopped talking, scared it would drip from my lips like tar but also too nervous to swallow the rancid stuff.

Boma looked at me strangely and when I remained silent he finally said, 'Very well, Josef, I'll leave you to it. But call me if anything arises.'

I nodded – the fluid sloshed – and Boma drained his glass, crushed my hand, then marched out of the office. I leaned forward, opening my mouth, and pale-red fluid, the consistency of egg white, pooled on my desktop. I stumbled out of my office, slurring at Beatrice, 'Call that dentist, I need the appointment now. Now!'

My tooth was weeping and I was spitting blood into a tissue when I parked up and jogged to the building, stepping off the littered street into the orderly surgery. The radio was playing a tinny guitar song, people sat reading magazines, most of which had pages cut out and the remaining pages were crisscrossed in black censorship marks. I growled at the receptionist, 'You know who I am. I need to see the dentist.' Flustered, she jumped up and disappeared behind the door. I felt many eyes press against my back but when I turned around, all heads clicked down to their shredded magazines. After a brief moment of restrained whispering, a woman rushed out of the surgery, her mouth stuffed with bloody cotton buds. Then the receptionist appeared, 'This way, minister.'

The dentist, a Bwalo man with a nervous smile, explained I had an impacted tooth, infected and dangerous, which had to be pulled. The gas caused my head to swell and the world became a soft painless place. The dentist worked at my mouth with pliers – disconcerting internal tugs – as I drifted in and out of consciousness. When I first came to, he seemed to be pulling at my tongue, as if turning me inside out. In my daze I had a strong sense that this was not my tongue at all; it was the slimy tail of a demon curled and hidden inside me, its tail hanging from my mouth. As the dentist yanked, I smiled, childish gurgles bubbling up my throat, happy someone was at last helping me abort it.

Then came a deep sound, the soft crunch of a nut, and a sour stench caused me to sit up straight and puke, expecting to see my tongue flop into the bowl like a twitching fish. The nurse rinsed the dish with purple disinfectant. Next time I came to, Tafumo was there, leaning over me, still young, strong, but as the fog cleared I saw it was a portrait. Watching, watching, always watching. As the dentist dived back inside, armed with needle and thread, I remembered a time when, as children, Tafumo and I had been warned not to go to a bend in the river. Our elders had said bad spirits lingered there. Tafumo had to go and of course I, his ever-willing shadow, followed. I remember that feeling of fear as we crested the hill – expecting dark shapes to be shifting over the sand – then looking down and laughing. Our laughter racing uncontrollably until tears came to our eyes, we held our knees, fighting for breath between giggling fits. For there on the sand was a hippo: inflated by anthrax, comically bloated into a stuffed toy with legs jutting up. Tourists think hippos are slow, harmless creatures, but they're vicious, killing more people than any other animal in Africa. The terrifying beast was made funnier by its ignoble end. Clearly they had warned us that spirits lingered there to keep us away, for fear of infection. But standing there, we felt we had seen through the adults' game; we were wiser than everyone, even our elders. We had more courage than them, no longer just children but men. Our laughter made us brave as we walked towards the hippo, daring each other to get closer, when the wind turned, whipping the stench of the carcass at us, the thick smell like tongues tunnelled deep into our bodies, filling us with pus, until we folded over and vomited. All that had been funny a moment ago was now repulsive. We stumbled back, gagging as we ran, until we were free of the stench. Then we slowed down and walked silently back to our village feeling foolish and childish once again.

The dentist gave me painkillers. I threw money at the receptionist – Tafumo staring up from the notes – and broke out of the surgery into the sharp light, my tongue snaking around the soggy crater, as I drove to the address Patrick's maid had given me.

When she opened the door, though I'd never met her, I could tell from her elegant features, her slim almost oriental eyes, that this was Patrick's mother.

I said, 'You know who I am,' and she nodded. When I enquired about Patrick's whereabouts she looked around me, searching, and I assured her, 'I'm alone, Mrs Goya. I'm Patrick's friend; we were at university, uMunthu members…' I noticed her head was bobbing to some unheard rhythm. Her body was struggling against a current, afflicted with dementia or some degenerative disease, her dress quivering like silk in a breeze. I wondered if she was all there. But as I spoke, she smiled gently – some code passing secretly between us – as I said, 'He's OK, isn't he?' It was hard to tell if her nod was in response to me, or to the tremble of her body, so in an attempt to confirm this I said, 'Yes, he was always a clever man, your son. And I'm happy he's safe, I'm glad that…' Her hand shot out and snatched my wrist, her grip impossibly strong. And in a dark transference, I felt her tremors infect me; a tingling sensation ran up my arm like ants. And before I could pull away, I realised I was shivering helplessly as she began to still. Standing for a moment, tall and static, staring as I quivered before her, she whispered, 'Patrick is dead, his wife is dead, his children too. I'll never know what happened. Can you imagine? Your son? Gone. Nothing left but a terrible emptiness to fill with horror.' A repulsive moan escaped her mouth, then she said, 'I know who you are.' And when she released me I ran but I felt her hand, as if still there, the ghost of her grip tight around my wrist.

Charlie

WHEN THE ALARM SHRIEKED, everyone stopped still but I was off: sprinting down the corridors, hammering doors, shouting, 'Tafumo's coming!' Didn't matter if the Do Not Disturb signs were swinging on the knobs because Dad said Tafumo could disturb whomever he wanted to.

Wayne filmed the dancers being herded out to the road where soldiers handed out flags. A few women were in bikinis but Dad shouted, 'No bikinis!' It was the only time Dad ever shouted at guests. Then Wayne filmed Truth and his bodyguards zipping past like a chongololo in a rush of legs and bald heads.

On the other side of the road, the staff kids emerged from the *kaya* and Aaron came over for a chat. The kids lined one side of the street and the colourful celebrities and drunken locals lined the other. Us locals looked scruffy and homemade next to all the slick celebrities.

A soldier told Wayne to stop filming but Wayne shouted, 'You can't bloody stop me filming?' But the soldiers with rifles stopped him filming.

I stood next to Sean and told him, 'The great Tafumo is Bwalo's saviour.'

'Is that so,' said Sean, in a way that sounded like it wasn't so.

'It's in our textbooks,' I replied.

'Then it must be so,' said Sean, in a way that sounded like it mustn't be so.

'It is so, Sean. Tafumo is so powerful that even my headmaster has to wave a flag when he passes.'

Sometimes you have to explain so much stuff to adults.

Then Mum gave me *the eye*, which is when Mum talks without her mouth, so I turned and said, 'Sean. Um. I'm sorry about the thing I said last night about Stella,' forgetting the words Mum had told me to say, I muttered, 'that word that I can't say...' Waving his hands as if shooing flies, Sean said, 'No problem, chief.' I held out my hand, 'Still friends?' and Sean shook it. 'Won't get rid of me that easy, Champ.'

Then Sean and I stood in one of those hot sticky silences, where you feel like you might burst, before Sean nudged me and said, 'Hey, check out your man over there.' Across the road a council worker in ripped overalls was painting a rock and Sean said, 'Now, is it my eyes or is that fella painting a rock black? Is that what I'm seeing? OIA, man, OIA!' Sean always said OIA when something weird happened. It means *Only in Africa* and he said it quite a lot.

Things got hot and boring until Solomon arrived in one of his dad's Mercedes and came over and asked if I had any new recordings. First of all I played them something funny that Mum and Dad had said over breakfast.

Click!

Mum: Oh, hey, remember John whatshisname? Marlene was talking about him last night. You know? John somethingorother?

Dad: No.

Mum: Dutch guy was manager at the textile place up past the lake.

Dad: What's his surname?

Mum: Evans, or Ettes, something Dutch, you know the guy, you played golf with him, his wife was a primary teacher at...

Dad: No, I don't, Fiona, as usual you've not given me enough. How can I remember a John-someone from years back who may have been Dutch?

Mum: Well he was your bloody mate! So you should remember him!

Dad: Well I don't know who the fuck you're talking about!

Mum: Well stop fucking shouting at me!

Dad: OK. God, relax. Sorry. Anyway, what about the guy?

Mum: He's dead.

Dad: Oh.

Mum: Yes, well I better get to work, it's starting to get mental. If that bloody Truth fella asks for one more dumb request like blue sheets or bloody distilled pomegranate juice, I'll kill all his bodyguards then strangle the little teenager myself!

Dad: I love it when you're mad.

Mum: Get off me.

Dad: Just give me a kiss.

Mum: Bugger off.

Dad: You never used to say that.

Mum: You never used to annoy me so much.

Dad: Fine.

Mum: Fine.

Aaron and Solomon giggled.

'Now this one is a bit weird,' I warned. I'd left my Dictaphone under Dad's desk, thinking I'd catch Dad and Sean swearing up a storm. Instead Mr Horst and Willem had gone in. 'Ready?' Solomon and Aaron nodded and I pressed play.

Click!

Horst: I can't loan you more money, Willem. It's not enough that I've flown you out and put you up and given you a free holiday to get your shit together…

Willem: Stop, Eugene, hey, just stop talking, man…

Horst: You only get so many chances and you've burned through yours. Buggered the farm, ruined the security firm, you've been a mess since you left the army…

There was silence, like the Dictaphone had stopped; our ears touched as we placed our heads close to hear what sounded like a cat licking, soft and watery. Aaron pulled back first, then Solomon looked disgusted as he realised Willem was sobbing like a baby. We stared at each other until Solomon said, 'Yah, that's really messed up, eh,' and I pressed delete. That recording would get me into so much trouble and I never wanted to hear Willem crying again.

When some kids started playing football with a ball made from plastic bags, Aaron and I joined in but Solomon didn't want to because his shoes would get dirty. Solomon's shoes came from the UK. The rest of us got our shoes from Bata Bata. I painted a Nike Swoosh on mine but you could still tell that they were cheap Bata Batas. Also the real reason wasn't his shoes but that Solomon thought the staff kids were smelly. They did smell but it was a nice smell. It was the smell of Lifebuoy soap, woodsmoke and Vaseline. So Aaron and I left Solomon with his silly shiny shoes. But just as the game was getting good, the soldiers shouted, 'Everyone up,' and motorcycles and Mercedes materialised through the haze at the end of the road, zipping past the celebrities who looked stunned but soon joined in, whooping and cheering like the rest of us knew to do.

The locals sang the Bwalo anthem as the cavalcade sped past dragging a cool breeze behind it, then came the Rolls-Royce and I got a glimpse of Tafumo waving his fluffy fly swat.

Sean whispered to Dad, 'The whole bloody country's just an audience for the Great Tafumo Spectacle. We live in the world's most expensive reality show.'

Once they'd passed, leaving us in a cloud of dust, a soldier raised his eyebrows at Dad who shouted, 'Back to your gin and tonics, everyone.'

Walking to the lobby, Sean said to Dad, 'If that spring chicken was Tafumo then I'm Mary fucking Magdalene.' But before Dad could reply Sean answered his mobile and when he finished talking, Dad asked if everything was OK with Stella and Sean said, 'That wasn't Stella. Worse. It was the Big Man's Little Man, Josef Songa. Wants to see me right away.' Dad and Sean gave each other *the eye*. Though it was hard to read what their eyes were saying, it definitely didn't look good.

Sean

I SAT OUTSIDE HIS OFFICE like a naughty boy. Could this really be about the bookcase? Surely that was below the great man. Since becoming a minister he'd delegated most of the day-to-day university work to lackeys but he kept his old office. He was dean of the university when I first met him, when he offered me the job in the English department. Even back then Josef was a man about town. Dapper and stylish, the best-dressed man in the university by a clear mile. The rest of us were still in kipper ties and flip-flops but he looked like some sort of black male model. In the eighties when he became a minister his suits got sharper, the respect people had for him turned to fear, and he was met with fawning admiration wherever his Mercedes took him. His gleaming car, shining shoes, were a sort of miracle to me, in a country covered in dust. But he aged fast. Though his suits remained sharp his face thinned, his knowing smile took on something sad and his luxurious style slipped into a louche gear. Clearly the recent death of his second wife devastated him but it was something else too. He was a man trying too hard to be clean, trying too hard to hide the dirt within. As Beatrice waved me in, I smiled at her. She frowned. Never a good sign. It had been a while since I last saw him and I was so stunned I had to stop myself staring. It looked like someone had taken to his face with a scoop, carving out pockets of flesh. One cheek hollow and, as if in compensation, the other billowing out like a sail. I almost asked after his health but decided to forgo false pleasantries. We were beyond small talk. Strange to think that at the start, we were almost friends. Right up until we realised we were better suited as enemies.

I wasn't long off the plane from Cork, still pale as butter, when he'd invited me over for a welcoming dinner. I remembered the day I arrived in Bwalo; I managed to shock myself with my own idiocy. Not as rare an occurrence as I'd like to hope. I was surprised to see cars, roads, shops. Not entirely sure what I was expecting. People swinging from trees? Lions chasing Zulus? Idiotic, I know. That's just what I thought when I thought of Africa. I was young, dumb and a bit of a gom, a skinny Irish lad who'd never left Cork, a recently published author with the world at my feet. I remember it was my first time inside a real African's house. Fresh from Ireland, I was ready for my exotic adventure, my Hemingway phase. I was prepared to observe deep cultural differences. Not that I thought the guy would live in a mud hut; I wasn't a complete idiot.

But nothing was quite what I'd expected. For a start his house was huge and a Mercedes sat fat in the carport. His sitting room was an absurd mix of heavy African furniture and refined European art. Chairs carved from cedar, carpets of earthy threads, yet on his walls hung delicate Constable prints. Over time, he had become more sophisticated but back then he was still young and a touch rough around the edges.

When he poured me a whisky, he pointed to his TV and said, 'Panasonic.'

He said it like it was his framed degree. So much pride: 'Panasonic. Nineteen inches,' squeezing extra vowels into the word, *Panasoonic-e.*

A bit baffled, I replied, 'It's grand. But I thought there was no TV here?'

'True,' he said, as if I'd asked just the right question and, like a magician with a flourish of open palms, he said, 'My new Sony. VHS.'

'Lovely,' I replied. Then he added, 'I get my shoes from London,' and showed these fantastically expensive brogues polished enough to reflect my bemused expression.

I didn't know it then but Josef had recently divorced and was a bachelor. So it was just the two of us for dinner. His cook, Ruby, served an Irish stew. I'd been hoping for goat curry, plantain, even a blob of *nsima* and beans, the dish of the Bwalo everyman. It was a lovely stew, mind. And he was a great host. We drank and spoke and, as different as our backgrounds were, we found common ground. He loved *King Lear* and when I raised my fork saying, 'Am I a man more sinned against than sinning,' he quoted back in his rich voice, 'The art of our necessities is strange, that can make vile things precious.' Odd moment when men from different worlds effortlessly reference authors and playwrights. The empire's curriculum briefly bonded us but the glue didn't hold. When I asked about a wife, things turned, and he fell into a sulk. I had to ask. It was impossible not to sense the female ghost in the trim of the curtains, the way the carpets shared some subtle pattern, something a man could sense but not articulate.

We made up over another whisky but it was obvious from the first weeks at work that we didn't see eye to eye. Soon he stopped inviting me for dinner, the novelty of the funny Paddy fading fast, Irish stew wiped off the menu. Then, before I knew it, we were faculty enemies. Men who disagreed on education policy, teaching and life. As dean he'd let the place fall to ruin. I taught classes with sixty students, ten chairs and three textbooks. For months there were no working toilets anywhere on campus and all the while his Ministry of Spies gleamed like a diamond.

So now I sat before him, awaiting my latest reprimand, a new laptop – *Samsung-e* – on the desk. I considered confessing to throwing out the bookcase, maybe even faking a little remorse, but before I spoke he threw a book at me and it flapped open in my lap. It was in a bad state, as if he'd been kicking it around the office before I arrived.

'The wilderness found him out…' I quoted. 'Whispering things to him, echoing loudly within him because he was hollow to the core…'

'Very poetic,' he snapped. 'Sean, we're not friends, you're not protected here, so tell me: what gives you the idea that you can teach a banned book, subversive material?'

'Conrad's disturbing *Darkness* and Achebe's sublime response: these two greats form the literary hinge of African…'

'Spare me the lecture!'

'I was only trying to educate.'

'Exactly. Educate. Educate my students the way I want you to. You will have all of these books returned to my office on Monday.'

'Why? So you can burn them?'

His head snapped up. I thought he might jump the desk and throttle me. For years the teachers warned me about Josef. It's bad to make an enemy of a peer. Far worse when your peer becomes a powerful politician. Everyone said that Josef was connected to the Big Man and had shot through the university ranks with the speed of a nepotistic rocket. Yet here he was, permanently furious about his place in the world. But even after he got his fancy and ludicrously long ministerial title, I treated him just the same. Far as I was concerned he was still just a man running the university into the ground.

So I protested, 'Education is not indoctrination…' but I noticed his jaw throbbing like an angry little lung and decided that maybe some capitulation might be in order. 'Josef, I'm sorry, but I wasn't teaching the book, swear to God. I just had a few students around my place, few beers you know, and one of them saw the book and, hey, I lent it to him, that's it. I know it's banned but really, come on, is it that big a deal?'

'You've done nothing but undermine me and also you have directly questioned the integrity of the King. This isn't Ireland, Sean, this is Bwalo and you are a visitor here.'

Having been at the sharp end of a few of these things, I knew this preamble well. He went on for a bit and then, exhausted or bored, he tossed out the conclusion like an afterthought, waving his hand. 'You are, of course, fired. Effective immediately. I'd be surprised if your visa remains valid. You're dismissed.'

'And you're a fucking disgrace,' I shouted. 'You can't fire me.'

'Pack up, get out, you're no longer welcome at the university. I suggest you leave the country soon or I'll make your time very uncomfortable.'

'You wouldn't fucking dare.'

'Try me.'

I considered punching him but knew that would dramatically shorten my time. I'd be on a plane before I had a chance to grab Stella or say bye to Stu. But though I managed to cool my fists, my words poured out before I could stuff them back in. 'If we are going to start burning books it should be your book, your history, *fantasy* of Bwalo, hagiography and disgraceful fucking propaganda. You should be ashamed. Ashamed of what you've done to your people, ashamed of this mockery of a university that you care so little about, destroying the future of your own country. I don't care who the fuck you are or who you know, I know this much, Sonny-Jim. You'll die a lonely man who only has one thing to look forward to and that's fucking rotting in hell!'

Before he could reply, I walked out as fast as my legs would take me. Beatrice's face was tight with shock; she was crouched, half standing near the door, as if she'd been eavesdropping.

And I wish I hadn't seen it but I did. As I was storming down the corridor, it caught my eye: through the glass door, the edge of it peeking out: the bookcase, returned to its spot. Someone had dragged it from the skip and placed it back and I don't remember getting my keys out, don't remember unlocking the door, don't recall where I found the fire extinguisher but I do recall how good it felt raising it up like an axe and bringing it down so it smashed the first shelf, then again the second, and again and again, until I'd beaten it flat – who knew violence could be so uplifting, so purifying, so satisfying – then I yanked the extinguisher hose and blasted the remains until it was hidden below a foam-mountain. The extinguisher hit the floor with a solid clank and I was gone, out the door, blinking away sunlight, riding my motorbike home.

The first thing I did was check all the rooms; thank God Stella was out. I couldn't face her right now. Then I sat on the *khondi* and punched a hole into a bottle of whisky, until my irritation got so hot it blew itself out and I realised something. I wrote my first book out of sheer rage, when all my options were gone, and now look, here I was again, against the ropes, the very spot where Sean Kelly comes into his own, this is where I shine, where I tear and claw my way out of the very knot I've tied myself into, and I'm not missing this opportunity to take a breath, focus my fury, sit at my desk and…I ran to the study, pulled the cover off my typewriter, sat before it puffing like a boxer, then…nothing. Like a fish escaping the hook, the line fell slack and I stared at the wall, and waited and waited, breaking the monotony by screaming, *Why can't I fucking write?* Outside the cat replied with a sarcastic meow. When I was young my brain effortlessly translated booze and experience into witty prose. But now booze collects into a clot that my rage brings to the boil and all it gives me are headaches and weeping jags.

I'd spent a fortune shipping my typewriter over from Cork. Having poor Mum with her bad back get up into the attic. I wrote my first book on her: my dusty blue Royal. She's everything I'm not, functional and gorgeous, and together we made a rare team. At times it felt as if Royal wrote the book with me looking on, gently encouraging her, *That's a great bit there, Royal, on you go, don't let me get in your way.* Yet now I stared at her keys and they glared back like a mob of disappointed eyes. But then, right at the deepest point of despair, my fingers suddenly began to dance, black bloomed on white as I hit a rhythm of fluid words and a gang of letters leapt up and stuck in an arthritic clump! I yelped! Fumbling desperately, prising them apart, returning my fingers to the keys, but…no. *No!* It was gone. I raised Royal above my head and threw her – imagining her sailing through the window in a blaze of glass – but she fell short, hitting the floor and chipping a concrete shard that shot into my ankle like a bloody full stop. *Facken Christ!* Yanking it out, I rinsed the blood with whisky to see the wound wasn't as spectacular as the pain suggested. I took deep breaths, the steam of my rage escaping, leaving me flat and exhausted as I hobbled through the house and sat my sorry arse on the kitchen stoop.

Hope

THE ROOM FELT TAUT – a trap was set – I wheeled him into it. Ministers rose, old men with aching bones. A standing ovation for the great performer. I sat in the shadows, searching for some hint of revenge or reckoning, some suggestion that these men were finally going to overpower their king. But for all the blood and corruption flowing between these men, they didn't have it in them. Most of them were harmless academics or businessmen appointed for their greed and malleability. They hoped time would do their bidding, would finally stop the crocodile rising each morning to feed off his starving nation. These ageing yes-men would prefer that death, in its guiltless way, take Tafumo and leave no blood on their soft hands. Their eyes caught the shining wheelchair; it brought false hope. It was a ploy. Tafumo was using it to throw them off guard and to spare his energy.

Patrick's seat remained empty, a missing tooth in the circle of chairs. Josef never spoke in meetings; he was smarter than that. Many ministers who'd spoken out were now gone. But today all eyes moved to him and mine followed. His neck was skinny as an egret, his face and hands fleshless. Against my will, my heart beat for him, as he cleared his throat and began, 'Excellency. With the utmost respect, the demands of the IMF aren't entirely unreasonable. Could we potentially start by…toning down the Big Day festivities to show…' Sympathy worked like a spark, our old love flickering to life, urging me to take Josef away to safety. The other ministers looked like schoolboys who'd escaped a beating, who'd sent Josef to do their bidding. There was fear in his eyes as he spoke. He'd lost that shine he once had, that suggested he knew things that others did not. That brightness that Essop, Boma, Levi, Patrick and I were once drawn to.

The only other man as scared as Josef was Essop, who knew his friend was making a grave error. Terrible things stirred below the surface of this dull meeting. For as beautifully delivered as Josef's speech was, I knew that Tafumo didn't hear any of it. His hearing was now so bad that crucial words lay camouflaged in silence, sentences collapsing as he tapped his hearing aid, only for it to squawk like a bird nesting in his ear. I saw the light of his hearing aid wasn't on; he'd given up even pretending to listen.

Just as Josef's speech was gathering pace, 'Even minor concessions would…' Tafumo cut him down: 'Minister Songa. I'd hope that you of all people know I've no intention of being bullied by the world. We fought hard for the freedom to rule ourselves.' Tafumo stopped abruptly and moved his eyes from minister to minister. 'It pains me to look at you all. Pains me that our great ancestors have become you: a table of fat, pathetic men.' He gave the cruelty of his words time to sink in.

'Do any of you have anything more to say to me?' He let the silence stretch, as if daring them to respond – thin microphones craned from the table to their mouths, taunting the ministers to speak – before releasing a bullying laugh, then proceeded to deliver his favourite speech about how as a boy he had walked with bare feet from his burning village to fulfil his destiny. Josef, who wrote the speech, stared with strange blankness, unconsciously mouthing the words as the others squirmed. Tafumo continued to rant. His mind was weak today; lucidity like water through a net.

I watched Essop's fingers dance nervously on the tabletop and I noticed how all the fidgeting ministers accentuated Boma's stillness, as he sat staring at Tafumo with undisguised disgust. Once his greatest supporter, Boma now looked at Tafumo with the disenchantment of a son discovering his father was a fraud.

Boma caught me watching him and, like the film on a snake's eye, he hid his hatred behind a glaze of boredom. Boma the big man. The big man who I'd known since back when he was still just a boy, a student, the youngest uMunthu, a naive kid with a wild Afro, who wore tight cowboy shirts. But now Boma thought himself the big man. Now he treated me as though I were a ghost. He ignored me; ignored me like a man who'd never drunk my beer, eaten my food, or come to me for a sympathetic ear after one of my friends had broken his heart. Now he was playing soldier. A man who'd never fought in a war, chest emblazoned with medals granted for valour on imaginary battlefields. He wore his false medals with real pride. Where had all those young caring men gone? Drowned in the fat of pitiful old men? A sharp bang broke my concentration. A fidgeting minister had knocked over a glass and water flowed across the polished table as they leapt to absorb it with their suit sleeves, damming it before it reached Tafumo, who talked on as if nothing was happening. Grown men leaping up, bums in the air, faces full of fear: it made me sick. His speech droned to an end, he snapped his fingers, and I wheeled Tafumo out as the ministers rose for a final standing ovation.

Jeko was waiting in the corridor, his skin as grey as his suit. He said, 'Please excuse us, sister?' I walked away, back to the door of the cabinet room, and peeked in on the ministers standing in clusters like women in the market, chattering excitedly. Josef sat alone, hands clasped in his lap. Boma and Essop stood together away from the others.

Tafumo waved for me and, walking back, I was overwhelmed by the ordinary moment, as if studying a significant photograph from my past. Everything shone with a clear and anxious clarity: me walking towards them; Tafumo sitting motionless in his wheelchair; Jeko getting smaller as the corridor swallowed him down its deep red throat.

I wheeled Tafumo back to the bedroom where he got out of the chair and waved me away, revived by the meeting, his performance, by turning the trap set against him on to those who set it. Walking fast, I broke out of the cool palace into the heat and there was Josef: standing by his car, staring dumbly at the sky. He said drowsily, 'Hello, Hope.'

'Josef, listen, I'm not sure what's happening but there have been things going on...' I noticed the guard at the gate looking over at us and Josef said, 'Thank you, Hope, but I can take care of myself.' I wanted to slap him out of whatever dream he was in. Grabbing his hand, I whispered, 'Josef, I think someone is coming for you; in his sleep Tafumo talks of a man, he whispers his name. The man's name is *Sefu*.'

I noticed he was shaking slightly, like a leaf in a breeze, but he seemed not to have heard me, and when he replied it was as if we were simply having a pleasant chat, 'Take care, Hope, take care.' He got into his car but, before driving off, leaned out and asked, 'Can I give you a lift to your tree?' He saw me flinch. 'I didn't mean to startle you, Hope. Just happened to see you there...'

I said something, I can't remember what, as I turned and walked quickly to the kitchen. When I got there I was still flustered and I felt a disproportionate sense of disappointment when I noticed Essop wasn't around. The young rage against routine as the old cling to it. And today of all days I needed my routine to hold me together. Reading my reaction, Chef said, 'Essop's at a meeting,' and I replied, 'Of course. I was at the same meeting. It's just...Well, he's usually here when I come.'

As he handed me my lunch, Chef explained in a tone of mild frustration, 'Are you so blind, Hope? Essop is always here because he is always waiting for you to come here.'

I stood with the brown paper bag hanging from my hand, until Chef added, 'There's plantain in there. I popped a spoon in. Be sure to bring it back. I think it's solid silver.' When I finally found my tongue I said, 'Thank you, Chef,' and he grinned and replied, 'My pleasure, Hope.'

Josef

MY SECRET FRIEND, A boy I'd carried on my back and elevated to power, sat before me stewing in his own dementia. Tafumo's was a mind ripe for madness. Never questioning his own judgement, his opinions flowed unhindered by self-doubt – he'd long ago disposed of such tedious checkpoints – and now senility slipped through the gates. Instead of replying directly to my pleas for concessions, he recited a speech, a speech I'd written for him many years ago. There wasn't much left of him now, this man made up of scraps of speeches tied together by lies.

As Tafumo rambled, I remembered the day our friendship finally came to an end. One of the last times he'd come to my house, last time we'd sat together without ministers or aides. It was a few years ago, on the day of Rebecca's funeral. Everyone had already left by the time he turned up. He was splendid, saying all the right things, giving a moving performance. And performance it was. He talked to me like he spoke to people on the streets, revelling in his own reflected glory.

In the early days, when he first took power, he would drop by my house, we would drink and talk. He rarely mentioned our past but I knew those get-togethers were his way of reconnecting with it, escaping the cronies and sycophants. But those times were long gone, and as we sat together on the *khondi* that day, I realised my old friend now only traded in epic emotions: in life, death and power. He only came because he knew it was worthy of him to come, that he could bestow his presence upon me in my time of need and that I would be eternally grateful.

He had not once come to see Rebecca when she was sick. He had paid for our flights to Switzerland but that was different to spending time with my dying wife, as he should have, as he would have done before, when he was still a real man not a false god. But at first I'd been pleased he'd visited. I thanked him and we drank together. When Ruby nervously served our beers, her head bowed so low, Tafumo grabbed her hand, 'This beer is the perfect temperature, thank you, sister.' Bending even lower, Ruby muttered, 'Thank you, Excellency, thank you.'

By then my access to Tafumo was non-existent. The time between our informal meetings had stretched so much that I rarely saw him. So I didn't waste these moments and, knowing I was in a strong position to ask a favour, I used the opportunity to explain that some small changes were required. To soften the walls and enable some freedom of expression. He nodded as I spoke, he wasn't angry with me. I explained that many students were talking of democracy. That David had spies in student cells that were being encouraged by the democratic movement sweeping the world. That if we didn't bend a little, then soon we would snap. He grinned as if about to agree, then said, 'Did I tell you I saw Father Lane a while back?'

Confused by this non sequitur, I replied, 'Oh?'

'Yes. We fished together at the lake,' he said. 'It was splendid seeing him again. We sat on warm rocks, fishing lines shining in the sun, and I told Lane my life was full of stress and power struggles. Lane was just the same, a simple man, with his strange ear. And when I watched him staring out to the lake, thinking only of the fish he might catch and fry with salt and oil, I knew I'd never be like him. I'd never be free of worries and ambition and I envied this poor man fishing for his supper.'

This was an old, entirely fictitious, story that Tafumo told his public. It was his way of explaining to his people their lives were truer than his, that they should be happy with their lot, should worry only of fishing and leave him to suffer the stress of running the nation. I was furious. Now he was patronising me in the way he patronised his people. We sat in silence until Tafumo pointed at the lawn that rolled out before us and said, 'We've come a long way, my friend. Pretty good for two barefooted boys from the bush.'

'Thanks to you,' I replied.

'Rubbish,' he said. 'You are the brains, always have been, listening for me, taking care of me, polishing my statue as I make a fool of myself behind it.'

This brief flash of self-awareness was ruined when he said again, this time more pointedly, 'But you have indeed come a long way. Now listen, I've had these toilets imported from Italy, finest in the world, you should take one; also there are some incredible tiles. I'll have them sent to your house with some men who will fit the toilet and lay the tiles.'

I wanted to shout, 'Your toilets may be imported but your shit stinks same as everyone else's.' It's what I'd have said years ago but now I said, 'Thank you, Excellency.' Inside my reply was a test; a word I was sure he'd dismiss. When it was just the two of us, if I threw in an *Excellency* he'd scoff, 'Enough with the *Excellency*.' But now he didn't. He smiled, basking in his generosity, a man who rules a nation and comes to his mourning friend to offer him a toilet. Power is a drug that makes the baboon forget he's foolish. And sitting there, next to Patrick's empty seat, I suddenly had a vivid image of the toilet and tiles Tafumo gifted me. Tiles that he'd sent along with two men who laid them on my bathroom floor. Hope suddenly stood up and I watched as she wheeled Tafumo out of the room. It was all over.

I remained seated, looking at the old men holding together this exhausted nation; their ugly reflections glaring and trapped under the table's surface. When he took power Tafumo declared, 'So far as I'm concerned, there is no Ngoni, no Tumbuka, no Chewa. There is only one tribe: Bwalo.' More lies. In fact, he hired heads from every tribe, inviting generations of blood and war to sit together. He wanted them divided and impotent. He differed from other leaders in one respect. He cut people arbitrarily, no one was safe, it mattered not who your father or brother was, anyone could be swiped out by a listless swat of his hand. Was I next? I stood and drifted through the palace as if sleepwalking – neither awake nor asleep but lost in the border between – considering if the man snooping in my office, the man following me, wasn't just David. Was David working with Jeko? Was Tafumo the invisible hand behind everything? Was my time up? Is this really how all of it would end? One night soon I'd look outside my window and on the lawn, standing in the silvery light, would be the figure of Jeko in his silly hat, waiting.

I was surprised when Hope came out to the car park. I hadn't seen her up close for years and the sight of her made me sad. Her skin, once a shiny pearl, now soaked the world into its greyness. Her sparkling eyes were now dull stones. What happened to us? It was a strange conversation. When she grabbed my hand, it had been so long since a woman had touched me that it felt forbidden. When she spoke my old name – *Sefu* – it was as if she'd electrocuted me, it sounded illicit on her lips, this name I'd never even told my first love. This name Tafumo whispered in his sleep, bubbling up from within. She was warning me about threats I was already aware of and the moment our hands unclasped, my sadness became almost unbearable. And wanting to stretch our time together, I offered her a lift to her tree.

'No,' she said, flustered. 'I like to sit there. I didn't know anyone…knew. I thought it was my own place. Do you still follow me? How do you know about my tree?'

She was terrified of me. She used to look at me like this when I was violent, when I blamed her for everything. That fear never dies. It lives in everything I touch. This woman I loved, this woman I ruined, this woman I beat. I beat her; beat this woman so many times bruises lay below her skin like storm clouds. When all along it was my lies that tore us apart. In my youth I believed secrets contained power; now I know they're poison. Poison that prevented Hope getting pregnant, killed our love, killed Rebecca and now pollutes my life. Nothing will make you lonelier than a lie. My lie sliced me in two. Two names, two lives, two wives, two of everything in a life that was still so empty. I wanted to wipe the fear from Hope's eyes, explain all the things I was thinking, but my clouded brain could only muster, 'I didn't mean to startle you. Just happened to see you there. It looks peaceful. Everyone needs a place to hide sometimes.'

Like drying mud, her expression hardened and just before she left, she said, 'I don't hide from anyone.'

As I drove home my mind cluttered with thoughts: thoughts of Tafumo, of Jeko, thoughts of Hope, thoughts of Sean and our meeting, of the anger that rose up when Sean told me I was a disgrace, that I wasn't educating my people – that truth – that anger that propelled me to lash out and fire him. I'd had no intention of firing Sean, I'd only planned to scare him a little, to get him in line so that he wouldn't rouse David's paranoia, so that he was one less problem to deal with. But when he had shouted at me, when he dared question me, my anger flared.

Ezekiel opened the gate, the security camera winked. I went to see Solomon who was asleep. I sat on his bed, wanting to lie down and let his breathing drown me to sleep, but a pain gripped my stomach and I rushed to the toilet and sat expecting a great evacuation. Nothing came. Sitting there, trousers puddled around my ankles, I saw my milky reflection swim in the tiles; the tiles Tafumo had gifted me.

I flushed the toilet, pulled up my trousers, and placed my ear on the tiles. Once the belch of the plumbing ceased, a hum continued. It was a sound I heard sometimes in the Listening Room in the Ministry, the soft static of a microphone recording empty space. I went to the garage to get a chisel and a hammer then returned to the bathroom. Quietly I chipped the grout between the tiles, then levered one off but there was nothing below but pasty cement. After pulling up many more tiles my floor looked like a crossword puzzle. I worked until my arms were drained of strength and then I lay down, the tiles cool on my back, waiting for energy to return. Out of habit, my tongue pried the sodden cavity of my molar but the dentist had pulled the nerve and no pain came. So I took the small penknife I kept in my pocket. Unfolding the blade, I laid it gently into the soft skin of my forearm, pushing down until it bit. The pain offered a fresh jolt of energy. I stood and walked into the warm silence of my wardrobe, got to my knees and extracted the folder from under the floorboard. The fog of sleep, which normally clears after a few minutes, now clings all day, drowsy and persuasive, seducing me back into slumber. Staying on the floor, elbow propping up my head, I heard Ruby cleaning downstairs. I wrote until I couldn't stay awake any longer, laying my head down and finally falling asleep. Ruby must have found me there; when I woke, I had a pillow under my head and a sheet over me.

Charlie

*C*LICK . . .

'Sean, did you know dung beetles prefer herbivore poos to carnivore poos?'

'Sorry, Skipper, I've not got time to talk, you caught me on a bad day.'

'Is that why you are sleeping on our couch again?'

'Exactly, yes.'

'Did you know cicadas stay underground for ten years then only live for a day?'

'Sounds like my muse? Gestating for ever and only lasting a moment.'

'What's a muse?'

'It's what I need to finish my book.'

'Can't you just buy one of these muses?'

'I tried that but it didn't work out. Turns out she's frightfully expensive.'

'Are you excited about the safari? Safaris are the best and the worst. They start with so much excitement but then they end with a dead animal. And how excited are you about the Big Day? Do you think it will all go well this year?'

'Never rule out the farce factor.'

'The fart factor?'

'*Farce*, Charlie, *farce*, although one must never rule out the fart factor either. Africa does farce like Italy does pasta or Amsterdam does dope.'

'What's dope?'

'Go ask your father.'

Click!

Charlie

THE MIRAGE MINIBUS WAS full of guns, beers and sand-wiches. Mr Horst, who normally shouted at black people, was actually talking to Truth politely, 'This your first safari?' Truth shrugged, 'I know guns, I can shoot.' But Bel said, 'We don't have insurance, you can watch but you can't shoot…'

Truth took the rifle from Horst and said, 'Stop acting like my mom, Bel,' but I could tell by the way he held the gun that he didn't have a clue what he was doing.

As Bel had a quiet word with Truth, I asked Mr Horst what *not having the right insurance* meant and he whispered, 'Means the boy doesn't have the balls to shoot a buffalo.'

On the way to the safari lodge, Ed drove us to a watering hole and everyone glued their faces to the glass, screeching each time they saw an animal. They acted like they'd never seen an antelope before.

Even when some ugly warthogs strutted about, tails shafting up from their bottoms, the dancers squealed, 'This is so *real*.' Next a group of giraffes came strolling by, moving their long legs in treacly slow-motion. And when some elephants plodded in for a bath, everyone in the bus got crazy-excited, looking at the lovely elephants with their wise old faces and old man's bums.

The animals were great but the watering hole looked sort of sad, drier than I'd ever seen it, little more than a black puddle.

That was because of the drought. The drought was a beast, Ed said, thirsty as hell, that sucked the water out of everything, turning the earth to dust. But Ed also told me that I wasn't to worry because Tafumo was going to bring a great rain, which would drown the drought and save us all. So that was good.

As we drove on, Dad explained to everyone that we couldn't have a whole entourage stomping about scaring off the animals. So we stopped at the safari lodge to drop off Bel, the bodyguards and dancers, who sat in the cool tent drinking beers, as we got ready to go. Mum hated me going on safari but Dad said it was *all good experience*, which was what Dad said whenever we did anything Mum disapproved of.

As guns were loaded and water bottles filled, I looked across the park, wondering if we'd get a kill. The grass rippled like a giant was running his hand through it. Then, as if the tall grass had woven itself into a man, a shadow broke from the savannah; slim and slow he moved like a leopard towards me and I shouted, 'Fantastic! Howzit?'

His arm shot up, face cracking into a bright smile. 'Hey, Charlie! Howzit!'

When we shook hands we did it the cool Bwalo way, grabbing each other's forearm, his skin rough as a rhino. He wore a T-shirt with *Team IBM '93* on the front, shorts, and no shoes. Fantastic was the most important man on the safari, the scout. He was the greatest in all of Africa. Mr Horst said Fantastic could track the day-old fart of a flea.

Fantastic led the way, touching broken twigs and sticking his finger in poo, Truth behind him crinkling his nose, then Willem and Sean, followed by Mr Horst who whispered to Dad, 'Fantastic does that shit for show, eh. For the tourists.'

But I think he does it for real because not long after, we were looking down the wavy distance at a herd. One of the bulls was huge, with its black-rubbery nose and horns curled like question marks. Though Mr Horst called himself the Great White Hunter, Dad said only a third of the description was correct: the bit about him being white. Mr Horst took three shots and none of them killed the buffalo, which was getting really mad.

Truth looked the most scared but, running alongside, I assured him that although buffalo had a great sense of smell they actually had terrible eyesight and bad hearing, so we were safe as long as we were upwind from him. But part way through my explanation, maybe Dad and Fantastic realised we were downwind, because they were suddenly really rough with me, dragging me so hard that I grazed my knees. And when we stopped running, I had two bloody knees covered in grit.

Finally, Mr Horst shot the bull dead. That was the saddest part. When a bull that had been happily grazing with his family was cut up into hairy chunks. Fantastic butchered it expertly. The bull's neck was twisted like a thick root, eyes pretty as a cow, its pouring blood churning the dirt into dark soup. I was going on about how the hair looked like broom bristles but Dad looked so unhappy, so I said, 'Don't worry, Dad, you didn't hurt my knee that much.' Dad gave me a weird hug and that was when Truth threw up and Horst laughed about what a pansy he was. When Fantastic asked if he could keep the bull's balls, Horst smirked and said, 'Sure, put a little lead in your pencil, eh.'

Dad called Ed on his walkie-talkie and he drove the minibus to us. We threw the bits of bull into the trailer and returned to the lodge, where Truth went off with a bodyguard who kept rubbing his back, as all the dancers poked at the bull and said, 'Jezzz-sus! That's like, so gross.'

Then, amazingly and incredibly, Sean met up with an old friend, right there at the safari lodge, which is like in the middle of the bush, in the middle of nowhere.

So Sean kept shouting, 'OIA, *only in Africa! Only in Africa!* OIA!'

Sean's friend caught a lift with us and on the way back we were stopped by soldiers who waved their guns about, and Dad said, 'Everyone keep calm.'

Sean

BLOODY SAFARIS. CAN'T STAND them but time away from this frazzled town was in order. There weren't enough hours in the day to fit in all my fuck-ups and being far from Stella would be good. Also it allowed me to interview Truth and, being officially unemployed, this was now my only source of income. But when I sat next to him on the bus, Truth grunted, hiding in the shadow cast by his cap. He didn't peel his eyes from his phone as my unanswered questions bounced off him. Only thing he said was, 'I wanna make a difference.' I couldn't stop myself saying, 'By giving CDs to starving kids?' The ever-hovering Bel took me to the back of the bus and said Truth wasn't in the mood, and I kidded her, 'I thought it was going great.' Professional to a fault, she responded with an automatic and un-heartfelt apology.

I stayed in the back of the bus, sipping beer. It was noon, hottest part of the day, the scorched centre, and town reeked of tar, paint and bananas. Even the beggars had retired to the shade of the jacaranda tree. Only the women kept working – keeping the country fed as men played politics – pounding mealie in big drums, like a diorama setting the day's rhythm, pestles jacking in syncopation, tossing them up and driving them down.

When we arrived at the lodge, as they sorted water and guns, Bel approached with a servile smile. 'Can you not include any of this safari stuff in your piece?'

'But I was hoping to write an entire article about what Truth is wearing. Where did he get the powder-blue safari suit from?'

'From Armani,' she said. 'Is it too bright? Will it blow your cover?'

'I was more worried the animals might fall about laughing.'

Hands on hips, she waited for a straight answer. I said, 'Fine, I won't write about it. But how will you stop the Australian tornado filming it?' She hesitated, determining if she could take me into her confidence again, then pulled a plastic cube from her pocket. 'He can't film without a battery.'

When we left the lodge, Wayne was hopping about screaming like a child. I walked behind Fantastic, feeling fat and pathetic. Looking at my belly, then at Fantastic's gleaming blackness, lean as jerky, I marvelled that we were even the same species. If Fantastic was evolution's optimal design, I was its offcut. And it wasn't long before Fantastic lived up to his name and Horst was squatting, fondling his gun like a shining cock. In the second just before the shot the world seemed to hold its breath – as if it knew it was soon to lose a soul, even the savannah seemed to stop swaying – then Horst pulled the trigger and birds burst from trees as the herd heaved into the grass in dark waves.

Horst had botched it. Fantastic told me a perfect shot acted like a blade, spinning through one shoulder, smashing the spinal cord then exiting the other side. Horst hadn't even hit a limb; the worst sort of shot, as it left the buffalo furious yet still capable of running you down and expressing its fury with a bloody good goring.

Injured and baffled, it swayed, then slowly turned its head towards us. Its horns were immense, black eyes staring down the distance to where we squatted. On my first safari, Stu gave the best advice: Don't worry about the animals, just watch Fantastic. He's a stone-faced tracker, so the only time he'll look scared is if something bad is about to happen. I saw the infinitesimal twitch on Fantastic's face as Horst botched the second shot. This time the bull charged, hooves chomping the distance between us.

Buffaloes are terrifying but not nimble; they stay the course, lowering their horns and shunting their bodies down the line. We had plenty of time to move, so when the bull stopped and looked up: we were gone. Fantastic pointed to trees up ahead, 'If we're missing him one more time we will run up those trees.' But Horst barked, 'I've got this,' and took aim. The world paused. The shot, sounding like a snapping branch, hit the bull's behind. Twisting in a sad-funny way, it tried to flick off the pain, to outrun its own backside, stumbling then vanishing, swallowed by savannah. Fantastic flinched again. There's only one thing worse than watching a buffalo expand as it charges towards you and your own spectacular death: and that's losing a buffalo. Fantastic whispered, 'This is not being good.' I wondered if that euphemism was the last thing I'd ever hear. Fantastic gathered us close and advised Horst, 'Mr Horst, now it is time for the rest of the group to go to safety, over there, a long way away to the trees. I am worried that the bull is no longer in sight, this is being dangerous for everybody.'

I was nodding like a madman, already grabbing Charlie to walk away, but Horst said, 'Hold your fucking ground, you lot. Trust me, I have this.'

Fantastic shook his head slightly, not enough to get into trouble for defying Horst, but just enough for me to see we were all in grave danger. Stu said, 'Come on, Horst, you and Willem hold your ground, I want to take Truth and Charlie to a safer spot and…'

'This is a safari,' said Horst. 'Truth is loving it.' Truth looked so scared I was sure he was swallowing his own vomit but he nodded like an idiot and said, 'I'm cool.'

Dead cool, I wanted to shout, as I realised that some sort of humid machismo was permeating these men, a sweaty madness had set in, and we were all going to have to stay here when we should be running for our lives.

Willem said, 'Nah, come on, Eugene, the rest of the herd will soon find this bull again and they'll group up to protect it. Then we're in real trouble. Let's you, me and Fantastic just track from here, let the other…' Horst looked at Willem, in that terrible way that an older brother can, and Willem, who was far bigger and stronger than Horst, backed down, like a turtle retreating into its shell. And I realised that Horst had bullied us all into holding our ground. Charlie was just out of earshot, as I whispered, 'You better fucking shoot it dead this time, Horst, or you will have a lot of blood on your hands.'

He snorted. 'Yah, yah, you pansies need to calm down and watch the Great White Hunter at work,' as he got himself in position and the rest of us tried to stand back, away from where we thought the buffalo might be. Stu and I shared an anxious glance as we all waited for the bull to move again, to give away its position. We stood and listened, listened to every sound, listened so hard I thought I could actually hear the sun scalding my skin, heat fizzing in the grass, bugs skittering in the soil, but the buffalo didn't budge. We formed a tight knot, backs to each other, looking out in every direction, searching the area for movement. Tiny flies dive-bombed our faces, supping at the moisture from our wide-open eyes, as time stretched into something agonising and unbearable. I wanted to scream at Horst for putting us in danger and, as heat beat against my head, I sensed that there wasn't a bull out there at all. But that Horst's baboonery had so enraged Mother Nature that she'd condensed her fury into a dark ball of vengeance and here it came, rolling through the grass to crush us. The world began to shake: the bull was charging. Fantastic's arms spread like wings, holding Charlie, Stu, Truth and me in place. Every fibre, every impulse, screamed to run, but Fantastic was right: we had to keep in as small an area as possible, until we knew where the beast was. The rumbling got louder, then the savannah yawned open and, like a whale cresting the surface, a flank broke out of the grass then vanished. It stopped, realising it hadn't hit anything, then, just like that, trotted out, not ten feet from us, facing away. He was so close I saw blood pour like ink down his hide. He turned and looked at us with an almost casual curiosity, at these strange crouching beasts.

Horst raised his gun but Willem held the barrel, hissing, 'He'll see the movement.' Horst pulled the gun free, and so it was: the bull saw and he was coming fast, faster than it seemed possible for a beast that big to move, closing in as Fantastic and Stu yanked Charlie and we ran, scattering across the land. Truth and I both tripped, fell and lay panting in the grass, the bull racing past us. Fantastic and Stu dragged Charlie, their ankles snapping and rolling on the uneven ground, and Stu tripped but the bull passed him – locked in on the smallest of us: Charlie – leaving Stu in the absurd position of chasing the bull, screaming at it, with the trees swaying up ahead as if calling Charlie to safety. Fantastic gave Charlie a last push, then turned and stood his ground in the centre of the bull's line, waving his hands to steal its attention away from Charlie. It was the bravest thing I've ever seen a man do. I watched Willem snatch the rifle from Horst's hands, raise the gun to his eye and hold his aim so long I nearly screamed, 'Fucking shoot,' only to realise Willem had the bull, Charlie and Fantastic in his line of fire. A crowded shot. Finally, he squeezed and – for a beat – nothing. Then, as if a giant had swiped its backside, the bull jackknifed, the sound of the shot reached my ears, and its horns tipped and ploughed the earth. Willem ran, gun lightly grasped, and I caught up just in time to hear him whisper in the way you would to a dog, 'Good bull,' before he shot him in the head.

Horst arrived screaming, 'Idiot! Not the head, not the skull! I want it clean!'

When Willem turned to his brother, I thought a fistfight would break out. Willem started shouting, 'You put us all in danger, Eugene…'

But Stu's face quickly stopped the brothers short. Even through his thick skin, Horst knew what had just happened, what had nearly happened; he knew he'd endangered Charlie's life. But being the king prick that he was, Horst immediately began revising history. Joking and thumping Stu on the shoulder, he said, 'Now that was a safari.' I'm no clairvoyant but it was crystal clear that Stu was about to lose his job by throwing a sucker-punch at Horst. But before he had time, Charlie caught up with us, looking exhilarated, and we all jumped on board Horst's revision train, making sure Charlie didn't pick up on just how close he had come to being gored to death.

Truth glided towards us, pale as a black man can be, and Horst shouted, 'Bet you don't see that shit in the States, eh.' It was clear that Truth had been in his own hell, his mouth speckled with dried spit, vomit on his trainers, his safari suit crosshatched with grass stains. He pulled the brim of his cap as low as it would go and Horst let him be.

I said to Charlie, 'You just beat the hundred-metre record there, Chief.' And Stu gathered him into a tight hug. 'You were like lightning, son. Let's not tell Mum what happened here, right?'

'How do you mean?' asked Charlie. And we all breathed a sigh of relief – realising Charlie had missed just how much danger he'd been in – as father and son went off to sit on a rock, where I saw Stu couldn't stop touching Charlie, his head, his knee, his cheek, his back, touching and rubbing him as if to ensure he still had a living son and not a ghost.

Horst barked on about what a great day it had been but, with Charlie out of earshot, no one was playing Horst's game any more.

When Stu returned, without hesitating, he hugged Willem and said, 'Thank you.'

Willem replied, 'It was not as close a call as it looked.'

'Close as it could be without me losing my only child.'

Unable to ignore the force of Stu's words, Willem nodded.

I went for a piss, expecting the panic to have boiled my urine blood-red, so was surprised when the normal seedy stream dribbled out of me. I zipped up and went to watch Fantastic butcher the bull so it could fit on the trailer, slicing open its stomach, slopping out its intestine. It's something to watch, how clinically and swiftly a beast can be deconstructed into strange, bloody parts. The good stuff was loaded on the flatbed. All that remained was the shadow of blood in the dirt and the thick rope of guts and partly digested grass, which was left for the vultures.

Jack

A SIMPLE PLAN. FANTASTIC WENT off to track for a hunting group and in the excitement of the returning safari, I was to slip out and hand over the case. The time alone was torture. Crouched in the bush, about a mile from the safari lodge, my hands slick with sweat. Reviewing the damage done to the case, I tried desperately to fix the fliplocks. But every time I pushed them down they yawned back open. I squeezed chewing gum into the slits to glue them. A pathetic solution but it would buy me time, even a few seconds. He'd hand over the money, take the case, start to check it and I'd bolt. Surely he wouldn't shoot me in front of a group of tourists? My stomach boiled. The anxiety was a feeling well known to me. I experience it moments before all my major mistakes. Even when my dumb head was too slow to figure things out, my body was forever warning me exactly how much trouble I was in. Even as a kid I remembered this cold dread. The time I dismantled Dad's watch. As dirt-poor farmers, that watch was the only object of any worth in our lives. Probably cost more than our house. It lived in its own box, a golden oyster wrapped in tissue. I twisted off the screws, prised a knife into the gap and shucked it open as springs and cogs spewed out, rolling and vanishing under furniture like silvery ants. I knew in the instant after the fact that I couldn't fix it. The harder I tried to get it back together the more pieces I snapped, lost, broke. Knowing it was broken was bad. But the waiting, waiting for my father to come home and beat me, my guts churning endlessly over themselves, that was the feeling I had now.

And this would end in worse than a beating. This guy Willem was an ex-soldier with a rough reputation; he'd make me pay. Would he kill me? You can't be sure what a man will do until the time comes.

I waited until I saw the minibus vanish into the bush, driving a few feet from where I crouched. When it returned with the kill, I took a breath and walked down the road, following in its dust. I assumed a few people would be there, maybe a party of three hunters. So I was stunned to see a large group, big men with walkie-talkies, tall girls in tight jeans laughing and smoking, people standing around with mobile phones, one guy even had a film camera. I nearly turned and ran but in the distance Willem had spotted me. He jogged over, pulled me into the fringe of the bush. 'Yah, you made it, howzit, Jack? Everything go well? Let's have a gander?'

I held out my hand and he nodded. 'Sure, sure, here.' He handed over a fat white envelope, tied with elastic bands. I tore the edge, saw the notes, and he said, 'It's all there, eh. Good job, Jack. Come on, come on.'

I handed over my backpack and said quickly, 'Just keep my pack, I don't need it.'

He looked at me, then looked back to make sure we were a safe distance from everyone. Their voices travelled over the bush to where we crouched, and for a moment it seemed as if he might just turn and go. Then he pulled his case out of my backpack, squatting down, saying, 'Let's just check the chemicals didn't leak, eh.'

As I watched his thumbs turn the locks, my tongue swelled and filled my mouth. I reached into my pocket for my knife. The heat of the sun pressed down on me, something fragile in the centre of me snapped, my heart thumped so hard the world shook, and Willem's face reared up so close I felt his spit against my cheeks as he was forcing the case and backpack into my hands, hissing, 'Fucking act calm, hold this, I'll deal with this, act calm!' And there, walking towards us, with his wire-brush beard and Hawaiian shirt, was an Irishman I used to sell weed to when I lived in Bwalo. I'd never have thought I'd be so happy to see that old drunk again. He used to buy a bag of weed then stay for days and smoke half my supply for free. Well all was forgiven as he stumbled towards us waving, his face surprised and happy, shouting, 'Jack! Fuck! Who'd have thunk it! Jack the lad,' then he was all over me, hugging me, and I gave him an almighty hug back and shouted, 'Shit, Sean. What the hell you doing here?'

'I'm trying to interview some poptart,' Sean replied. 'More's to the point: what the hell are *you* doing here?'

'I'm just on a bush trek, you know,' I said.

With his hand still on my shoulder, Sean stood back and stared at me, acclimatising himself to the coincidence. I watched as Sean took in the scene, weighing up what he was seeing. Me clutching a backpack. Willem standing in the bush with a tight smile scratched over his face. Sean muttered, 'Wait a minute here…'

Willem's fists curled and for a horrifying moment I saw Willem leaping on Sean, beating him unconscious then dragging his body into the bush. Panicked, I said, 'Sean, listen, um…' but then Sean interrupted, he let go of my shoulder and he did all the hard work for me. He tapped his nose, winked and whispered in a tone heavy with implication, 'I get you, Jack. You mean you're out *cutting some bush*?'

Then he turned to Willem and said, 'Will? Why didn't you tell me you worked with Jack? I thought there was something suspicious about you.' He thumped Willem gently on the shoulder, like they were old drinking buddies.

'What? No,' Willem protested. 'We don't, I don't know this man…I just noticed this idiot crawling out the bush and I came over to check.' Willem actually pointed at my face like a schoolteacher reprimanding a child. 'You should not be walking around a safari park. Dangerous place to be.'

Everything we did and said felt stiff and false. I checked Sean's face to see if he was buying it. He didn't believe it for a moment. He waved Willem's lie away, saying, 'Sure, Will, sure, your secret's safe with me, buddy. Hey, far be it for me to stop a bag of gold making it across the border. So long as you share. Don't worry, Will, you got the right man for the job. Jack of all trades, master of none, isn't that right, Jack?' and Sean shook his head and shouted up to the sky, as if talking to God, 'OIA, man! Only in Africa would you of all people pop out of the bloody bush. Hey, come back with us on the bus, plenty of room for one more. We can catch up on old times.'

That was when I realised Sean was the saint who had come to save me. I knew if I stuck to Sean, and held on to the backpack, then at least I could postpone giving it to Willem. In town, when everyone got off the bus, I could simply leave it under the seat for Willem to take away. I would be long gone before he got to his room and opened the tampered locks and saw the torn false top. I already had the money and now I just had to sit tight in the bus, stick with the safety of the crowd, and I knew I'd live through this. Grabbing Sean's shoulder, I said, 'Bloody good idea. Thanks, mate.'

As we walked, Sean ran ahead to tell Stu about the crazy coincidence, giving me time to whisper to Willem, 'I'll leave it under my seat when the bus gets to the hotel.'

Willem seemed to have gathered his nerves and, looking straight ahead, he said, 'Good, good, just stay calm.'

On the bus, drinking beer with Sean, for the first time in days I had just allowed myself to relax a touch when I felt the vehicle shunt to a stop and watched soldiers surround us. They weren't much to look at. Little more than stoned teenagers. One of them wore a pair of Bermuda shorts instead of army slacks. But even these untrained youngsters would know, the moment they saw it, that the long-range rifle in my case had nothing to do with shooting buffalo, and in Africa was used only for one very specific purpose.

Sean

HEAT HAD CAST A drowsy spell on the party but the arrival of the kill gave them a jolt. Dancers circled the trailer, prodding the carcass, saying, 'That's so disgusting.' I marinated my shot nerves in cold beer. And as the adrenalin left my body and the beer slowed my brain, I thought my mind was playing tricks on me when I spotted a man wandering out of the bush. Not just any man, now. But a man I knew. A man from my past. He wore snake boots, olive shorts, a grey shirt, and his hair was still curled up in a grey quiff.

For a surreal second I watched the man give Willem a bag. Though I was shocked to see this old friend of my mine, I wasn't surprised in the slightest by what he was doing. I knew the fella from way back. He had lived in Bwalo and we'd become friends. I say *friends*. He was my dealer and I was his best customer. As good a grounds for friendship as any. He was that rare sort of dealer who delivered. Spent a lot of time around my place until I met Stella, who told me she didn't want some 'no-good stoner' in her house. I explained that was difficult, seeing as she was engaged to a 'no-good stoner', but she refused to see the logic.

Jack was the first poor white African I ever met. Decades ago poor whites didn't exist; now there was a whole underclass of them, fallen through the cracks of a society that no longer favoured their fair skin. Jack and his wife Sally had lived day-to-day in Bwalo and Jack's 'couriering', as he called it, got them by. Then one day, as too often happens with good dealers, he just upped and vanished. I jogged over, snuck up on Willem, placed a finger into the small of his back and whispered, 'Don't move a fucking muscle.'

The fear on Willem's face was priceless. I spilt my beer, laughing. 'Only joking, Willem. Relax.' Willem stood speechless, as Jack and I fell into that funny sort of shouting conversation that occurs in the midst of a coincidence. And all that '*What the hell are you doing here?*' '*No way! What the hell are you doing here?*' meant it took me a while to spot Jack trying to hide his backpack. And when I finally twigged and busted the two of them, they laid on this hammy shtick, the very worst schoolboy acting, with Willem so freaked out I had to say, 'Don't worry, Will, your secret's safe with Sean.'

As we chatted, I considered how slim the chances were of bumping into Jack again. Though it had to be said that Africa is a coincidence-rich continent. Once in a bid to finish my book – and escape Stella – I'd travelled in buses and leaky boats to the most remote part of Bwalo, walked three hours to the only guesthouse, sat at the bar and who was the only other fella there: a Cork schoolfriend I'd not seen for ten years. Needless to say no writing was done, only heavy drinking and sweet reminiscing.

So we walked back to the minibus and I said to Stu, 'Look who it is? OIA, man!'

Stu shook his head in mild amazement. 'Wow. Nice to see you again, Jack. It's been a long time.'

When I asked if it was all right if Jack hitch a ride back to town on the bus, Stu nodded. 'As long as you can handle a vomiting pop star and a load of hot dancers.'

Jack laughed and we both sat together. I tried to get Willem over to sit with us but he gave me this bruised look. I responded with a big obvious wink to assure him I wasn't the sort of man to stop a sweet bag of the green getting over the border. Weed was not a major issue in Bwalo; it was semi-illegal, generally tolerated by a police force and army who themselves thrived on a healthy diet of the stuff.

When Jack asked how I'd been, I shook my head and said, 'Jack, you wouldn't believe the time I've had. One calamity after another, man. As if each new disaster is trying to top the last. You know?'

'I hear you, man,' said Jack. 'Oh, yah, I hear you.'

It was hard to talk properly because the bus was so loud and Horst was standing in the aisle, swigging beer, impressing everyone with tales of his great kill. Willem didn't even contradict Horst, so I thought the least I could do was set the record straight. Horst looked off into the middle-distance and said, 'Yah, you really have to admire the spirit of the beast. My dad always said, if you don't respect the thing you kill, it will kill you.'

'Did your dad also tell you lying is a sin?' I shouted, but Horst and his enthralled audience ignored me. I suppose, to outsiders Horst cut an impressive figure. A leathery brute with his shirt stained by blood and dirt. Bel, who sat behind, leaned over and whispered, 'What an ego. And I thought Truth was bad.'

'Horst is nothing more than a liar and a racist,' I said.

Bel flared her eyes, then asked the incendiary question that every tourist eventually asks, 'So is there actually much…' her voice dipped to a whisper '…*racism* here? It seems so peaceful, I haven't seen anything really…'

I pointed to Truth sitting up the front and replied, 'Well, look, Bel. The only black man on this bus who's not a servant or a driver is richer than God. So, yes, there's still racism. Bwalo is better than some but still worse than many. Personally, I don't believe that cultures ever integrate. They grate at each other until one wears the other down.'

My timing wasn't the best. Having finished up his glory story, Horst had been eavesdropping, and he sneered, 'What bullcrap, Sean. You've integrated with Stella.'

Refusing to take the bait, I just said, 'Great safari story there, Horst, you should write a book one day.' But the bugger got me again: 'I'd write a better one than you.'

Jesus, I was being slaughtered. Bel gave me a sympathetic look, Jack smiled awkwardly, and before I could muster a comeback, the bus stopped and Horst grumbled, 'Bloody checkpoint,' waddling up the aisle. Jack tensed up so tight I whispered, 'Easy, Jack. Horst knows these fellas, no problem. They won't dare search us.'

Having said that, I had my own cold sweats to deal with, speculating as to whether Josef had already put me on a blacklist. Watching the red-eyed soldiers climbing on board, I considered if this was the moment my charmed life turned tragic: the moment I was handcuffed, beaten and deported. I'd made enemies in my life with just as many men as women but this was the first time I'd offended an entire country. So I lowered my head as Stu bribed them with beers but they were persistent. And suddenly I realised, as the air tightened around my throat, that they were actually going to search the bus.

That changed things considerably. Normally a bus full of tourists was waved along; Tafumo knew the importance of projecting a postcard image to the outside world. Tourists were never searched or touched; backstage blood was always carefully hidden. The soldiers began barking at us to get off.

Once outside, they conducted us into a line with flicks of their rifles and, just to add a pinch of freaky to the situation, a troupe of kids emerged from the bush to stare at the spectacle. Why was there always a group of skinny kids everywhere you stopped?

One of the soldiers had a clipboard; it had Mickey Mouse grinning on the back. Very deliberately he moved his chewed Bic down the list and I imagined my name and mugshot with the word '*Execution*' scribbled next to it.

The dancers were squealing with fear, soldiers were taking the pistols off Truth's bodyguards and even Wayne, the cocky Aussie, was cowering. The one time the prick should've had his camera out, should've pointed it like a gun at their guns, threatening to show the footage to the world, and the bloody guy was standing there pissing his pants.

Of course, this was not my first roadblock. They're a day-to-day nuisance in Bwalo but something about this one was strange, something about the hostility in the eyes of the soldiers, the twitchy way they handled their guns. Then I realised what the real problem was: these guys were not actually soldiers; their uniforms were ever so slightly different. These were not Boma's boys. These guys were far worse: they were Young Pioneers. A bunch of psychopaths led by a sinister freak called Jeko. A man who shadowed Tafumo. And though he looked faintly ridiculous in his Homburg hat, something about the guy still sent the fear of God up me.

Jeko's young hooligans existed in that grey area, somewhere between the police and the army. They were Tafumo's dirty little force; the men who made people vanish, who made accidents happen. People called them the Magicians because they made all of Tafumo's problems disappear. Soldiers were bad enough, but when you were stopped by these boys it usually didn't end well. Naturally, my rational core presumed this could never happen; that a bus full of tourists couldn't just be shot dead on a bright sunny day. But another, more seasoned part of me knew that this was a country where anything can happen to anyone at any time. The Young Pioneers shouted at us and shoved us hard against the bus. Our own panic seemed to redouble in them; a few of the younger ones aimed their rifles at our faces. They seemed as scared as us and I sensed that the dancers' squeals were soon to be silenced.

Jack was clearly in the grip of a panic attack, his pupils flitting like trapped flies, searching out a gap through which he could bolt. I wondered just how much weed he was smuggling in. I wanted to assure him everything was going to be fine but all I could manage was, 'Stay calm, Jack.' And that was when I heard one of the men arm his rifle, that oily sound of sliding metal – *click!* – and I turned to watch Willem start to completely freak out. A soldier trained his rifle on Willem, who was gesticulating wildly, shouting unintelligibly. I assumed Willem must have a touch of sunstroke, or that he thought he was about to be busted with so much weed that even the dope-smoking soldiers wouldn't be able to turn a blind eye. In all the noise and chaos, I realised that Willem was the hero one minute, saving Charlie's life, and next minute here he was acting the fool and about to get us all shot. I was shoved by a soldier screaming, 'Back! Back!' waving his gun in my face. Jesus, this was it, shot to death on a sunny day. What a way to go. He yelled, 'Back, you, with the beard, over there!' Stumbling to the side of the road, I felt suddenly calm; I realised I should try and die with some dignity. I'd survived most of my life without the stuff so I hoped I'd have plenty in reserve, might as well try and muster a little at the end. I took a breath, turned to look my killer in the eye and saw the soldiers grabbing Truth, shoving the dancers, screaming at Bel, 'Take the shot, take it, this is good! Say cheese!' They were posing for a photograph. Bel, with shaking hands, was trying to take the shot on one of the soldier's phones. I realised that Willem had been shouting to the soldiers that we had Truth on board the bus, that we had an international superstar with us. And the soldiers had switched from killer squad to grinning fanboys in the blink of an eye. Jesus! Willem was the saviour of all of us today. First Charlie, now he goes and saves my sorry Irish arse, and Jack's too.

I owed that fella a serious drink, I thought, as I watched the scene. Soldiers monkeying about, touching the dancers' bottoms, Truth standing frozen in the centre, a rictus smile cut into his face, as village children squealed, '*Mazungu! Mazungu!*' Only in Bwalo would you be boiling in your own piss and panic, awaiting death. Then next minute, you're surrounded by dancing children, while a teenage millionaire grins at soldiers singing into their beer bottles, '*Beautiful Aaaafricaaaa!*'

Looking at that scene, I realised I'd never convince people of this place. Writing was the wrong medium. I'd been a fool. I shouldn't be struggling with a book. I should be composing a musical with a catchy title like *Bizarre Bwalo*. I could see it now, West End posters on the backs of buses: *Bizarre Bwalo*: It'll have you ululating in the aisles!

Ed came and stood by me, watching with blank disinterest. He smoked a Life and I grabbed a beer from the coolbox and drank it down in a few gulps. Something sharp kept catching my eye and I saw in the distance these blazing circles, odd fruit hanging from the trees. Ed and I walked closer to investigate and saw the silvery suns were CDs.

After many more photographs, Stu herded us back to our seats and bribed the soldiers with the remaining beers. But before Truth got on the bus, he noticed the CDs and shouted, 'Hey man! They ruined my albums!' Ed smiled as he explained, 'But this is good, Mr Truth. For they are using them as scaring-crows, to protect their crops. Keeps the stupid birds away.' What I'd have given for a photograph of Truth's face.

For the remainder of the drive, we fell into a silent trance; shock and farce will do that to you. Ed dropped me at my door. I shook Jack's hand and he smiled; calm again, now his dope was through the roadblocks. I winked at Willem too but he pretended not to see.

When I waved the bus off I noticed a bull's legs sticking out the trailer, something comical and grotesque in the way the hoof was pointing to the sunset. I looked up and staring at the sky, pink sediment decanting on to the horizon like glowing ash, I thought: Another crappy day ending in another heart-aching sunset.

After I'd checked every room of the house, I breathed easy. Stella was out. And I knew what I needed to do. The safari, singing soldiers, the fluky reunion with Jack: all sweet inspiration to break my block. At the very least I was determined to rattle off a puff piece on Truth. It wasn't until I entered the study that I remembered I'd abused poor Royal, her keys bent like a palsied face. I contemplated resurrecting my laptop. I'd once dabbled in the twenty-first century, purchasing a laptop thinner than a thought yet stuffed with more technology than a spaceship. But it resulted in no inspiration: only intimidation. When I finally found the 'on' switch, it asked me a slew of increasingly personal questions: age, sex, thoughts on genetic modification. The silvery brilliance of this machine built by machines made me feel fleshy and foolish, so I'd slid it like a puck into the spidery kingdom below my bed.

However, looking around me for inspiration, I realised I'd been unconsciously holding – and fiddling – with the answer all along. I didn't need retro typewriters, nor space-machines. I'd everything I needed right here in my hand: the humble Bic. Tenderly I rubbed the callus on my finger that had risen like a celebration when I used to write longhand. It had remained ever since, standing to attention, a memory formed in flesh, reminding me this was the secret all along: the simple pen. And as soon as the tip hit the paper, sentences – as if compressed within the black tube – poured out in wondrous, powerful order. And I was grinning like a kid when, half a page in, a brutal pain stabbed my hand, my fingers cramped into a claw and I tossed the pen across the room. Jesus, the pain! I winced and my little callus glowed bright red. In my frustration, I wanted to slice it off with a scalpel. But I was more squeamish than I was dramatic. So I glared at it: to think moments ago I'd been rubbing it like the clitoris of my muse. It was just a build-up of useless flesh. I tried to avoid the thought that I was the same. My autobiography: *Sean Kelly, A Build-Up of Useless Flesh*. Instead I took to staring out of the window, hoping some resolution would arrive. But in place of a resolution another problem stormed towards me. A gecko flashed across the ceiling in green panic as Stella stomped through the house, swung the study door open, and sneered, 'What are you doing, old man, still trying to write this greatest novel of the world ever?' then spat out a cruel little: 'Ha!'

'Look, Stella, calm down, I've some bad news, come sit with me a moment.'

She remained in the doorway, arms braced and legs apart, as if the bad news might blow her over. 'I'm afraid that for reasons which are utterly unjust, I've been fired. And…' I was getting sloppy; should have frisked her at the door: first her purse sailed past and landed with a thump on the floor. 'Now, Stella,' wobbling to my feet, her right shoe spun past me, followed by her left, which struck my belly. I shoved my desk towards her, causing her to move enough so I could squeeze past the door, her claws catching my neck as I jogged down the corridor, out the door and on to my motorbike, to ride to my oasis, the Mirage.

After a few fast drinks and in the mood for a fight, I think Horst and I went at it. Something happened, the details remain fuzzy, but a moat formed around me, people moving away creating a space into which rushed Stu, gently persuading me out of the bar. I asked if I could crash on the sofa but Fiona had put the kibosh on that.

So Stu, saint that he is, gave me the key to my regular room, one I hid in when things were too hot at home. Overcome with emotion, I hugged him, 'You're a good man, Stu,' as he manoeuvred me into the lift, where I was relieved to have so many walls to lean on. Attempting to assure him – and myself – that everything was somehow going to work out, I said something like, 'It'll all blow over, Stu. This sleeping elephant is vast enough to absorb the bickering of men. You and I both know that most of what is meant to happen here turns out to be little more than rumours; the plans of mice and men rarely ever happen. And even the few things that do actually happen are rarely finished. So let the world get on with its noise and let us sleep in peace a moment longer.' Stu shouted through the closing doors, 'Shut up and get some sleep.'

Charlie

AFTER THE SAFARI, AARON and I went to the back of the kitchen to watch the buffalo being strung up to bleed out. Its head was dunked in a nearby river, where fish would nibble and clean the skull so Mr Horst could put it on his wall and bore guests about how he shot it. But the body was strung up on a tree, hind and front hanging like a pantomime horse, black blood striking the soil like pepper. The staff had taken all the organs they wanted but Ed was annoyed Fantastic had taken its balls, as they were the best part apparently. Ed said that they made a man a man, whatever the heck that means. Tomorrow the bull would be sliced into strips, soaked in salt and spices, then Aaron and I would get to hang them on the washing line like bloody socks, so the sun could bake them into biltong.

When we got bored of watching blood drip, Aaron and I went to the bar where the adults were arguing. Why do adults drink and repeat everything all the time? Mum called it the Great African Dilemma. She said a dilemma is a question without an answer. But why Mum calls it *Great* I've no idea, as I'm pretty sure it was the most boring conversation in the whole world. Sean always looked like a kettle about to boil as Mr Horst told a dull story about corn or something. We snuck past the adults and, since Mum hadn't noticed I was still awake, went to play in the office.

We kept rucksacks full of water and biscuits in the office cupboard. Dad said they're in case we have to leave the country fast one day, but most of the time Aaron and I just raided them for biscuits. I was doing my impersonation of Mrs Horst when she's drunk, which is most of the time.

Marlene is South African, so when she's sober everything's a bastard – this *bastard* heat, the *bastard* car, that *bastard* maid of mine – but when she's half-cut everyone's her *bokkie*, which means *sweetheart* in Afrikaans.

So I was saying, 'Hiyaaa *bokkie*, whisky please *bokkie*, kiss me *bokkie*,' when Mum and Dad rushed in. Dad looked at Mum, Mum looked at Dad, then Mum said, 'How many times have I told you not to eat the emergency biscuits!'

Before I could come up with a good excuse, Mum gave me a peck on the cheek and snapped, 'Bed! Both of you.'

Aaron ran, then I ran too but I left the Dictaphone running. *Click!*

Mum: I thought he'd gone to bed hours ago. Close the office door, close it, lock it! Listen, I just heard: they think they found Patrick Goya.

Dad: And?

Mum: Well they found his body. Dr Todd said he saw the body. Said some heavies came to the hospital and forced him to sign the pathology report saying it was 'accidental'. Todd said he was terrified; he could be struck off for signing a false declaration, but he was too scared to refuse.

Dad: And?

Mum: Well, Todd said there was no way his wounds were from a car accident. Not unless the car had bashed one part of his skull again and again and tied his hands with rope and cut off his ears and lips.

Dad: Jesus Christ. Was it definitely Goya?

Mum: All I know for sure is that we need to get out of here. Things are closing in fast, darling, and we don't have much time left.

Dad: Sure sure. OK, OK, OK. OK look, look, let's just get through this Big Day and we can talk and sort out a plan and…

Mum: You say that every year.

Dad: Trust me.

Mum: My mother warned me never to trust a man who said trust me.

Dad: Your mother was a fucking nightmare. Look, listen, everything will be fine.

Mum: Will it?

Dad: Trust me.

Click!

THE COCKROACH

Bwalo Radio

D J Cheeseandtoast speaking to *you, beautiful Bwalo people, on the eve of the Big Day. Now we have much music to play and many things to look forward to today, but before we begin, remember this: beware of who you help, keep your ears peeled, for the cockroach can only rule the hen if he persuades the fox to be his bodyguard. Yes yes! And you get two sayings for the price of one today, for I am feeling so very generous. My mother always warned me never to trust a naked man who offered me his shirt. Can anyone tell me what this means? I still have no clue. Call in and tell me what it means and I'll give a carton of Life cigarettes to the winner. OK, now let's get on with our show. Ha! So for all of you out there suffering a bout of Saturday Night Fever, fear not! For I have the muti, I have the medicine. Doctor Cheeseandtoast is in the house to cure all ills and the tonic is a dose of Big Day muti. For on the Big Day the sun will shine, the wind will sing, and all your aches and pains will be washed away! Now to get us in the mood, here's 'Freedom' by Bwalo superstar, Zomba. Ha! Tomorrow we sing, dance, laugh and praise our glorious Ngwazi.*

Jack

I SHOULD HAVE HITCHED MY way out of the country. I should have walked across the border. I knew the moment he looked at my passport that something was wrong. He smiled. Maybe I should have paid a taxi or a bus to get me to the border. But I also knew that as soon as Willem got that case into his hotel room, and saw that I had buggered it up – that I knew what was inside it – he'd come after me, or send someone to come get me. Whatever his plan was, I could tell from the size of that gun that it was not the sort of plan that allowed for untidy loose ends like me. So I'd decided that an aeroplane was the only way, the fastest way, to get out. If I'd tried to get out via the bush or the border he would have had time to come for me. But I saw now, as the man slowly placed my passport into his own top pocket, that the airport had been a bad idea, that there was probably no route out of this country that would have been fast enough, or safe enough, to ever save me. That everything had been impossible, that all my options were exhausted the very first moment I'd said yes to this terrible job. I knew it all now; now it was all too late it was all too clear. Two big fellas materialised either side of me. And, without touching, gently moved me out of the queue into a room with peppermint-green plaster walls, a desk, and a chair where I sat under the crab-eyed gaze of a camera.

Hope

*I*PUT ON MY WEDDING ring. It only just fitted my finger, which had thickened with age. When I went to pick up my breakfast, Essop was there, and as we spoke of dull things much travelled between us, I felt a strange excitement, an old feeling of being wanted by someone, someone I'd seen so often that I'd forgotten to notice them. Chef winked at me when he handed over my food. Essop spotted my ring and said, 'Who is the lucky man who has breakfast with Hope every day?'

'Too old for all that,' I said, but I felt my face go hot like a silly girl.

Essop shook his head so hard his glasses slid down his nose. 'Never too old, Hope.' And his eyes were held by the shine of my diamond ring.

'I just like to look nice for my sun,' I said.

'Well it's a lucky sun,' Essop replied and I smiled and left.

I walked out the palace gates but when I got to my tree, two boys were lounging under it, cooling in its shade. The nearest village was far away and few people came this close to the palace, scared of guards and soldiers. But these boys seemed not to have a worry in the world. I felt like a dog whose territory was threatened. I wondered if they had looked inside the tree. Where had they come from and why had they sat here? Under my tree, the one piece of land in this world I considered mine alone. I calmed a touch when the boys both politely said, 'Morning, mother.' The endearment caught me out; if ever you forget you're an old woman you can count on the young to remind you. It was a polite term and I sensed they weren't mean. They were just boys, with all their awkwardness and bravado. I sat near, to show them, and me, that I wasn't threatened.

They immediately asked where I was from. 'I work for the King.'

I was pleased when the younger boy looked scared. 'The King?'

'Yes,' I replied. Hoping the less I said the more unsettling it would seem.

'As what?'

'Nurse.'

The older one smirked. 'A nurse? What does a god need with a nurse?'

His young friend giggled and I felt a childish rage in my belly. Children have a way of levelling you, reminding you that even though you're an old woman, once upon a time you cried in the playground in agonising sobs after being tormented by boys; once you were a frightened wife beaten by her bullying husband. Those old feelings live on.

Taking the fruit from my bag, I asked, 'Want a guava?'

They looked at one another, quickly checking each other's reaction, before the older boy shrugged, 'Sure.'

These skinny boys were not the sort to say no to food. He took a bite and the younger boy had the rest. For a moment we sat and listened to the crickets, until I said, 'You're obviously brave boys.'

'Yes,' said the big one automatically, before adding, 'But how do you know?'

'Because not many boys would dare come here. To this tree.'

'Why?' said the younger boy, wiping juice from his mouth.

'This is a witch's tree,' I said. The young boy stopped chewing. 'Don't you see the scratch marks?'

The young boy's eyes flared but the big boy snorted. 'Those are animal marks.'

173

I knew I was fine because he hadn't said, 'There's no such thing as witches.'

Although these boys went to school in town and were brought up Christians, maybe seen computers, maybe even been to the cinema, I knew they still had a living, breathing, fear of witches in their hearts. I knew their mother warned them about certain women. I knew I had them when he questioned the origin of the marks, not the fact of witches. Now on solid ground, I said, 'So you say. Well, I'm glad you're so…confident. I wouldn't be. I'm not nearly so brave as you boys.'

'Why aren't *you* scared?' the big boy asked with the fast intelligence of a bully.

'Well, the witch and I, we have an understanding,' I said quickly, convincingly, leaving the remark in the air between us, hanging, before adding to it. 'But she loves little boys, their hair, teeth, toes, earlobes.' And I stared at them for some time before saying, 'She uses guava to drug them, trap them, slice off their…' The young boy was up and sprinting as if the devil himself were at his heels. The bully took a moment longer, he made a brash exit, spitting near me before jogging away, not too fast, he didn't want me to think he was running scared. Watching them weave through the maize, bare feet nimble through the corn, limbs shining in the sun, spitting out guava, I knew they'd never return. When I finished eating I placed the bag into the hole in the tree, my arm dipped in coolness, deep in the living thing. I carved another line down the bark, wiped the blade on my top, then made my way back to the palace.

Charlie

THE POOL WAS ALREADY packed with people. The right side was lined with celebrities, all wearing big shades and sun hats, and also lots of dancers with their long licorice bodies. The left side was lined with blotchy white-and-pink locals, sunburnt hippos, hiding behind shredded magazines, trying to catch glimpses of celebrities across the water. I went to the bar and asked Alias if he had seen Aaron anywhere. Alias pointed up to one of the hotel balconies and said, 'He was helping Ed carry cases for Mr Truth.'

I walked past the pool, up the stairs to the balcony. Truth was staying in the Tafumo Suite, which was more of a house than a room really; it was by far the fanciest part of the hotel. I wasn't allowed to just go inside but I could see that the door was open a bit and, thinking that Aaron and Ed might be in there, I peered through the crack and I saw something amazing. Since Truth had stepped off the plane, he had been constantly surrounded by bodyguards and assistants who whizzed around him like a cloud of midges. But this time it was just Truth and only one bodyguard, the one that was always by his side. I could only see a slither of what was happening and it seemed like Truth was just looking down at his hands, but when I moved to get a better view I saw that Truth was holding hands with his bodyguard, like boyfriend and girlfriend, only this was boyfriend and boyfriend. Then the big bodyguard tilted his head towards Truth and they kissed. I had to cover my mouth to stop myself making a noise. I should have run right then, but for just a second I couldn't move. I'd never seen two men kissing. It looked really weird. Dad said in Bwalo no man is allowed to love another man, but in other parts of the world it is allowed. That makes no sense. How can you stop loving someone just because you move to a new country? When I asked Mum she explained that the only man that Bwalo men were allowed to love was Tafumo. That Tafumo does not want all their love for him diluted. Like love was some sort of liquid, like adding water to Fanta to make it less sweet. Solomon knows nearly as much as anyone about Bwalo laws because his dad works in the government and drives a Mercedes. So when I asked Sol about men kissing other men he said very seriously, gayness is against the law, Charlie!

Finally the bodyguard stopped kissing Truth and they smiled at one another, and before I realised it I'd touched the door and it creaked. They both glanced at me. It was funny in a way because for a second they both still had that goofy love-look all over their faces, then a second later they were so mad, so angry. But I was already off; running down the corridor hoping the bodyguard wouldn't chase after me and blow me to bits with his gun.

I didn't look back and the closest place I could find to hide was a room down the hall that was used for meetings and conferences and was always empty. It had a Please Do Not Disturb sign on it but I knew it was empty as usual, so I quickly ran inside and waited, my back up against the door, wondering if the bodyguard was going to get me.

I was thinking about how much trouble I was in: if the body-guard didn't kill me then Mum and Dad would do it for him, because one of Dad's main rules was that guests always have complete privacy. Between Dad's rules and Tafumo's rules, it was like you couldn't get away with anything around here. I heard footsteps outside the door and in a panic I got on to my knees and slid under the huge conference table, lying flat and still as a snake as the door creaked open and I watched the feet of two men enter.

I knew immediately that it wasn't Truth or his bodyguard, though. Truth wore box-fresh white Nike trainers that were the coolest shoes I'd ever seen and his bodyguard wore black boots that were a little like army boots. But these men had different shoes. One had on snake boots, the footwear of the UWA, and wool socks pulled up to his knees and the other wore slightly scruffy Bata Bata shoes, the sort a teacher might own. They didn't talk at first, they moved around the room, and one of them checked outside of the window and then there was a funny silence, the sort that makes you itchy, before the man in Bata Batas whispered, 'What the hell do you think you are doing?'

'I'm telling you it's all under control, so calm down,' said the man in the wool socks and as soon as he spoke, I knew it was Willem, his voice smoky and angry.

'It's not under control,' said the Bata Bata man, who was definitely a local Bwalo man. 'They have a tourist at the airport under interrogation. And you're telling me it's all under control…Why did you use this man?'

'Well why didn't you let the army bring it in like I suggested in the first place?'

'Because,' said the Bata Bata man, in a furious voice. 'I have been over this before. We don't have anyone that we could trust, the army is tiny and also nothing about this can come back to us. This has to be an external job. This is why we hired you.'

'Well I could hardly sling that thing through in my hand luggage; I was coming from Scotland, for fuck's sake. And this man I used is the best…'

'He is not the best if he has been caught and we are all about to get into…I can't believe…' The Bata Bata man was sort of telling Willem off and I could hear that Willem was furious about this as he hissed back, 'Listen here, you. I needed a real…real equipment brought in. I can't use a peashooter for this. I know what I'm doing.'

They spoke in whispers and hisses, like their sentences were under pressure; they spoke like Mum and Dad spoke when I was in bed and they were trying to argue without me hearing, speaking in codes and spelling words so I wouldn't understand.

The Bata Bata man said, 'I expected something more professional. You nearly had all of us...I had to see to this man myself. I can't believe...Why didn't you tell the man to go over the border, the bush, he was caught trying to take a plane out of here with nothing but a pocketful of cash, I mean...'

There was another moment of sharp silence, then Willem said in a tired voice, 'Just deal with him and let me get on with my job. You are in control here, you deal with that shit. This is your country. These details are nothing to do with me. I have what I need for the job you have paid me to do. I'm only here to do my job. Now leave me the fuck alone and sort out your problems and I'll sort out mine.' Then Willem stormed out and slammed the door behind him.

My heart was racing so fast that I thought I might be sick as I watched the man's Bata Batas pace up and down the carpet for a moment. Then he made a strange noise, like he was clearing his throat, and he walked towards the door. Just before he slammed it shut behind him, I looked up from under the table and caught the back of him, a bald man in a funny old suit and cheap Bata Bata shoes.

I stayed under for a while, wondering what I'd just heard. It was very unusual for a local Bwalo man to shout at a white man like that, so I knew that this was something bad. Part of me wanted to tell Mum and Dad that I'd seen Truth kissing and that I had heard something strange between Willem and this Bata Bata man.

But although they always told me to come to them with questions, whenever I had lately they ended up shouting at me. And I knew that the trouble I'd get into for snooping and spying on guests was far too big for me to handle. I would be grounded for life. And also what would Mum and Dad do if they knew about Truth kissing a man? Mum told me that, although it was against the law to be in love with a man, the heart has its own law, and that is what we all abide by. I still didn't know what that meant but I think it meant that Mum didn't mind men kissing men. And when I tried to figure out how I would tell them what Willem said, it was like untying a plate of spaghetti, it just made no sense to me, no matter how long I tried to straighten it all out.

So I decided that I should tell Aaron and Solomon everything first and then see what they said about it. I ran out of the room, checking to ensure that Truth and his bodyguard were nowhere near, were not waiting for me. Then I quietly tiptoed down the stairs and went to the kitchen out the back of the hotel.

In the kitchen courtyard Alias was slicing up the buffalo, slopping the meat into a bucket reeking of salt and vinegar. When I asked if he'd seen Aaron he told me Solomon and Aaron were playing near the house. Which was weird because Solomon didn't like Aaron, and it was only when I was there that the two played together.

We lived at the far end of the golf course in a concrete house Mum called the nineteenth hole. As I crossed the fairway, Mum caught up, gave me a kiss and said, 'Hi, sweetheart, the hotel is out of butter already, I pray to God we've got some spare in our fridge. What have you been up to? You look like you've been running around, do you have a fever? Come here and let me check your temperature...'

Her voice was so concerned and gentle that I nearly told her everything. I was just trying to figure out where to start, and also just how honest I should be about the fact I was spying, but before I could get it all straight in my head, Mum spotted that our front door had been left open, and she started to scold me. 'Why didn't you lock it, Charlie! How many times have I told you about this! Christ. That's the last thing we need...'

'I did,' I said and that was when we noticed one of the windows was smashed.

Mum pushed me back. 'Run, Charlie, run and get your dad and Ed.'

Last time someone broke in they poisoned our dog, hurt Innocence, took everything, and when the police came they just drank tea and kept muttering, 'Ah yes, but it is such a shame.'

So I ran as fast as I could and when we returned, Mum whispered, 'They're still in there!' and Dad shouted, 'Come out! Come out with your hands up in the air. We're armed!' and Ed picked up a broom that was leaning against the wall and held it up like it was a sword.

We heard whispering, then we saw a child coming out of the door: it was Aaron, and behind him, Solomon.

'Quick, you boys,' Dad shouted. 'Get out of the house, someone has broken in.'

Solomon and Aaron looked at Dad strangely and then Mum said, 'Um, no, Stu, I think they're the ones that broke in.'

Dad said, 'Oh,' really slowly as if he was figuring it all out, *Ooooh*.

Mum grabbed Aaron, 'Aaron? What's going on here? What's happening?' as Dad asked, 'What are you doing in the house, Solomon?'

At first, Aaron and Solomon were completely silent.

Then Solomon looked straight at Dad, he looked mad as hell as he said, 'We were just playing with Charlie.'

'No you were not!' I squealed. 'I was at the hotel looking for you guys. He's lying, Dad! He is lying!'

Dad raised his hand. 'OK. OK. Everyone just calm down. Let's see what's going on. Charlie, come with me.'

I followed Dad into the house and we went to my bedroom. My mattress was overturned. My window was open and all of my special toys from the UK had been thrown out, scattered across the garden. It looked like Aaron and Solomon had realised they were caught. They must have heard Mum and I return and then flung everything out of the window, hoping to climb out and run away, but the white steel bars bent over the window meant they couldn't slide through them. I looked out at all my toys on the lawn.

Dad leaned out of the window and asked, 'Everything there?'

I checked: one *Batman* comic; one toy car, a red Ferrari; my cool wristwatch, which was transparent and showed all the ticking bits; and my Spiderman action figure, which was missing one arm that I'd lost a while back. 'Everything is there except the Dictaphone Sean gave me.'

Dad checked the other rooms and nothing else was gone. Back at the *khondi*, Dad told Mum what had happened and she said, 'How could you, Aaron? This isn't like you.'

Ed had run off to get Innocence, who now came across the golf course with a face so fierce even I was scared. She flip-flopped across the fairway right up to Aaron, and before anyone could say anything she slapped him hard across the face.

Then she grabbed his cheek and he started to cry as Innocence yanked his ear, stretching it like rubber. 'Say sorry to Charlie! Sorry to master and to missus-master too.'

Aaron cried so hard snot ropes fell out of his nose as he said he was sorry again and again until Mum said, 'ok, stop, Aaron, stop, stop.' Innocence and Mum whispered something to each other, before Innocence dragged Aaron off across the golf course by his ear.

Once they were gone, I turned back to the action, crossed my arms and waited for everyone to start shouting at Solomon. But when no one did, I shouted, 'Solomon! You have my Dictaphone and I want it back right now! Now! That's the coolest toy I own! I want it back! Give it!'

No one seemed to want to talk, so I stepped back a bit, giving Mum room to really scream at Solomon. I waited, wondering when Mum was going to start giving Solomon one hell of a telling-off. But Mum just said, 'Charlie, go get a Fanta from the bar, we'll deal with this.'

I shouted, 'But he stole! He took it!' and Solomon looked at me like he was trying to kill me with his eyes. Then everyone just stood around looking at one another until I screamed, 'How come Aaron gets told off but Solomon is just…'

Mum gave me *the eye* and Ed gently led me back to the hotel. 'Let's get you a Fanta, *bwana*.'

I was crying now because I'd lost my Dictaphone but also because it was so unfair that no one was telling Solomon off. None of it made any sense. As we walked away, I looked back and Solomon was standing there with arms crossed tight as a knot, Mum wasn't saying anything, and Dad was on the phone talking really fast.

Josef

WHEN I WOKE UP my body wouldn't move. I stared at the ceiling, fearing that exhaustion had finally paralysed me. Using all my strength, I reached to pull the penknife from under my pillow, placed the blade on my forearm by the rows of healing cuts. Skin bunched around the blade and, when it bit, blood ran down the sides like lips kissing the steel. Muffling my scream, I rose off the bed and got dressed. Ezekiel was dozing at the gate but roused when he heard the car crunching over the gravel. He pushed open the gates and saluted. As I drove to the office – endlessly checking the rear-view mirror – David called. Soon as he started to speak, I knew he had something for me, his voice pitch high with excitement. 'Morning, minister. We detained a man who says he is a tourist, trying to take lots of money out of the country.'

Tourism was part of my portfolio and I was responsible for potentially delicate situations. Anything involving white tourists was considered 'potentially delicate'.

So I said, 'I'm sure it's nothing but I'll check it out,' and over the static line I heard David waiting, waiting for some sort of compliment about his good work. I left him waiting.

When I got into the airport, the guard guided me through streams of tourists to the back of the building, down a corridor that led to a pale-green room.

Staring through the window at the tourist, I asked, 'How long? Has he had any water or tea?'

'Two hours, baas,' said the guard. 'No water.'

'Well, go make the man a cup of tea, for God's sake.'

I walked in smiling, hand outstretched, greeting the man. 'My friend, I hope you've enjoyed your stay in Bwalo, my name is Josef Songa from Bwalo Tourism.'

When he shook my hand, I leaned in, winked and whispered, 'Sorry, our airport staff are being overly protective. Big Day coming, we want it all to go without hitches. Yes?' I put on a thick African accent; it settled them, believing me to be a dumb bureaucrat. I mimicked Ruby's verbal tic of tying off sentences with a drawn-out and friendly, 'Yes?'

'I'm Jack Franklin. I'm a British citizen but resident of Kenya,' he said, like a soldier giving name and rank. His voice fluttered and he was too easy to read. The furrows of his brow told me he was a man in above his head, pushing what little luck he had, always owing more than he made. 'Now, my good friend Mr Jack, most importantly have you had the most splendid holiday in this our marvellous nation of Bwalo. Yes?'

He nodded. Power is an exclusive spirit, possessing only one person at one time. You can't see it move but, like wind, you can catch its effect. I watched it fill this man as he sat up, in control again; big men are used to being in control. 'Good good, this is good. We welcome tourists and hope you'll tell your friends of Bwalo's beauty. Yes?'

'Sure,' he said, patronising now, the spirit shining in his eyes.

'We're going to let you go but we would like to know about this money. Because you see, *bwana*, we're a poor people. We see a lot of cash-e, we think, goodness, so much cash-e. Yes?' Looking at his red eyes, I wondered if drugs might be the issue. 'Let me get you some tea and we can talk a little more as good friends do. Yes?'

'Sure,' he said flippantly, and I got up off my seat, turning as if to leave, then – using the back of my hand – slapped him precisely across the face.

184

He stood so fast his chair fell over behind him. Something shifted. The light on the security camera blinked. We stood, facing one another, watching for a brief moment. Then very slowly, he turned, grabbed his chair and sat back down. It's ill-advised to do more than a light slap. The world was watching, more than ever, but usually a slap was enough to open up the mouth of a scared man. Now, in my normal voice, I continued, 'Mr Franklin. You're trying to catch a flight out of the country and you say you're a tourist but you don't have a bag, only lots of cash. We've detained you for hours without a charge or legal explanation and not once have you asked for a lawyer or an embassy representative.' His eyes searched the space around me for the dumb bureaucrat who'd been sitting before him moments ago. 'Our country is beautiful but our prisons are not. So, here is what's going to happen. I'm going to get tea, then we'll talk properly and you'll tell me the full story of this cash. Cash always comes with an interesting tale and I know that you know what it is.' I could almost hear his heart thumping as I tied off the end of the sentence with a sing-song, 'Yes?' I stared at him a long time, observing his fear, before asking brightly, 'Milk? Sugar?'

'Four sugars,' he mumbled.

'Like we Africans,' I joked. 'You like your tea so full of sugar the spoon stands.' He didn't smile but his shoulders relaxed a touch. Tension must be relieved, like teasing a fish on the line. If it's permanently taut it snaps and you lose the catch.

In the corridor the guard was standing with the cup of tea ready and a fistful of sugar cubes. When I returned to the room, placing the cup in front of him, he spoke without prompting. 'I did a courier job for a guy. Don't know his name. Big guy, meaty, a yarpie or Zimbabwean, not sure, Afrikaans maybe, white guy.'

'And?'

'And he told me it was chemicals, not drugs, all very low-grade illegal.'

'What chemical?'

'Something to extract gold. Potassium something or other. I'm not sure…'

My phone began to vibrate, again and again, like an insect trapped in my pocket. Holding a finger up to silence him, I read the text, and it brought such relief that I smiled: '*Josef. Can you meet me at Victoria Market? PG.*'

Before considering the problems that this text invited into my life, I simply felt a deep and clear sense of relief. PG: Patrick Goya. Alive. I knew it.

He looked confused as I said, 'I have a colleague who will take over from me. You tell him everything you know.' Then I left the room and told the guard that I was sending David to finish the interrogation. As I walked down the corridor I texted back: '*On way.*'

When I called David, he immediately asked, 'Did he confess anything?'

'He's just small-time, David. But, look, something important has come up. Can you take over and finish the interview? You might be partly right about Horst. Sounds like this man has smuggled something in, chemicals, drugs probably, for a man who fits Horst's description.'

'Good, good,' he said.

'But listen, David. Don't hurt this man. We don't want any incidents. And get someone to tail Horst; don't let him out of our sight. But if it's some small drug deal, let it go until after the Big Day. We can't have any scandal, understand?'

I ran: out of the dark airport, blinking into the bright steel day, and drove in the opposite direction of town, waiting to see if a car materialised behind me. It was almost impossible to tail someone on the airport road where only a handful of cars moved sluggishly along the thin rail of tarmac that crumbled on either side. As I obsessively checked the rear-view mirror, I caught glimpses of myself, shocking glimpses, of a sick, old man. I'd aged enough now to see my father in my face. Though I'd no memory or photographs of him, I instinctively knew I was now staring at him. That I'd grown into him, with my sunken eyes, my grey-green skin, dusky as an artichoke. He'd have looked as exhausted as this after a hard life, a village life, raising children and farming a tiny scrubland until he died of malaria not long after I was born.

When I knew I had no tail, I turned towards town, driving via the back roads, wondering how I could help Patrick. Was he in need of a little money? That I could do. But what if he asked me to let him stay at my house, to risk my life, Solomon's life, to invite Jeko in to kill us all? But for all the fear, I still felt a strong sense of vindication that I'd been right, he was alive, and a small sense of assurance that all was not lost, Tafumo wasn't killing again, Jeko wasn't vanishing men and women and children.

My phone rang. It was an unknown number. Assuming it was Patrick – and about to warn him not to talk over the telephone – it took a moment for me to register that it was actually Essop, chatting brightly, 'My friend, how you feeling? Where are you? Did you get your bad tooth sorted?' Trying to get off the phone, without raising suspicion, I said happily, 'I'm much better, Essop, thank you, just busy.'

Essop wasn't the suspicious sort and he wittered away as I pulled the car into an alley, walking cautiously towards the market via the back streets.

'You sound busy, Josef, so I won't keep you. Shame we couldn't do sundowners in the end.'

'Soon as this Big Day is over we'll drink a proper drink together. I promise.'

'OK, my friend, till then.'

I put the phone back in my pocket and came out of the alley. The market was thick with hawkers and tourists haggling for carvings and batiks. Sugarcane husks carpeted the floor, flies swarmed around the hot yams, stalls lined both sides of the street, facing each other, packed with carvings of elephants, lions and warriors arranged on flax mats like some over-populated chess set. I was about to text Patrick to get a bearing on where he was in the market but through the streams of people I spotted the back of him, his tall frame towering over the short Bwalo people. I saw no obvious threats, no soldiers, none of Jeko's Young Pioneers. Patrick was dressed badly, no longer in a tailored suit but in a dirty T-shirt and embarrassingly tattered shorts, some sort of disguise. His feet were bare and exposed and he looked pathetic and primitive.

People moved into my path as I walked and I gently pushed them aside; one man started to protest but as soon as he saw it was me, the only man in a suit in this shabby market, he bowed and started apologising. I told him to shut up before he drew attention, then I saw Patrick – who'd noticed the commotion – moving away, skipping past people, panicking that he'd been spotted. I reacted fast, jogging through a tunnel yawning between us as the crowd parted, and I finally got within reaching distance and he turned, collapsing to his knees, prostrate, his face close to my shoes, begging, 'Sorry, minister, sorry, sorry, I do not know why I am running.'

I touched his dirty hair and when he looked up I saw that this man wasn't Patrick. He was just a man with Patrick's figure who'd seen me and run, like any man should when they saw the likes of me coming.

Patrick wasn't here – he wasn't anywhere – it was a trick. Looking around – expecting to see soldiers, or spot that Homburg hat bobbing above the crowd towards me – I felt faint, and in the dark swoop my senses retreated deep inside my body, the world stretching away, as I stumbled back down the alley.

Jack

THE FIRST MAN WHO came in was grey as death. He looked bad but smelt worse. His face hollowed out, the whites of his eyes bloodied like a burst embryo in an egg. His suit was expensive, shoes shinier than glass, but his face was wrecked. He had what we used to call as kids a nappy-head, hair dense and messy as moss. However, he came in smiling and shaking my hand, talking in this pidgin English about how everything was going to be fine and had I had a good holiday, and sorry about how heavy the airport officials were. Then just as I breathed a sigh of relief, thinking I wasn't going to go to prison, he stood and slapped me across the face. His voice changed and he was suddenly a well-educated official threatening me. In a panic, I told him half the story, the one I was told by Willem, no mention of names, or the gun. But before I really got started, he looked at his phone and left.

Josef

As I drove back to the airport, I considered calling my Ministry and asking them to track the text message that I'd been sent. But I knew whoever sent it knew what they were doing and it would be blocked. There was also the possibility that it was someone *in* the Ministry, someone high up, who had sent the text. Deleting the message, I tried to think why they wanted me to go to the market. Did they want me out of the way? *Who* was behind it?

Parking in front of the airport, I was relieved to escape the sharp daylight as I entered the cool building. I pushed through the crowd to the immigration rooms. Marching down the corridor I knew something was wrong as soon as I turned the corner: the guard wasn't there. Jogging to the door I saw through the window that the suspect was gone. My knees melted as I walked into the room and sat down, looking across the desk at the empty chair. I shut my eyes, placed my elbows on the desk and lowered my face slowly into my hands and in the warm silence, my face wrapped in my palms, I heard a mild electronic whirring and glanced up to see the security camera, its light blinking.

I stood up and stormed through the airport, screaming, 'Where is the guard that was at Room 6? Tell me! Tell me! Where is he!' Tourists looked bemused and airport officials tried to help, their faces twisted with fear, but no one had any idea what I was talking about. Then I spotted the guard, far across the concourse with many people between us. He looked as if he was sneaking away, so I shouted, 'Where is he?', my voice echoing across the large space as people turned to stare.

I ran over and dragged him back by his arm, taking him down the corridor to the small room where the suspect had been. I pointed at the empty chair. 'Where is he?'

'You took him, minister,' he said. 'The man came and told me you wanted to take him. I let him go with them. They said it was your order and…the man came and he told me…the quiet man, he had a document you gave him, a release form, it had your name on it and so…so…'

The guard backed against the wall, as I yelled, 'It was David. Was it David? Tell me now.' He looked at his shoes, as I screamed, 'Get me the tape! Get me the tape! From the security camera. Get it. Get it!'

He was shaking his head. 'Sorry, minister, but the camera in the room, she is broken.' I remembered the red light. He was lying: someone had got to him first, someone he was more scared of than me. 'Listen,' I said slowly. 'Look at me and don't stare at your fucking shoes…' I moved my face into his, almost touching him. 'Tell me who did this. Or I'll do far worse to you than David did…'

The guard and I both turned when we heard the footsteps and there stood David at the end of the corridor. I walked towards him so fast he instinctively retreated, stumbling backwards until I caught up, grabbed his shoulders, and David started talking: 'What's wrong, minister? I thought you were gone? Are you OK?'

'I'm in better shape than Jack Franklin, if that's what you are asking me,' I shouted and David did a passable impression of a confused man.

I shook him a little. 'Don't fucking play the fool, David. How dare you take him out of the room. Where is he?'

David acted well, I'll give him that. 'I have not touched him, minister. I'm only just arriving now. I had to make sure a guard was on Horst. I've just arrived, I'm telling you, minister, telling you the truth, please, please look at the tape.'

I shook my head, releasing David. 'What do you think you're doing, David? Do you think you're more powerful than me, that you can play games with me? I'll crush you, David, I will…' When he tried to defend himself, I screamed over him, 'I don't want to hear from you until the Big Day is done! And we will review your situation! I don't know what you are up to, David, but you are suspended with immediate effect. Now get out! Get out of my fucking sight!'

For just a second, I thought he might actually take a swing at me. He stood shaking with anger but instead of lashing out he suddenly looked broken, his body twisting as he slumped, exhausted. Then he turned. Watching him limp away, I felt my phone vibrating as texts and messages arrived one after the other. There was a list of missed calls from the Mirage and four texts from Solomon asking me to call him. I checked my voicemail: one from Stuart saying, 'Sorry, Josef, but something has happened with Solomon but um…I wonder if you…'

I called the hotel but the receptionist said she didn't know where Stuart was. I called Solomon; he didn't answer. The corridor tightened around me. Something had happened. Had the text been a test? Had Jeko sent it to see if I'd help Patrick? Had someone broken into my house and found my folder? Were people there now, tearing it down to find evidence of my sedition? Was I about to go to whatever place Patrick had gone and Levi before him? Was Jeko in my house, his grey hand wrapped around Solomon's neck?

I drove back to town with my hand on the horn, leaning out of the window, screaming at cars to pull over. They all did; no one stopped a government Mercedes. I drove erratically, heat beating off the road, twisting the world out of focus. Parking at the main entrance, I ran through the lobby and shouted at the receptionist, 'Where's my son? Where is he?'

She pointed to the office and there he was: Solomon sitting quietly at the desk. For a second I just took him in, sitting there, alive: my son. Soon as I entered the office, Stuart stood and launched into a stuttering explanation, 'Um, Josef, thanks for coming, look, um, Charlie has lost...Solomon may have been in our house and...so...we think some property might be missing from our house.' Needing more time to control my breathing, I didn't reply, simply nodded as Stuart stuttered, 'I-it's j-just a toy, a little recording device, a present from someone and we are not sure...' A large window dominated the office and daylight was streaming through, blurring everything; Solomon, Stuart, even the furniture seemed coated in a fine layer of glowing dust. Horst's idiotic portrait stared down. I noted that he had illegally hung his portrait higher than Tafumo's.

The brightness dimmed a touch as I fought to gain control of my breathing and – realising that Stuart was waiting for a reply – I finally found my tongue.

'Solomon. Did you steal it?' I stared at my son, playing the furious father when all I wanted to do was wrap him in my arms, ecstatic that my fears were not realised, that he was alive.

Stuart shifted awkwardly then said, 'That's fine, Solomon, it's all...let's just leave it and get on with our day, sure you and your dad are busy and...' I raised my hand to silence Stuart. 'Solomon, what do you have to say for yourself?'

There was a long defiant silence before Solomon pointed at Stuart and shouted, 'We are richer than them. Why would I steal from people who are poorer than us?'

In the shocked hush that followed, I saw the arrogant glaze on Solomon's face, my son, my blood, perfectly reflecting my own pride and cruelty.

I grabbed his arm and shouted, 'You say sorry to Mr Johnson! How dare you talk like that! How dare you!'

Ragged, wild and out-of-control, the sound of my voice brought tears to Solomon's eyes, as he muttered, 'Sorry, sorry, Mr Johnson, I am sorry, I am sorry,' his breath catching in his throat.

I left Stuart frozen, still standing behind his desk, mouth open with shock, as I yanked Solomon across the lobby, my brain churning the phrase over and over and over: burn the folder, burn the folder, burn the folder.

Sean

THE NIGHT HAD CHEWED me up like sugarcane, sucked me of goodness, and spat me into the dawn. I woke up exhausted and confused. Stu had kindly lent me some fresh clothes, which were perfectly folded at the foot of the bed, and as I changed into them I tried to remember yesterday. I glimpsed only slim flash-backs among vast tracts of blackout: being fired, fighting Stella. I was suddenly arrested by an image of Stella on the kitchen stoop, staring down a rifle sight, waiting for me to return. It was time to tidy my act up. I left the hotel room determined to have a sober day, to deal methodically and clinically with each of the many problems lining up in my life.

With a mobile in one hand, coffee in the other, Bel caught me sipping my morning beer at the bar and said, 'Morning, Sean. Truth would like me to offer his sincerest apologies for yester-day's failed interview.'

'Do you ever get bored of apologising for other people? Has he recovered from the safari?' Letting her tight smile slacken a touch, she sat down next to me and said, 'Look, Sean, he's nine-teen. He's one of those stars that went straight from his mum's house to his mansion. They're the worst. He can't even work a dishwasher.'

I nodded and then she said, 'Now here are the ground rules.'

'Oh, you mean like a safe word. How about *Eskimo*? If you're getting carried away with the handcuffs and whatnot, I'll just shout *Eskimo*. You should know I bruise easily.' Her eyes rolled, and I said, 'I thought all interviews ran a fairly predictable line. I ask questions he fails to answer. I go away and, with the god-like power of a hack, breathe life into the vacuous poptart.'

'Seriously, Sean. First rule is: no hint of what I told you about his,' her voice dipped, 'sexuality.'

'My lips are sealed tight as a nun's…' She interjected, 'And don't ask about his mother.'

'What about his mother?'

'That's what you're not allowed to ask.'

'I'm not allowed to ask about things I don't know about. Doesn't it defeat the purpose if I can only ask about things I already know?'

'Please ask at least three questions about the album.'

'What's it called?'

'It sold millions and you don't know what it's called.'

'Amazing, isn't it. Don't worry, I'll just ask the kid.'

'No you won't. It's called *Mirrors*. And don't run over twenty minutes.'

'I'd be shocked if I stretch to twenty minutes.'

'Are you drunk?'

'Of course. Are you stupid?'

'I'm just doing my job, Sean.'

'Can you believe this is actually your job?'

'Much as I can believe this is actually your job.'

'Touché.'

Then she brought our friendly banter to an abrupt stop as she snapped, 'At least I'm not squandering a considerable talent.' I returned a baffled look and she explained, 'I bought your book from the hotel shop. And can I just say: I love it.'

'You can say it to me every day. Please tell me again how clever I am.'

'Don't sleaze up to me; you'll ruin the whole thing.'

'So there *is* a thing,' I shouted triumphantly but she instantly countered with, 'Yes. A thing called your fiancée.'

'You got me there,' I said.

'So you writing another?'

'I'm attempting to break the record for longest gap between books. Presently held by Joyce who took seventeen years to complete a book. It was *Ulysses*, mind you, so I suppose it was worth the wait.'

'Are you working on the Great African Novel?'

'Achebe, Conrad and a thousand others beat me to it.'

'Great Irish novel?'

'I refer you to the aforementioned *Ulysses*.'

'Great expat novel?'

'I'm blocked. Can barely write a cheque.'

'It should be the Great Sean Kelly novel then,' she said, pulling my book out of her handbag. It always shocked me when I saw it again, this child I once loved with all my heart then abandoned. There it was, on the bar, gently abused by a recent reading.

'Would you?' And she gave me a pen.

I wasn't sure what to write. So blocked I couldn't even muster up an inscription. I stalled. 'You bought one of the only two copies sold. Mum bought the other but said it was nothing but rude words and filthy thoughts.'

'Well, I like rude words and filthy thoughts.'

'Got it,' I said, and wrote, *Where the fuck have you been all my life?* and put my phone number at the bottom.

She smiled, placed it back in her bag and said, 'Right. Ready to interview Truth?'

'I'd really rather not.'

'For God's sake, Sean, just come on and get it over with.'

In the centre of the Tafumo Suite, Truth sat like an atom surrounded by swirling assistants. Though I'd given my new digital Dictaphone to Charlie, I'd held on to my original, a huge old tape machine. I pressed record and it purred on the table like a cat. Truth sneered at it and, relaxing him with a little small talk, I said, 'Isn't she a beauty. Old as me. I like tape, I like analogue. It's got more integrity.'

He shrugged, 'I'm all about digital,' then he spelt it like he was singing a song, 'D.I.G.I.T.A.L.'

'Right you are then,' I replied. 'Well, how about we get S.T.A.R.T.E.D.'

He didn't crack a smile. Knowing how ill-prepared I was, and hoping to buy time, I asked, 'Do you think I'd be able to get a beer? I'm awful parched.'

'Truth is teetotal,' said Bel, who was now standing behind him with all the other assistants trying so terribly hard to look like they actually did something for a living.

'Shit,' I said.

'And no swearing,' Bel explained. 'Truth is religious.'

'Tough room,' I muttered. 'You're teetotal and religious yet you went on safari?'

'Just 'cos I believe in Jesus don't make me no vegetarian.'

Usable quote, I thought. 'Killing animals just seems a little unchristian.'

'I'm an entertainer not a priest. I'm full of contradictions.'

Full of something. But at least I had a second quote. Twenty words to work with, only a thousand to go. But after this brief burst, the poptart seemed spent; he slumped and stared at his phone.

I waited for him to look up until it became clear that I was to conduct the interview while he completely ignored me. I tossed out some puff questions: 'Why do you think Tafumo asked you to play the Big Day?'

'I sing about truth and Tafumo is all about truth.'

God give me strength. 'Is it because Kanye turned the gig down?'

This caused a brief flurry among the assistants but Truth wasn't taking the bait. 'Nah, I love Kanye and I love Tafumo.'

'Whole lotta love. So is it because you've got a song on your new album called "Beautiful Africa"?'

'Could be,' admitted Truth. If this was all I was getting I might as well make up the article from scratch. 'Will you sing that song?'

'Never reveal my playlist.'

'Oh? Well, now that's interesting,' I said, seeing something there. 'And why's that?'

'Just 'cos.'

Christ. The world is run by entitled creeps.

My foot started tapping erratically and I heard myself asking the question, 'Do you like Billie Holiday?'

'Never heard of him.'

I caught Bel suppressing a smile.

'Well, that's a shame,' I said and he snapped, 'Yeah, why's that?'

'Because she was the greatest singer we had. She gave so much of herself in each song that in the end her generosity, along with a huge smack habit, killed her.'

'You going to ask me about me?'

'Well now, of course I am. Isn't that why we are all here after all?'

Truth nodded: a king granting a pauper the gift of his time. Having asked some puff, I hit him with a real question: 'How can you take money from a dictator?'

'Don't know nothing 'bout that.'

'Don't you think you should?'

Like a media-trained Muppet, he repeated the line, 'Don't know nothing 'bout it.'

I attempted to hold my irritation in check. The importance of the interview pressed on me. I needed it more than anyone in this room. Needed to play the game, get the money to buy a ticket out of the country. I was a man without savings and that little voice, uncannily like my mother's, warned me, *Come on now, do your little interview, take the money, give yourself a rest from breaking the balls of everyone you meet.*

I nodded quietly, acquiescing with the voice in my head, then swallowed and said, 'One day, kid, when all your friends and assistants have vanished. When you're the last man standing in some spit-and-sawdust dive staring into a glass of petroleum you paid for by sucking off the bartender, you'll hear something so sad it'll make you want to die…' As the assistants went into a panic, protectively flapping their clipboards, I raised my voice to be heard over the flutter of outrage. 'So sad your gut will tighten like a trap to protect itself from the impact of it.' A bouncer was closing in. 'And that sound will be a song about your life and the lives of everyone on this fantastic planet you've worked so hard to learn so little about.' Bel was escorting Truth to the next room but he was twisting back, listening. 'The song will kill a part of you while bringing another part of you to life. And you'll ask the barman, who's this singing? And he will say, Billie Holiday, son.' The bouncer shoved me out into the corridor but I shouted through the closing door, 'Right then, kid, right there, you'll think, who was that drunk that interviewed me all those years ago, that man who tried to tell me how all of this would end?' The door slammed. Then immediately reopened. My recorder sailed out and cracked on the floor, its tape spewing out of it like shiny black guts.

Josef

WHEN WE GOT BACK to the house I instructed Ezekiel not to let anyone through the gates. Solomon's face, drained of expression, stared in shock as I shouted, 'Go to your room, lock the door.' I went to my wardrobe, down on my knees I pushed my shoes aside, pulled up the floorboard and stared into the empty space. My folder was gone. For a dumb moment I simply gazed into the hole as if my folder might magically reappear. First Patrick, then the tourist, now my folder: the world was evaporating before my eyes. And as I continued to stare into the space, I became aware of a sharp ringing. My vision vibrated to the sound, the world shivering out of focus, as all that had been solid now turned to dust. My hands left ghostly traces, thin as smoke, scrambling like frantic animals, grabbing the edge of the next floorboard, which I prised up, convinced the folder had slipped. But when it gave, all it revealed was more dust. The ringing reached a deafening pitch as I swept aside my ties, then tore the dry-cleaning plastic off my suits, smothering the floor in pale skins. I could barely hear Ruby, who was suddenly standing in front of me. 'Master. What's wrong?' I grabbed her so tightly her flesh squeezed out between my fingers. 'Ruby! The folder! My folder! Where's my folder?' Her petrified eyes floated before me as I suddenly became conscious of the source of the ringing. Placing my hand over her mouth, 'Sshhhhh,' I felt the moisture of her lips, my hand moulding her face into an ugly mass, as I pointed to the wall. 'Sshhhhhh!' I put my ear against the wall but the sound didn't get louder. Then I placed my hands over my ears and, with dreadful comprehension, realised that the ringing didn't change. It wasn't a sound coming from outside; it was a scream building from within.

I yanked Ruby out of the house, into the garden, where I turned on the sprinklers, knelt on the lawn, dragging her down with me, whispering as we got wet, 'Sprinklers will block out any bugs. They can't hear us. We can talk. We're safe but we must act fast. Tell me the truth. Where is it?' My jacket grew heavy and sodden and Ruby stared with such horror and confusion that I put my hand on her shoulder. 'Don't panic, Ruby. I'll protect you from anyone that threatened you.' Dark flowers bloomed on her uniform as her skin showed through soaked cotton. 'Now where's my folder? Did someone force you to give it to them? Was it David? If you return it now, Ruby, you won't be punished.'

Feeling as if a spotlight had been switched on behind me – a great heat beating against my back – I turned, and when I looked up sunlight was pouring down from the sky like honey and I laughed at how strange everything was, hearing my voice say vaguely: 'Why is everything so bright?'

Ruby's hands caught my head just before it hit the lawn and everything went black. When I came to I had the taste of vomit in my mouth and Solomon was standing slightly away from me, looking repulsed. Ezekiel was there too. Ruby jumped when I opened my eyes. 'Are you OK, master? You are acting strangely; we must call the doctor, I am thinking.' When I got to my feet the lawn slid under me. Solomon wrapped himself around my legs. The tick-ticking of the sprinklers lulled me into a hypnotic state, and as I tried to think straight each new theory disintegrated under the force of the next. Had David stolen my file? Had he taken it to a higher power? The sanctimonious man would have done just that; he'd have given it straight to someone above me, to Jeko, who was probably on his way to me right now. My phone vibrated and – as if he was plugged into my very thoughts – I looked at the screen and saw that it was David's number.

I waited for him to talk first. 'Minister, it's David. I have something you need to see.' I waited, waited for him to tell me more.

'Have you told anyone yet?'

There was a pause before his voice broke the silence. 'No, minister. Not so far.'

'Where are you? The Ministry?'

'We cannot meet there, not about this.' That was good news; maybe he was willing to negotiate.

'Are you still at the airport?'

'No, that is not safe.'

'Then where are you?'

'The Flamingo.'

'What? That whorehouse near the airport?'

'It is safe here.'

'Fine, I'm coming now. Stay where you are.'

I pocketed my phone and grabbed Solomon. 'Listen. Don't leave the house. Don't let anyone in.' Turning to Ezekiel, I instructed him, 'Make sure your gun is loaded, get your panga, close the gates when I go and don't open them until I return.' He came to attention. 'Yes sah.'

As I left, Solomon tugged at my leg and Ruby had to pull him away from me as I barked at both of them to get into the house and lock the doors. Ezekiel returned with the shining crescent of his panga hanging from his hand. And as he heaved the gates open, I shouted, 'Don't let anyone in, no one, not police, not soldiers, no one. Do you understand?'

I drove fast, shivering as cool air blew on my wet shirt. There was a terrible smell, sour and sharp, coming from somewhere. I checked my breath but it wasn't that. Smelt my armpit, and although they were bad they weren't the source. I drove a circuitous route to ensure I wasn't followed, and by the time I was closing in on the Flamingo the smell was overpowering. I stopped the car at the side of the road. Then clambering over, following my nose like a dog, I knelt on the back seat and sniffed right in the crease. Sliding my hand into the gap, the buttocks of leather squashing my fingers, I felt wetness. When I pulled my hand out it was covered in blood and in my palm was a small animal turned inside out, blue and red veins scribbled over pale whiteness. Then I saw that it wasn't an animal, this vile lump of flesh. And it wasn't turned inside out, it was an organ: the stomach of an animal, stitched with wire in Frankenstein lines, twisted and tied. The sound of my ragged breathing filled the car as I untwisted the wire, a stitch at a time, until the slit gaped like a mouth. I dipped into the red-blackness and my fingers found a sharp nugget. I pulled it out and there it was: my rotten molar, bloody and grey, in the centre of my shaking palm. I stepped out of the car and flung it as far out into the fields as I could.

Sean

*I*F SELF-DESTRUCTION WERE AN academic subject then I'd be
a PhD. I was not only boiling with disappointment in myself
but also, inexplicably, I was horny as a bull. Disappointment and
erections are close cousins in my body. I even – this is how deep
my madness ran – considered surrendering to Stella, hoping a
little make-up sex might be thrown my way. But a sharp moment
of clarity quickly dispelled that moronic notion. For any man
who goes out with a whore hoping to get sex on-tap is a pure
fool. And that'll be me. Also any man who finds himself in a hotel
room, bent over double, chatting to his aching balls, knows it's
time to do something about it. So I donned my Buddy Holly
glasses, struggled into some corduroy trousers and a clean white
shirt that Stu had lent me. I checked myself in the mirror – a fat
Elvis Costello looked back – and I wished my beard would grow
wisteria-like, covering my ruddy cheeks and smashed red nose.

I rode my motorbike, parked it a little way down the road and
then walked to the bar. And right there, in one of the most brazen
examples of false advertising, the sign declared: *The Flamingo
Bar: For Gentlemen and Gentlerwomen*. For it was a stone-cold
fact that neither a gentleman nor a gentlerwoman had ever graced
this bar. Below, it read: *Shake Shake Chibuku: To Go With The
Good Times*. And I could surely do with some of those.

I'd not been here since I met Stella a year ago, at last year's Big
Day celebrations. Having become too drunk for the Mirage, I'd

moved on to this more humble establishment, a place that prided itself on its moral elasticity. I remember it was packed when I got in, people cheering as I fell about, the novelty white man, the *mazungu*!

I spotted her on the dance floor, wearing this magically tight dress, printed with red chillies that shimmered as she moved. *Too hot to handle*; all the signs were right there for me to completely ignore. Before I knew it, I was dancing with this exotic panther, her liquid hips moving in a motion I could stare at for all eternity. And as if the night couldn't get any better, I charmed her into bed and we were together, inseparable and happy forever amen. Or not.

Of course people told me, warned me, that she was a paid hostess. One of my university colleagues, a nice Bwalo chap, got drunk one night and said to me straight out that she was a whore. Just like that. 'I'm so sorry, Sean. But Stella, well, she is a whore.' But I convinced myself that they were all just bitter; they didn't like the idea of an Irishman taking one of their finest women. And who could blame them? Yet deep down – and maybe not so deep – I think I always knew Stella was a Flamingo girl, that a few men had had their wicked way with her and maybe gifts, even money, had changed hands. But thank God my Catholic heart was big enough to forgive Stella her past transgressions. And her Bwalo heart was big enough to forgive me my drinking and permit me to play with her intoxicating body.

However, since that first wonderful night a year ago, life had become hard for Stella and me; returns had rapidly diminished. Our engagement party was a shambolic affair, held at the Mirage, with a worried Stu and Fiona looking on. Stella and I had never returned to the Flamingo. I didn't really like being reminded of her past. And Stella certainly didn't want to be hanging around her old stomping ground. Not when she could be sitting pretty at the Mirage, which for Stella was the very height of social success. Sometimes I think she only wanted to marry me for my Mirage membership.

Waving away those pesky memories, I entered the Flamingo and found a seat. My first drink vanished as quickly as it arrived and, looking around, I realised how much I'd missed this place. It was filthy. The air thick as soup, the heat of the day exhuming the stench of old nights. It was grotty as a pair of old Y-fronts and I felt right at home. The Kelly curse alive in me: only feeling I truly belonged when in the most alien of circumstances.

The second beer improved my mood as I drifted into cosy nostalgia. It was right here – well in the car park actually – that Stella offered me the sort of sex I could only have dreamed of when I was dating don't-touch-me-there girls from Cork. I smiled, thinking how Stella would laugh at the modesty of all those Irish lasses. And with this thought came a sudden and shocking image of Stella in Cork. Jesus. Just the thought of Stella and Mum in the same country, the same continent. Impossible. Unfeasible to unite such opposing forces. The tiny might of a tyrant, who brought up five kids in the moral straitjacket of the Church, meeting the awesome power of a violent, bloody-minded whore. My feeble imagination simply couldn't accommodate it.

Stella would never go to Ireland. And Mum would never come here. In fact I'm sure Mum never fully believed in Africa. Beyond the TV, she was a woman who'd never really seen black people. Surely there couldn't be a vast continent entirely populated with black folk. When I told her I was off to Africa, she looked at me as if to say, 'You're a funny fella, Sean. Just like your dead dad.' And each time she mentioned it, she said it in a tone of inverted commas, 'So, Sean, when is it you're off to "Africa"?' As if 'Africa' was a code for something. This from the woman who told me the moon landing was faked; whole thing was filmed in a ditch in County Kerry.

Undoing the good work of the second, the third beer swamped me with sadness. Feeling as if I'd been swept off a warm beach into the cold belly of the sea, I was overcome by my predicament. There's me engaged to a whore, having lost one job, ruined the other, and now wondering how long I had before being deported from this country that I loved with all my heart. This parched place I called home. I wasn't built to survive anywhere else. I knew now that a long stint in Africa prepares you for only one thing: a longer stint in Africa. To survive here you have to grow as eccentric as the environment. You adapt so much that you can't live anywhere else. Somewhere along the line, I'd shed my pale Irish self and I was now...what? Not an African, obviously. But an expatriate. Neither-here-but-not-quite-there, I was forever doomed to be an in-betweener. Sitting there, I realised for the first time, with immutable certainty, that my body would be buried in African soil. I prayed it wouldn't be too soon but at the rate I was going...

So as I met the bottom of my third beer, I resolved that the world was – as I'd suspected all along – an unmitigated shambles. And who was I to try and do anything useful about it and surely the very least I could do was soothe my boiling balls. I glanced over to the Madam. I feared she recognised me. She might tell someone I'd been here and the news would creep its way back through the Bwalo grapevine to Stella, who'd then drug me and in my sleep remove my balls with her ivory teeth. We had history, the Madam and I. I'd stolen Stella. Madams don't take kindly to the theft of their merchandise. If she realised it was me she'd have me beaten to within an inch of my life. But I'd not been here for a year and I suspected if she remembered me that I'd already be out on my arse. Also I presume we white fellas all looked fairly alike to her.

So after my fourth beer – fifth? – I tried my luck. I strolled confidently to where the Madam sat and knew, straight off, that she hadn't twigged. I laid the cash down and she said a room number, waving me through.

Up the stairs to heaven I walked, thinking as I ascended how the Madam was a fat, black St Peter for the sexually frustrated. Standing outside the room, cock straining against its corduroy cage, I held the door half open, considering the consequences. I nearly turned from temptation, honest to God I did. But instead,

I rushed into merry heaven, yanking my trousers down as I went. In the weirdest way, guilt is the great aphrodisiac. That's the kink of Catholicism: guilt adds an extra shine to your sin, guilt burnishes the thrill, God gets you harder than Viagra. So I threw myself at the lassie dozing in bed, all chocolate limbs and tropical curves, and me grunting like a pig, snuffling flesh, when I smelt something – something familiar – so I switched on the side light and, like a mongoose and cobra, we reared up to face one another. And I knew who'd strike first. With a sharp knee to the groin I rolled up, tight as a foetus, clutching my balls. She screamed bloody murder but it wasn't necessary; the Madam was already barging in accompanied by two enormous fellas.

'Problem?' said the Madam. And something about her tone, the smirk in it, gave away that the old toad had me from the get-go. She'd purposefully put me in with Stella. World's full of comedians and ain't the shame that I'm forever the punch line.

'Why are you here?' screamed Stella.

'Right back at you,' I yelled, trying to grab my trousers and some dignity, but missing both by a mile. 'I spend half my life looking for you, Stella, and here you are! Back to your old tricks! Is this where you've been the whole time?'

'You don't make enough money for me, old man,' she shouted. 'And now you're fired, what choice do I have? What choice but this?'

The big men pulled me off the bed and I thought, thank God my old mam can't see me now. Hung like a limp dick between two giants, an old fool caught in the act by his own whoring wife. Stella stood naked, not a stitch on her, and shameful man that I am, my cock still twitched hopefully towards her. Not many women can stand naked, legs splayed, face a boil of rage, yet still looking like the sexiest flesh God ever shaped. But her anger quickly blew itself out and with a sad face she asked, 'How could you do this, Sean?'

'How could *I*,' I protested. 'I've not had a shag in months, is it any wonder I was forced back here in search of easy snatch? I can't even remember what it smells like.'

Any hope of winning the argument through the sheer force of righteous indignation was scuppered when Stella rubbed her crotch then slapped me. 'Now you know how it smells, old man.' We were all stunned. Which, in a whorehouse, a house of shock, is no mean feat. But before Stella and I could resolve the ethical conundrum of who was more in the wrong, I was hustled out.

Everyone enjoyed the show immensely; me dragged along with my trousers trailing like a corduroy shadow. Me bellowing, 'Stella!' in my best Brando impersonation; the Tennessee Williams reference lost on the Flamingo patrons. It wasn't the first time I'd been persuaded out of a bar. So I knew the drill, which traditionally finished with a little flourish as they tossed me out the door. But this time they just dumped me at the entrance, and as I was pulling up my trousers wondering why they'd been so lacklustre, I saw that my own small problem was being consumed by a larger one.

Not known for their speed, the Flamingo regulars, soggy with Chibuku and lust, were running, galloping, shoving past one another. The source of their panic was a huge Mercedes, a government car. A guy seized me by the shoulders. 'Run, *bwana*, but you must run.' Streaming from the bar, people were pouring into the bush below, and before I knew it I was sliding down an embankment. I stopped, grasping a stilt that supported the bar's balcony. I wanted to keep running but I fell on my arse, and by the time I'd yanked my trousers on properly I heard footsteps above me and I froze. I saw men and women sprinting away and being swallowed by the cornfields. I wanted to be swallowed too. But I was too exhausted and far too out of shape to run for it now and so I lay back under the safe shadow of the balcony and decided to wait it out. I assumed a minister was just here to pick up a lady and then he'd be off. The music stopped. I heard more boots beat on the wooden slats above me. They were army boots, soldiers, two, maybe three, checking the area was clear. I lay back down slowly, noticing something shining between the slats. Jesus Christ Almighty. My heart raced before my brain could even find the right word. The shining things were machineguns. I realised too late that I should've run when I had the chance. That was when I started sweating and praying. The slats gave me some vision and I grew more terrified when I saw that another man was now on the balcony, a minister with exceptionally polished shoes.

Josef: my old boss. And he was accompanied by another man: a man who looked too badly dressed to be a minister; he looked more like me, a teacher, or an accountant. I didn't know the man Josef was talking to and the fluency of my Chichewa was tested, but I could translate enough to at least partly verify the nature of the shit storm I was about to be sucked into.

Lying low in the grass, my armpits and crotch dampened as my bladder swelled. I waited for Josef to stand up and take his goons away and leave me with a truly great story to tell Stu. But the story wasn't done with me yet. Worse still: they dismissed their soldiers. That was when my heart began to beat so hard I thought it might crack my chest. When a minister dismisses his own soldiers, his own trusted personal body-guards, it can only mean one thing: that he's about to share something so secret that even those closest to him can't be privy to it. I knew something terrible was coming. After the boots beat a retreat back into the bar, I lay there, praying harder than I've ever prayed: I know I've gone and fair loaded up your answer machine, Dear Lord, but please pick up. I'm begging you, Jesus. Anyone, even Jude, please pick up. It's Seanie here and I'm in a situation way beyond my ken.

I lay still as a dead man – practising for the inevitable – struggling to hear what was being said. But the bits that I heard – the words that floated down between the cracks – and that I could translate, I wished I could somehow un-hear. I didn't know which man was speaking but everything they said was bad. 'Who pulls the trigger? A white man, a soldier who is now a mercenary…not as expensive as one would think…It will be an insane white supremacist. Is he an insane white supremacist? He will be when the papers come out tomorrow…I've learned a thing or two from you.'

Finally, the men finished and left, the wood creaking under their shoes. I lay there a little longer, hearing the cars go and listening to the sound of people returning to the bar. I prayed to God, and all of his helpers, for sparing my life and thanked my bladder and bowels for holding true. I resolved to be a better man, to give more to charity, to care for the old and the poor, to love Stella like no Irishman had ever loved a whore before.

I crept out from that balcony a changed man, from the dark I emerged – the symbolism not lost on me – and as I got to the car park, reaching into my pocket for my keys, I realised I'd counted my lucky stars too soon. People were not returning to the bar; it was merely the sound of soldiers standing, chatting by the Mercedes. One of them spotted me sneaking out from under the balcony like an animal smeared in dirt. But I was a long way away from him and so, like a fool, I started to run. He shouted, 'Hey! You come back.'

I didn't like his suggestion. I knew I had a fair head start on them, I could make it to my motorbike no problems, but what I'd not counted on was outrunning a bullet. The report of their rifles sounded harmless, brief, like the crackle of a fire. And I prayed they were shooting warning shots into the sky as I jumped on my bike and was off. Not down the road but into a field, violently juddering down rows of corn, the organs of my body feeling like they might vibrate right out my arse as I tunnelled through flickering lines. When the field ended I risked life and limb, cutting directly across the road without looking, plunging into the next field, where I rode on until, after many shuddering miles, I finally slowed, breaking out into the next road, pointing my motorbike away from town towards the lake. I was too scared to face any of the roadblocks in town, to risk being caught by soldiers, too scared to go home; I had to get out of the country before I was shot dead by soldiers or thrown in prison by Josef. My brain didn't rope together a clear thought for a good half hour. All I could do was focus on the road, praying no roadblocks would stop me, praying the soldiers didn't know I'd heard anything, and had assumed I was just some no-good whore-mongering expat. My mind dashed back and forth over the conversation that I'd eavesdropped on. Did I overhear the whisperings of an assassination? Was Josef involved? You read about such things of course. Mercenaries, even the sons of British prime ministers, plotting the death of African dictators. But when you live in a spot like Bwalo, this slow, drowsy place, such things seem distant, somehow too sensational to be true. So, as I rode further away from town, my mind began to soften the conversation, to blur it, to suggest it was a lot less serious than I had initially feared. Maybe I was translating it wrongly – my Chichewa was far from fluent after all – maybe things were not as bad as all that. I smiled for a second, the wind racing over my face, and then, right at the clear point of conviction, pessimism suddenly overruled me, and I knew there was no hope, that some ugly violence was building in the wings and it was time to get out of the country and run.

Jack

By the time the next man arrived I felt as if I'd been left alone for an eternity and I was so petrified I could no longer stop myself crying, the sound of my sobs coming back at me echoing off the walls. But the second man didn't look as terrifying as the first. He had a gentle face and a wild ring of grey hair, reminiscent of a clown, surrounded his bald scalp. Still I assumed he was there to pull out my fingernails, or to beat my face until it turned soft and shapeless as mud. He didn't speak as he walked behind me and placed a blindfold over my eyes. I felt my breathing slow, my body taking over, short-circuiting my weary mind. He handcuffed me. We walked a long way, I felt us leave the building, the wind on my face, probably going to the middle of a field. I was sat down and waited for the small coin-shaped impression of a barrel to press into my temple. A terrible noise began and I took a deep breath and thought of my wife's face. A strap clipped tight over my waist, they pushed my head low, so it was between my knees, pulled my hands up painfully behind me, the cuffs clicking open, my hands falling free, the blindfold ripped off. I saw that the strap around my waist was a safety belt and the noise was the engine of a plane. I could see the pilot from where I sat. I looked around and we were the only two people in a small aircraft, which tipped up and took off.

Josef

WHY WOULD DAVID BE at a seedy dive? He was teetotal. I couldn't see him slumped at the bar sucking back Chibuku. Far too human, too disgraceful an act for a puritan like David. When I arrived my government Mercedes triggered a mass exodus of the Flamingo, drunken men and women racing out and vanishing into the fields below.

The Madam ran but I grabbed her as she tried to slink past. Realising she wasn't going to escape, she switched to fawning mode, smiling and purring, 'Minister, what an honour.'

'Seems your patrons don't feel the same way. I'm looking for David Cholo.' Her hands twisted in front of her as I warned, 'You've thrived for years due to me turning a blind eye to this place so…'

'He's here,' she admitted.

'Why did he come here?'

'He needed to hide.'

'Yes but why *here*? Are you friends? Are you related?'

'If I was related to a government man do you really think I'd be working in a place like this?'

'Then why would David come here?'

'He used to come to use the bar, minister.'

'He doesn't drink so I know you're lying.'

'No, I mean he came here for the other reason men come here.' She smiled, pleased that she'd shocked me.

'Are you sure we're talking about David? Bent back, hunched a little.'

'He used to come here. But this year, not so much. He fell in love with my girl Stella. Came often for her, only for her. Then we lost Stella to an expat and for a time he stopped coming. But today he asked if he could hide, he was scared, said people were after him.' For all my years of reading men, I was surprised. But something about it also pleased me. David: human after all. Not puritanical, nor perfect, just a man. His vendetta against the Irishman was nothing to do with principle or Tafumo. It was, like so many things, a petty and personal thing: a woman. I released the Madam's arm and said, 'Run!'

The room contained the anxious silence of a recently vacated space. Tables crowded with beer cartons, smoke rising from ashtrays, spiralling in currents left by departing bodies. Thinking a man was behind me, I turned. But the man was just me: my reflection in a mirror above the bar. I stared at this man, his suit streaked with mud, looking so ill and scared, telling me to run. Expecting at any moment a hand to cover my mouth, or a bright smack to my skull, I started to walk quickly back towards the door but a voice shouted, 'Stop, minister.'

Making his way slowly across the room, that painful gait, he stared at me like everyone does now, fear tainted with revulsion. But it wasn't his expression I focused on. It was what he held in his hand: my manila folder. Scared my knees would buckle and betray my fear, I went and sat on a stool, reaching over the counter to grab a bottle of whisky and two glasses. My hand shook as I poured the shots. David stood close to me, looking as if he was about to reject the drink, then he took a slug and sat down, his hump heavily pronounced as he placed his elbows on the bar.

When it became clear that he wasn't going to start the proceedings, I said, 'So is this where the righteous drown their sorrows?'

'I'm not a righteous man, minister. I'm a grateful man, grateful that you took pity on me, hired me, made me a man of importance when so many others mocked me.'

I checked to see if he was being serious, only to find he was. 'Well you shot yourself in the foot, David. Ransacking my office, taking this tourist, what the hell!'

'I never moved him. I was racing around to find you.'

'Racing around a brothel?'

'No, I had to hide, hide when I found this.' His fingers tapped my folder. 'I didn't know how to tell you what I am going to tell you.' And he flipped the folder open.

My pounding heart rattled everything out of focus, and initially all I saw were pale pages floating in a manila blur. Flicking through the folder, my vision gradually clearing, I struggled to find Patrick or Levi's pages and then, when I couldn't see my spidery handwriting anywhere, a powerful relief rushed in. This was not my folder. My heart calmed, and exhaling a long-held breath I smiled as I stared at one of the photographs. As the image came into focus, my relief turned to queasy confusion as I realised I was looking at Essop. A grainy photograph of Essop sitting opposite Jack Franklin in the interrogation room of the airport. David pointed at Essop as he said, 'This man, this man took the tourist. Your friend from the palace, Essop.'

'You're wrong! Again you've got it all wrong! This man has nothing to do with any of this,' I shouted, but David pounded the bar with his fist and I flinched, surprised by his anger.

We sat in silence, until his tight fist opened, and when he spoke again it was in the embarrassed tone of a youth, reluctantly explaining to his elder that he has been mistaken. 'No. You are the one who is wrong, minister. The guard was lying about the camera. I forced him to show me the footage.' As I stared at the photograph of Essop, I understood that everything I thought I knew was wrong. David wasn't the enemy. He was trying to impress me; he'd always been trying to impress me. I remembered Essop in my office, helping me up when I fainted. Showing me that old photograph of uMunthu. Had he been trying to warn me to run? I remembered him calling me on my way to see Patrick at the market. Then my brain, like some weary teacher, recalled Essop's favourite saying: we never look for the devil in the right place. This made me laugh hysterically, which caused David to look at me as if I'd lost my mind. David said, 'Something is happening, minister. The airport guard was terrified. He told me that your friend Essop is part of something terrible.'

I turned to him. 'David, listen to me now. Go home, get money, clothes and get out of the country.' David nodded, obedient to the last, and I said, 'Tonight the roads will all be blocked. But the weak point is first thing tomorrow when the army and the police will have to man the stadium. Go first thing. Do you understand me?'

When he stood, I expected him to leave but realised he was waiting, with his hand hanging awkwardly between us. I shook it. David walked out the door, swallowed into the bright light. I heard him get into his car and drive away.

I finished my drink and stood to go but stopped when I heard the sound of a car arriving. I listened to the clunk of doors, the whispering of men, and watched a shadow form in the glowing mouth of the entrance. 'Josef? It's me.'

'I'd recognise the crappy sound of your car anywhere,' I said. 'Anyone else here?'

When I said, 'Just me,' two more figures broke through the light, men with machineguns, soldiers, Boma's boys. 'I didn't realise we needed to bring guns,' I said.

He walked towards me, saying, 'Let's go outside, my friend, on the *khondi* will be safe.'

'Safe? With you? Safe as the tourist who vanished?'

Essop smiled awkwardly and I followed him, taking the whisky and two glasses. The soldiers came with us, checking the balcony and the fields below, then Essop said, 'Both of you, wait at the main entrance.'

We sat at a wooden table. Essop removed a smouldering ash-tray, placing it away from him at another table. I poured the whisky, we didn't clink glasses. I drank as Essop said, 'Sorry it has come to this.'

'Come to what?'

Essop observed me closely as he replied, 'The assassination of the King.'

As Essop continued to talk – 'You should have listened to David: he's smart' – I tried to focus, fumbling to make sense of everything, but my concentration was too weak to hold together my thoughts, which kept separating and disintegrating, leaving me with nothing but a blank frustration into which I shouted, '*You* sent the false text? To get me out of the airport? Is the tourist a mercenary? Is he going to kill Tafumo?'

'He's just a courier,' Essop said. 'But when Boma found out you had him...'

'Boma? You're working with Boma? He's a drunk and a fool. Boma believes only in Boma.'

Essop's tone was stern. 'No. That's you, Josef. Boma isn't a refined man but he knows Tafumo has to be stopped.'

'So it's a coup.'

'No. It's not a coup. If it's a coup Boma's military government might only last a month or two before the world interferes; there is no legitimacy to that. Boma is not the brightest man but he knows that much. So we are using an outsider, a mercenary. Then Boma will step into Tafumo's vacuum with clean hands to save Bwalo and start afresh. That is why Tafumo will be shot by a white supremacist.'

'Is he a white supremacist?'

'He will be when the papers come out tomorrow,' replied Essop. And he grinned at my shocked face. 'Yes, Josef, I've learned a thing or two from you.'

'You'll make Tafumo a martyr.'

'He should consider it our parting gift.'

'Then what? You'll take over?'

Essop laughed. 'An old translator won't amount to much in politics. No. Boma will form a government. I'll have some minor administrative role, then go quietly into the wings.' I felt an odd mix of confusion and fury building in my gut. I looked across at my friend and said, 'You're a fool, Essop. You know Boma is just Tafumo's dumb spear.'

'Sometimes you have to choose between devils.'

'But why kill Tafumo now?'

'The land is rotten. We should have done it years ago. You and I, all of us should have done it the day Levi didn't turn up at your wedding. Should have forced Tafumo's hand, forced him out of office. But we did nothing. You did nothing but make excuses...'

'Don't pretend you are better than I am,' I shouted.

He cast his eyes down, too embarrassed to even look at me as he confessed. 'No. I'm no better than you. I knew what was going on. I am culpable. We all are. Though we had different reasons for not doing something, we're all still guilty of doing nothing. Some of us were ambitious, Josef. Some of us were weak and optimistic, ever hopeful that the killing would stop.'

When he finally looked up, I couldn't hold his gaze. Two old friends who'd suppressed the most important conversation of their lives – a conversation buried under years of silence – now too embarrassed to look each other in the eye as we finally spoke it.

'There will be chaos,' I warned. 'People will rise up to destroy Boma. Many still love and would die for Tafumo.'

'Few things are as bitter as thwarted hope. So, yes, there will be violence. Boma may only burn bright for a short time. All I hope to do is finish Tafumo. The least I can do as my conscience grows heavier each day as I stand by and do nothing for this country that I saw come to life. And the young care not for *kwacha*, that word we sang, we fought for; that taboo word has sunk back to its base meaning. For young people today it means nothing more than sunrise. For a short time we made it mean something more but look where we are now. Two old men in a whorehouse untying our mistakes. It's time to clear the earth. Kill the old, let the young remain.'

I felt my confusion resolve into anger and, trying to claw back control, I shouted, 'That won't happen, Essop, I'll stop you. I will call Tafumo, I will call Jeko, I will call David, and we will stop you and Boma and his pathetic little army and…'

Essop shook his head. 'No, Josef. No. You won't, you will let it happen. Isn't that what you do best? Let bad things happen.'

'I'll do everything to stop you,' I said, but my anger was already fading. Essop continued to shake his head, as I spoke. 'What? You will kill me here? Boma's soldiers are here to kill me?' I glanced at the soldiers stationed at the door, as Essop said, 'Calm down, Josef. Trust me when I say that it's no longer in your interests to save Tafumo's life.'

'And why is that?'

Essop waited a moment, sighed, then said as if it were all so self-evident, 'Tafumo has turned on you, Josef. He wants you dead. You had your suspicions, surely? Jeko has orders to make you vanish, to murder you and Solomon and…' As Essop spoke, the world slowly, rather elegantly faded. Sound drained away like water, leaving Essop silently moving his mouth; shadows slipped from their moorings, puddling like oil, as shapes collapsed and colours bled to black. I could not see, hear, nor feel, waiting – suspended in darkness – until, just as gently, the world seeped back like a stain, colours blooming, shadows rising, and as if from some great distance, Essop's voice came to me: 'I didn't understand why Tafumo would target you, his golden son. It puzzled me.'

Placing my head in my hands, so tired, so confused, I was embarrassed to hear in my own voice how close I was to tears. 'Can you help me, my friend?'

'No,' he replied sharply.

'But you must. Please, don't let me die; don't let them take Solomon. Jeko will murder all of us. Please, Essop, please help me. We are friends.'

'No.' His head shaking slowly, the motion of it heavy with disappointment.

'You are my friend,' I said with desperate insistence.

'You're not capable of friendship, Josef.'

'How dare you,' I shouted but Essop shouted back in a voice I never knew he had. 'How dare I? How dare you! You sold our friends for little more than some pairs of shoes. You're a disgrace to all we stood for, fought for, to uMunthu.' As he spoke I realised that my hand, as if by its own will, was inside my pocket, curling around my knife. And Essop said, 'So is this how it ends? You stabbing me in a whorehouse? But are you going to actually get blood on your hands for a change? Are you really going to plunge your little blade in me, *Sefu*?'

My hand emerged from my pocket, empty. 'How do you know that name?'

Essop pulled a brown bag out from inside his jacket. He reached inside the bag, then he placed my folder on the table and slid it towards me. 'You told me, *Sefu*.'

I stared at it, feeling nothing; my nerves snapped like the filaments of burst bulbs, incapable of conducting shock. The emptiness brought with it a sensation of detachment, as I listened to Essop, talking away as if delivering a lecture. 'It is interesting that the Chichewa word for report, *mbiri*, also means story and rumour. Ours is an incredibly economical language, which from a starving nation should be no surprise. Don't waste food, don't waste words. Well, now, this *mbiri* of yours is truly fascinating. It explains so much about you, *Sefu*. It seems you've been pulling the strings for some time.'

'You came to my house and stole my folder?'

'Nothing so dramatic. Don't you remember inviting me for sundowners? When I arrived Ruby let me in, told me you were writing in your study, but I found you passed out, snoring in your wardrobe, clutching this confession, atonement, story.'

That morning I'd awoken to find someone had placed a sheet over me; I'd assumed it was Ruby. Then the image came to me as clearly as if I'd actually seen it: Essop standing over me, slipping the folder out from under my arm, then gently spreading a sheet over my curled body. 'When I showed your folder to Boma he said it was the scribblings of a madman. Boma wants you to become a public example of a regime that, from tomorrow, will be gone. He wants you, Jeko and many other ministers strung up for all to see, an example, a scapegoat, put on public trial. You, Josef, the old guard, Tafumo's bad man. All of it to show that Boma is sweeping away the past.' Essop left me hanging, watching me twist in my own panic, before he continued. 'But you're lucky I'm so persuasive. I told Boma that it's better to spare you. That one of Tafumo's closest men telling the world the truth about Tafumo will pave the way for a new regime faster than a lengthy, expensive trial of redemption against you and Tafumo's cronies.'

'Thank you, Essop, thank you. I'll do anything if you spare me, spare Solomon. I am in your hands.' He looked uncomfortable, maybe a little disgusted, as he said, 'Get out of the country, talk to the international press. Discredit Tafumo. It's the least you can do for Levi, Patrick, for Hope. A pathetic absolution but a start, I suppose. Certainly more than you deserve.'

'You must understand me when I say that I did what I had to do…'

'You lie so effortlessly, Josef.' Then a silence stretched between us before he added, 'Remember the god Tambuka? He sent a chameleon to tell man he'd be reincarnated. But also sent a lizard to tell man death was permanent. Well the lizard arrived first and man accepted the permanence of death. You, Josef, you are the lizard. You brought the lie that people believed. Now see if you can undo it.'

It wasn't until my voice got caught on a sharp sob that I realised I was crying. 'I didn't kill anyone.'

He studied me academically, as one might study a difficult question, nodding at some internal dialogue – as if I was proving all of the terrible things he'd assumed of me – then he said, 'Hold on to your delusions, Josef. I believe it is your only protection now. For if you faced up to what you really did, you would die of shame.'

I wiped my tears. 'How will I leave?'

'Boma has instructed a number of his soldiers to let you go. Leave in the morning before sunrise, when the country will be distracted and most of the force will be at the stadium. Take the lake road, the old dirt one.'

My fatigue was so strong that I felt my head nodding obediently as Essop said, 'Your *sing'anga* gave you powerful *muti* but it is not the sort you need.'

I took the tonic from my pocket and stared at the muddy liquid. Essop shrugged. 'Sorry, Josef, but you're a very smart man with a lot of spies out there and the last thing I needed was for you to figure out what we were doing. She's my cousin, the *sing'anga*. A good woman. I suggest you stop taking the drops. It's bad *muti*, my friend, bad *muti*.'

'Will I die?'

'No, you'll just be weak for a time.'

'And the fetish? The tooth in my car?'

Essop had a grim smile as he said, 'No, my friend, that's not my style. It seems you are rich in enemies. I'm Tambuka, you know? My relatives slowly overpowering the Ngoni with education, and now we're sweeping the next great tribe away, your Chewa tribe. But of course, I see that even that was a lie. You and Tafumo are not Chewa, not even Bwalo. Tafumo is the great refugee King. Which makes you what? You and him are boys from across the border, some weak Nguru tribe, little more than migrants. Funny to think that in fact you, Tafumo and I are all the children of slaves.' I watched him watching me and saw that his expression had shed its academic dispassion, which I now realised was a sort of foil, a disguise. He was just as scared and emotional as me, his face soaked in a fatigue that I knew only too well. 'It's not just that you lost your ideals, Josef. The world is a complicated place, after all, but even when your ideals were tested I prayed, I always hoped, and now I see it was foolish, that you and I were once truly friends.' He seemed to be awaiting a reply, some sort of explanation, but I looked away from him, over to the blood-orange sunset, shaking my head. 'I wish I'd listened more to all your silly stories, Essop.'

'No one listens to translators. I'm the voice of other men.' Then he smiled properly for the first time, that gentle smile, and I felt a terrible sadness that I'd never see it again, that everything was coming to an end.

When we stood, Essop said, 'Get out of your house, stay somewhere safe with Solomon tonight, then leave first thing, before the sun rises, by the lake road, the old one, the dirt one.'

I was so light-headed I could barely walk. Sensing this, Essop tucked himself under my arm and helped me through the bar, back to my car, where he placed me in the driving seat and said, 'Good luck, *Sefu*.' I watched as sorrow swam over Essop's face and, as if attempting to escape his sadness with speed, he turned and walked away.

Sean

*I*RODE THE LAKE ROAD a long time before my blood cooled enough for me to think straight. Not that straight thinking helped; it merely clarified how buggered I was. My wallet was lost in the Flamingo. My mobile was gone, probably vibrating in some cornfield. The seat of my trousers was wet with sweat and piss and darker matter. And I was travelling without a destination. Another great title for my book.

My plan was to ride until I hit the border and pray that they hadn't got my name on a list yet, to get out of Bwalo before the soldiers or Josef caught up with me. But what about Stu, Fiona and Charlie? I had to tell them something was about to happen. Maybe I could just phone them from across the border, I thought. And then what about Stella? There was no doubt that we had experienced a violent run and the Flamingo incident was undeniably a low point. But we had both pushed one another to the edge before and peered over the precipice, only to relent, and drag one another back to safety, cradling in each other's forgiving arms. And at the very least – if all was truly lost between us – I had to pick up my books, the few meagre bits of writing I had at her house, and my…*passport*!

Jesus! I didn't have a passport. I was never going to make it over any border without my passport. And so my panicked plan to break for the border fell completely to pieces. And I knew I had to return to town, see Stella, pick up my passport then ride, either with or without her, via some dirt road that was hopefully not festooned with soldiers stoned out of their minds and armed to the teeth.

But before I turned around, my motorbike made a terrific choking noise, lurching so sharply to a stop I nearly flipped over the handlebars. Out of fuel. Lights twinkled in the dusk ahead and I pushed my bike towards them. When I arrived at the lights, there was nothing but a jetty and some shacks with a sign: Port Tembo. There was, however, a bar. I went inside where all eyes fell on me. As a bar aficionado, from the majestic to the dingy, it was immediately apparent that this place was off the seedy scale. A few fellas were face-down on their tables, which were old wooden crates. The bar itself was just a stolen Coca-Cola billboard balanced on oil drums. It was a forlorn place of men who shared bad habits and the burden of heavy debts. It made the Flamingo look like the Ritz. The bar lady laughed and said, '*Mazungu*.' That won a few giggles and I said, 'Yes yes, I'm a white man, no hiding that. Would I be able to use your telephone?'

On the bar, like a museum piece, sat a Bakelite telephone. I found a few coins in my pocket and gave them to her. As I turned the circular dial the men in the bar trained their blasted eyes on me.

Beauty, the receptionist, answered. 'Good evening, the Mirage, how may I help?'

'Beauty, it's Sean.'

'*Muli bwanji*, Mr Sean,' she said, her voice like some happy song from a past life before I was beaten by pimps and shot at by soldiers.

'I need to talk to Stu, can you get him?'

'Eh but Master Johnson he is so busy. Can I be taking a message?'

I considered the message: *Dear Stu. There's going to be a coup. Run! Love Sean.*

'Is Fiona there?'

'Eh but everyone is running around all over the places.'

'Tell me about it.'

'I think I have just told you about it,' said Beauty.

'Is anyone there?'

'I am here,' she replied, brightly.

'Look, Beauty, find Stu and tell him. Tell him…' my voice lowered to a whisper '…the praying mantis is coming.'

Without a scintilla of suspicion, as if white men always spoke in code, she said, 'OK, Mr Sean, thanks for calling.'

I put down the phone and asked the bar lady, 'When's the next bus to town?'

'No buses for three days because of Big Day.'

I sensed people encroaching upon me, so I turned and said hello. They laughed in a strange way as the bar lady said, 'They want to help you stay here.' Noticing a commotion building behind the wall of men, I craned my neck, but they blocked me as one of them explained, 'We're friends, my friend. Stay in my house and we shall be friends.' But when he placed a heavy arm on me, another man warned me, 'This man is a bad man! But I am your friend, my friend. I give good price. You stay with me.'

I gently pushed them back and said to the lady at the bar, 'I need a real drink.'

She handed me a waxy carton of Chibuku. Throwing my last coins down, I took a sip of the rancid stuff and they laughed as I gagged. They stood awkwardly close, this sloppy audience of drunks, staring at me with cold and disconcerting candour. In an attempt to lighten the tension, I raised my carton and said, 'Cheers, fellas,' but a man grabbed my arm, shouting, 'These are bad men but I am safe.'

I pulled away from him but someone slapped me and – before I could register if it had really happened – someone hit my hand, causing the carton to burst on the floor. 'Get back,' I heard myself shout, as fresh scratches ran down my arm and they laughed like demented children. In an animal panic, I shoved and squeezed through a tunnel of them, breaking out into the street, and there – where my motorbike had been – was a mess of footprints and the tracks of my wheels snaking off into the bush. 'Where the fuck's my bike?' This provoked an eruption of more demented laughter, and as they thickened around me I saw the sum total of my life reduced to a headline: *Paddy slain in Bwalo*. The oddest things strike you when you're about to die. Africa is a continent brimming with cautionary tales and I remembered when I told a mate I was going, he joked, 'Careful, Sean. I knew this fella had a friend went there and he was drugged and killed, then this witch doctor brought him back to life, just so they could kill him all over again.' Strange stories crowded in as the men plucked at my pockets. The bike was just the start. Once they knew I didn't have two tambalas to rub together, things would get really ugly. I'd be sliced up and tossed into the port to join the other pale bones down there in the silt.

We're programmed to believe in our own immortality but eventually it's tested and here I was in a situation bigger than myself, screaming and flailing about punching air. I fell, the floor rushing up to smack me in the face, and as I curled into a defensive knot, sharp kicks taking divots out of my back, a crisp light cut through the crowd. The men shielded their eyes, giving me time to unfurl, crouch low as a bull and charge a hole through them, tumbling out towards the light. The blaze came from the headlights of a truck and I didn't care who was in there, could've been the devil himself, I was getting in.

The driver was a thin man with snowy hair, who looked at me and deadpanned, 'Need a lift, son?'

The bad men cowered in the light but a persistent one came to my window. 'Friend, don't go. Do not go with this man, he's a bad man.'

I shouted, 'Fuck off,' and tried to wind the window but it jammed. The driver said something in Chichewa and the man slinked back to the bar.

For a time we drove in silence, me quietly checking my arms and legs for cuts, until the man said, 'What in God's name were you doing there?'

'It's a long story.'

'It's a long drive,' he said and I shouted, 'Wait a minute! Is that a Cork accent?'

''Tis? Well, 'twas once, I suppose.'

'Two Cork men in a truck in the middle of nowhere. OIA, man, OIA!'

'He works in mysterious ways.'

'Jesus Christ, you're damn right there,' I said, feeling the elation of my escape. 'Fuck. Felt a little dicey in that bar. Sure I'd have been fine, though.'

Looking ahead, the lights of his truck carving out the dark, he said very seriously, 'That place is the end of the road for most of those guys, highest murder rates in the country. They'd have torn you apart and fed you to the crocodiles.'

I took a moment – a sharp aftershock of panic ran through me – before I said, 'Well what were you doing there?'

He reached over me and popped the glove compartment open. I flinched, thinking he was pulling a gun. Inside was a white collar smiling under the light. I picked it up and I suddenly clicked. 'Jesus Christ, you're a priest.'

'Paul's my name.'

Immediately falling into altar-boy mode, I confessed, 'Sorry, Father, for taking the Lord's name in vain and for all of that stuff and, my goodness, I mean, saved by a Catholic priest. Wow. Like, do you think God is trying to tell me something?'

'Food for thought, certainly.'

'Right you are, Father,' I said. 'So what brought you to the port of no return?'

Slowly, reluctantly, he replied, 'Well, last night a man came asking for shelter. I turned him away. I often take people in, you see, put them up, give them breakfast, but this man scared me or I wasn't in a charitable mood. Whatever the reason, I sent him into the night, and soon as I did it ate me up. Felt guilty all day. Last night my heart was cold, so I went in search of repentance and there you were being eaten by the wolves.'

I didn't talk for a long time, just watched the headlights stretch ahead, thinking. I'm a lapsed Catholic but sitting there I felt something. Not God, certainly not proof of the worth of organised religion, but I felt a force that, for a brief moment, was working in my favour. This was my crossroads and I knew what to do. I was going to tell Stu what I'd heard; he could do with it what he wanted. I was going to tell Stella we needed to give our relationship another go. Then we were going to start afresh in Zambia, or Kenya. And finally, even if I died trying, I was going to write my second book.

I was so lost to my thoughts that the Father had to jab my ribs to get my attention. We were stopped. He pointed through the window. 'Walk as an arrow flies through the field till you hit sand. Des's place. Tomorrow Des will ride you to town. It's a backpacking place. There'll be a carload of them wanting to see the Big Day. So you can hitch a lift.'

God it made me feel like a kid again but I had to ask: 'I'm ashamed to request even more of a man who's already saved my skin, but Father is there any way I could bludge a *kwacha* or two?' He went into his pocket, pulled out some notes and I promised, 'I'll post you the money back. Give me your address and ...'

'Rubbish you will. Cork men are bad liars. Take the money, God be with you.'

I leaned over and hugged him. He tried to wiggle out of it but I held on tight and I noticed his right ear was missing, nothing there but a hole. 'Father, listen,' I said. 'I don't know exactly what's going on but something bad is about to happen, possibly to Tafumo and others. I suggest you try and get out of the country before it's too late.'

Staring straight ahead, nodding as if he heard such things every day, he replied, 'He was always in trouble, that Tafumo. God be with you, son,' and drove off.

Bar the stars, all I saw was black to the left, right, top and bottom of me. Riding the high from my rescue, without a worry in the world, I tramped into the oily night, strolling through the rows of maize, right into another pit of uncertainty as the great scale of nature swelled about me, animals screaming and squawking to a terrifying crescendo. My smile hardened as I thought: maybe those drunkards at the port weren't so bad, maybe they'd just have cut off a finger but still cooked me breakfast in the morning and sent me on my way. Maybe this was worse, to be found dead, killed by a pack of lucky lions that happened to be strolling by. But as fear took hold, up ahead I saw lines of lights doing a dim impression of the stars. I jogged, hoping they'd get bigger, but they didn't. All of which made me feel as though I wasn't moving at all, just jogging on the spot, stuck in treacle, until finally my feet crunched against sand and I saw what they were: strings of Christmas lights set into the thatch of a bar. Des's place.

I'd escaped death, found God, and was somehow in a bar full of Scandinavian men who all looked like Axl Rose, drinking beers like the world was coming to an end. And maybe it was. After the greatest five beers any Irishman ever drank, I met Des, gave him some of the money that the Father had given me, and he set me up with a sleeping bag and a small tent into which I crawled and proceeded to sleep like the dead.

Josef

I RANG RUBY. 'ARE YOU safe?'

'Yes, master, no one is here but Solomon, myself and Ezekiel.'

'Don't put down the phone, Ruby, leave it on, leave it on!' I placed the phone on the dash and drove, occasionally shouting, 'Still there?' hearing her small voice call back, 'Yes, master, we are safe.'

I cut the headlights, then parked the car in the bush. I walked, holding the phone to my ear, hearing Ruby breathing. I looked back at the palace, so brightly lit that the fields around it shone in its ivory glow. When I got to the mango tree I touched it. I took out my folder and looked at it for the last time, thinking of all the things Essop had told me, things I hated hearing because I knew them all to be true. Here is my *mbiri*, my report, my story. Terrible to think that this small folder represented more truth about me than all the words I'd ever spoken to everyone I loved. From my pocket I took out a small wooden London bus I'd once carved for Hope back when she accompanied Tafumo on a trip to England, back when life was sweet. I considered what Essop had said about the economy of the Chichewa language. The English have many words for guest, each one carefully distinguishing the character of the guest, whether they be a relative, some sort of refugee, a friend, stranger or enemy. But in Chichewa we use just one word, *mlendo*, which offers no detail as to whether they are someone to be welcomed, invited in, rejected, someone to be loved or feared. And in all its multiplicity, that word is exactly what I am; I am a *mlendo*, a refugee, a guest and a threat.

Deep scars ran down the bark of the tree, reminding me of Hope's intricate braids. Sometimes late at night or just before I woke in the morning, I remembered them. My fingers, the slim muscle within, remembered the weight of her braids, the sensation of them slipping through my hands and the warmth that radiated from her head. I slid my folder deep inside the tree, placed the bus on it and stood there just a moment longer, imagining Hope. I didn't see her as the old Hope of today; I saw her briefly and clearly as a young woman, looking up at me with tears in her eyes, our wedding ring shining in the sun, the two of us hugging as we returned home, planning our lives and laughing, as if the rest of the world were merely a backdrop to our love. I made my way back to the car. I placed the phone on the seat beside me, shouting, 'I'm coming, keep the phone on.'

When I returned, Ezekiel was still standing to attention, as if he had not moved, his panga in one hand, his other resting on his gun. He opened the gates and I nodded as he turned and quickly closed them. I went into the sitting room; only one light was on in the corner, near the bookshelf where I saw Solomon was sleeping on the sofa. Poor Ruby sitting next to him with a carving knife in one hand and the phone in the other. I handed Ruby an envelope with money. 'Ruby, it is time for you to go, return to your village and stay there until the dust settles.'

Roused from his sleep, Solomon stood and hugged me. Ruby didn't ask any questions, she simply nodded at me, then she grabbed Solomon and gave him an awkward hug. He instinctively struggled against it, still half-asleep, confused. She broke the hug and placed her hand on his head and held it there as Solomon let out a little grumble.

'Solomon, listen,' I said softly. 'Run to your room and grab some clothes, only one bag, put what you need in a bag, we're going.' He looked angry, still sleepy, wanting to ask questions, but I shoved him towards his room. 'Go! Now!'

Ruby went with him and I heard them packing and muttering together, deciding what to take, what to leave. I went to my room and grabbed my emergency bag, full of passports, money and clothes. When I got back to the sitting room, Solomon was standing with his school backpack. Ruby was crying quietly as we got to the front door. Then I ran to the gate and looked through the bars; there was a car, a few metres up the road, waiting.

'Ezekiel, come with me,' I said. Solomon and Ruby looked confused as they followed us back into the house. I took Ezekiel into the bedroom and said, 'Take off your uniform.' Solomon and Ruby stood in the doorway looking scared. I grabbed my best suit from the wardrobe and handed it to Ezekiel. 'Get into this.' He nodded and stepped into the bathroom. When he emerged he was smiling; the suit was far too small for him, the jacket sleeves stopping abruptly just below his elbows and his sharp ankles jutting out under the trouser legs. Ruby said, 'Very handsome, Ezekiel,' and we all laughed as Ezekiel stood uncomfortably fidgeting with the suit.

'Now listen, Ezekiel,' I explained as I tied a tie around his neck. 'They're following us so I need you to drive my Mercedes. Can you drive?' He nodded and I continued. 'Drive it all around town, don't go near roadblocks and after you have driven for an hour or so take the car out to the airport, leave it there in the car park, then you must go home, to your home, to your village. Don't come back. Take a bus from the airport. Here is some money for it.'

I handed him his envelope thick with notes. 'This is too much, master,' he said and I shoved it back in his hand. 'No it's not. Now if anyone stops you just tell them you are dropping the car at the airport on my behalf. You are under my employment so you will be fine. Do you understand?' He nodded and I said, 'Now wear these shoes,' and I gave him my newest shoes, shiny as glass, which he looked at and, as if it was just a little too much to take, shook his head and said, 'No, master, not your shoes, I cannot.'

So Ezekiel sunk his huge feet into his Wellington boots, my suit straining against his body like a shrunken school uniform, and we all crept down to the garage. I handed Ezekiel the key to the Mercedes. 'Drive carefully; drop Ruby wherever she wants to go. Don't stop for anyone unless you're forced to. Keep them off my tail as long as possible.' Ezekiel shook his head, as if he simply could not take the keys of this precious car. 'Take it, it's an order!' I snapped and when he came to attention I heard the plastic clap of his wellies tapping together.

As I explained to Ezekiel how an automatic gearshift worked, Ruby ran to the *kaya* and brought back two bags, the sum total of her and Ezekiel's lives stuffed inside them. She threw them in the car and then gave Solomon a last hug. This time he didn't resist but hugged her back. I was helping Ezekiel push back the seat so his large frame fitted comfortably, and when I turned Ruby was standing waiting in front of me. I held out my hand. She shook it and I said, 'Thank you for…taking such good care of us,' and she got into the passenger seat.

Ezekiel moved the steering wheel a bit then nodded and started the car. Before he reversed out, I saw his long hand extend out of the window and I shook it, and Solomon shook it too.

'Drive slowly and normally,' I said and he reversed and headed out of the gates. The car on the street quickly followed and I breathed a little more easily. Then I turned and opened the boot to my old Peugeot, a car I had held on to for years since I'd been a poor lecturer. I had kept it so that Ruby could drive to the shops or taxi Solomon around. We drove in silence. I was checking my rear-view mirror, when I heard a soft sound and I looked at Solomon and said, 'What's wrong?' He was crying, looking ahead as if too scared to face me. 'Solomon, don't worry, we're just…everything is fine, don't cry.' But he kept crying and said, 'I am sorry, Father, is this my fault?'

'What? No, this is nothing to do with you.' He began to weep uncontrollably and I saw he had something in his hand. He held his fist out, then it slowly opened and inside it was a Dictaphone. 'I am so sorry, Father, I stole it and it is full of terrible things, this is all my fault...all my fault.'

'Solomon, no this is nothing to do with you, this is more complicated than I can explain right now, calm down...'

But I couldn't persuade him, couldn't pacify him and I didn't want to risk stopping.

Solomon was fiddling with the Dictaphone and he clicked a button and suddenly I heard the hotel manager, Stuart, and his wife, Fiona, whispering: 'Listen, I just heard: they think they found Patrick Goya...'

I snatched it from him and mashed the buttons on the Dictaphone, trying to stop it, but not before I heard Fiona say: 'Well they found his body. Dr Todd said he saw the body. Said some heavies came to...'

Then I grabbed Solomon and pulled him close to me. He sobbed, his face buried into the side of my body, as I said, 'It's not you, Solomon, you're not responsible for anything, we are fine, we are fine, we are fine.'

'So Patrick is dead?' he asked and for a moment I was incapable of saying the words as Solomon sobbed against me.

Then he asked, 'Are we going to be killed next?'

'No,' I said. 'You are my son and we will survive this. Now we must be quiet and careful and everything will be fine, Solomon. Fine.'

I pulled into the back entrance of the Mirage; the staff gave me a fearful look.

I said, 'Can you please get Master Stuart.'

Stuart came out of the building, his eyes smudged with sleep. When he saw us, and our bags, he didn't talk. He touched Solomon's head, guiding us into the kitchen as the staff turned away from us, acting as though we were not even there.

THE BIG DAY

Bwalo Radio

Yes yes! Ha-ha! It is here, beautiful Bwalo. Dawn is breaking on this our greatest day. Your day! My day! Our day! The Big Day! So sing with me, Bwalo, sweet soul of Africa, sing with all your heart. Kwacha! Kwacha! Kwacha! And never forget what your mother told you: If you have, give; if you need, seek. For I am shaking, yes, vibrating, yes! People, people, listen! Can you hear the sound? Yes! That's the sound of beautiful beating hearts. The wondrous day has arrived and we are born again because of our great and glorious King. So get out of bed, comb your head, wash your face, buy a pack of Life and come celebrate this day of splendour. Yes, my friends, yes! The Ngwazi is great!

Charlie

THERE IS ONE ROOM in the hotel without a number. The other rooms are decorated in what Mum calls *Africhintz* and Dad calls *Africrap*. Marlene Horst decorated the whole hotel and Mum said Mrs Horst thinks that the height of good taste is an elephant-foot ashtray. So all the rooms have mounted animal heads, ebony carvings, and lots of paintings of elephants. But not this room. This room was totally bare. Only a bed, sink and toilet. This room didn't even have a number; it just had a clean white door. People who stayed in this room never had their names on the register, never stayed more than a day and were never seen again. The room always had the Do Not Disturb sign hanging off the door. And it was the only door that, even when the King was coming, I was still not allowed to knock on. Once I saw a man going into the room, a man I recognised. And when I asked about it, Dad pulled me back to our house by my arm, and told me I was never to tell anyone I'd seen the man, not ever, no matter who asked. I was especially not allowed to mention it to Solomon. Dad had never looked so serious, and at the end he didn't even make a joke like he normally does. He just stared at me, checking I understood, and I nodded, pretending I did.

Very early in the morning, as the hotel was buzzing – waiters rushing about, wet with sweat – Ed took two meals to the room. And one was a kid's meal. Though I knew I was never supposed to go down there, I was so curious about what sort of a kid would stay in that room that I followed. Standing a safe distance away, I watched Ed go straight in without knocking. Something we were never to do; you always knocked on all doors before entering. That's one of Dad's laws.

Ed came out with the empty tray and walked back to the kitchen. I crept up to the door and I laid my ear against it. I heard footsteps coming towards me and in a panic I ran, but knew I'd never make it down the corridor, so I hid behind a laundry basket. When the door opened I saw Solomon's dad peeking out, then quickly closing and locking it. I went over and even though I knew I'd get into trouble, I knocked. There was a long wait, some whispering, I felt someone on the other side of the door, looking through the spy hole, heard them breathing, the lock clicked and there stood Solomon's dad. His eyes flicked up and down the corridor before he said, 'Charlie, hello.'

'Hello, Mr Songa. Happy Big Day to you.'

He smiled strangely. 'Happy Big Day to you too.'

'Why are you in this room, Mr Songa?' He turned and closed the door. When the door opened again Solomon was there. He looked tired, his normally shiny skin was dull; his hair, which was usually neat, was misshapen and spongy.

'Howzit Sol. What's happening?'

He didn't reply for ages; we both just stood there. So I said, 'You look funny, eh.'

'Sorry, Charlie,' he said and held out his hand and there, in his dark purple palm, was my Dictaphone.

I took it and said, 'But I knew you stole it, though.'

'Sorry,' said Solomon and I just shrugged. 'Fancy coming to play, Sol?'

Solomon shook his head. Then, not knowing what to say next, I said, 'OK, then, well I'll check you later.' But Solomon kept shaking his head, then he explained, 'We're leaving, Charlie. For ever.' I didn't understand what was happening, and even though I knew it didn't make any sense, I still said, 'OK then, Sol, see you around.'

Solomon closed the door and I went to find Mum, to ask what was happening. I raced past the pool, across the golf course to the house where, before running through the door, I heard screaming. I stopped, waiting on the *khondi*, listening. Mum was shouting, 'And you protect that man! That man who put so many people in prison.'

'That man and his son, who is our son's friend, could be shot dead. Is that what you want?' Dad yelled back.

'What about us! What about Charlie! We'll all be next, get rid of him, get them out of that room, out of the hotel. Now, Stuart! Now!'

Dad tried to shout over her. 'They'll be gone in an hour, it'll be fine.'

And it made me want to cry when Mum said in a mean voice, 'You always think everything's going to be fine, don't you.'

'Yes, I do,' said Dad but he didn't sound sure and Mum said in her cold voice, 'Well that's not always how it goes, darling.'

'What the hell are you going on about?'

Then Mum spoke in a really scary quiet voice I'd never heard before. 'I'm talking about two naive people who went to live in a strange place, and when things fell apart they overstayed their welcome and were slaughtered in a bloody mess along with their child.'

'Calm the fuck down,' Dad shouted and when I walked into the sitting room they froze like musical statues. Then Mum ran over and grabbed me into a weird hard hug. 'Sweetie, don't cry, we're just talking...Listen, there's nothing for you to worry about, but after the Big Day we're all going to have a chat because your dad and I think it's time to return to Scotland, it's time to go back home.'

I didn't say anything and so Mum looked briefly at Dad then she said to me, 'Come on, Charlie, that will be fun, right? What do you think? Won't it be such a great adventure going back home?'

I said, 'How can I go back to a home I've never been to?'

Then they both gave me that look I get when I've either said something really silly or really smart.

Josef

*F*OR THE FINAL TIME I saw Tafumo's kingdom. Shops shining
bright and clean; even the roads, usually pitted with holes
and carpeted in sugarcane husks, were now immaculate. But
beyond centre stage, past all the perfection, we hit the outskirts,
the dirty backstage. We saw Tafumo's monuments; each commis-
sioned and unveiled on previous Big Days. Each year a new
edifice erected to prove Bwalo's good health and Tafumo's great
power.

We passed the newest Big Day commission: the Tafumo Stadium. The previous stadium had been perfectly good but
Tafumo had declared that it was time for a new one. The new
showpiece was unnecessarily big and hysterically expensive, I'd
been privy to the budget, a spreadsheet of corruption. David
had shown me a subversive cartoon of it: cash, food and humans
falling from the sky into the hungry round mouth of the stadium. I imagined Patrick's bones embedded in the foundations,
to be discovered long after the structure had collapsed and
decayed back to dirt. Ministers joked that the stadium wasn't as
expensive as feared, as it was built from cheap bones rather
than expensive concrete.

We passed another Big Day monument: Tafumo's Academy.
An exclusive school for the intellectual elite. Children were tested
and taken from rich and poor families alike, taught an Etonian
curriculum of Latin and Greek, and expelled if they were caught

speaking Chichewa. This from the man who'd declared, 'My food. My tongue. My soul.' Yet here he was repeating the colonial crime of slicing out our tongues. Tafumo's surreal oasis, in the style of King's College Cambridge, complete with spires and gargoyles, yet populated by black children wearing bow ties and straw boaters in the blazing heat. The truest testament to his demented relationship with his adopted nation.

Other Big Day monuments didn't fare as well. Many lay abandoned like carcasses of old feasts. I passed Tafumo Avenue, unofficially named Nowhere Avenue. A Big Day project loudly launched before, a month later, being quietly forgotten. A road to nowhere, curving off then stopping, its silver tarmac crumbling into the bush. On the outskirts of town we passed Tafumo's Polo Club. Once green and lush but now bald and brown. The horses, those finely tuned creatures, were toiling on farms as labouring animals. Those that were not put to work were put to death and eaten. And a mile on, an abandoned Roman amphitheatre, a giant dust bowl, its rings of seating plunging into the earth like a ribcage. I breathed a little easier as we pulled away from the town, pushing the accelerator, feeling myself catapult into the future, safe somewhere beyond here, but my body twitched at the sight of a roadblock. As we slowed down, Solomon sat up, but the soldier saw my face and without even asking for ID he smiled and waved us on. Essop was true to his word.

We turned onto a dirt road. Solomon and I had to stop often to move fallen trees but otherwise we drove without impediment. As the sun rose I wondered if we'd survive to see it set. I knew Essop and Boma would have me covered but what would happen when Jeko discovered I was gone? All ministers were expected at the palace, the full cabinet, before dawn, at six am to wait for the King. Then my absence would be noted and I knew nothing would stop Jeko taking matters into his own hands. Phone calls were being made, orders racing down wires, outpacing our car, spreading like a web to the corners of the country as

I gunned the engine to outrun them. Was a prison cell ready for me, a blade sharpened, bullet loaded? My paranoia bled into reality and I saw up ahead another roadblock. The shine of oil barrels in the dust, a pole between them, soldiers playing cards by a shack.

As I slowed the car, I thought how simple my task was: get Solomon and myself across a few metres of dirt and we would be free. But when the guard leaned in, I could tell something was wrong. Either Essop hadn't paid this man or I'd not outrun Jeko's orders. Jeko had got to this man and told him to hold me at all costs, or worse.

His fingers reached in to pull the key from the ignition. I knew too late that I should have risked everything and driven through the barrier. The guard pointed his finger at me: 'Out.'

Solomon and I followed him to his hut and there, behind a school desk, sat a guard, the man in charge, with glowing red eyes and filthy boots. The room stank of sweat and beer. Solomon cradled in close to me. The man behind the desk ate a mango, slicing off segments, juice staining an orange patch in his beard. He waited. I knew the game. I'd played it on many men. I waited. Giving nothing more than I needed to give. Finally, he popped a slice into his mouth. 'Well today just got interesting.'

'You know who I am,' I said with a firm voice. 'Now let me through.'

More guards came in behind us, making excitable hyena noises, tightening the space in the room. Clearly relishing his moment, the head guard said, 'If you had been here yesterday I would have nodded and bowed and waved you through but today the world has changed, my friend. There is a rumour that you vanished and Tafumo does not like vanishing ministers.'

'I know that Boma called you yesterday and told you to let me through.'

'That was yesterday. Today I had a new call. From another man. Jeko.'

'I'll have you fired and thrown into jail.'

He blinked, a touch less assured, then said, 'Your threats don't scare me. You were a big man yesterday but today you are nothing, an invisible man.'

He placed his pistol on the desk, its barrel staring in the direction of my stomach. 'What am I to do. I'm a soldier. I follow the last order given.'

He was playing a game. This was good. I just needed to ascertain the rules. He hadn't immediately picked up the phone to Jeko to tell him that I was here. Unless, that is, one of his men was outside making the call and the buffoon was buying time, entertaining himself by wasting the last moment of my life and the life of my son.

'I can tell you are a thoughtful man,' I said, and he smiled to show me he knew I was manipulating him but was also open to false flattery. 'What do you need, sir? What can I get for you and for your men?'

'That's better,' he said. 'I like that. *Sir*. And that from an ex-minister no less.'

'I am not an ex-minister. I am your superior.' My voice held, no cracks in it. 'This is merely a misunderstanding with Tafumo and I.'

His smile was greasy with mango juice. All these years my actions had gathered into a dark force and here he sat before me in his filthy boots. Demons are not the slick spirits one hopes. They are this: a brute with a brain just fast enough to enjoy terrorising you before he kills you and your son. Solomon was shaking and I held his hand to calm him.

'I have an idea of what you can give me,' said the guard.

'Yes?'

'Everything.'

'Meaning?'

'Meaning I am under strict orders to return you to Tafumo. If I don't do that I risk my job. So my loyal men and I need incentive to not fulfil my orders. I am a soldier, my friend, and I like to take orders. So your car, everything in it, the money stashed, the cash strapped to your body, no man with a face as thin as yours has a belly as fat as that.' His hyenas giggled. 'Possibly even the money strapped to the body of your child, and your jacket too, I want that, it will look far better on me.'

I raised my hand to say something but his men grabbed Solomon, tearing at his clothes. He was screaming, 'Daddy,' and I was shouting, 'Stop, stop, stop.' I took off my jacket, flung it on to the desk, opened my shirt and pulled the packs off my belly. They thudded to the floor. The guard seemed satisfied that Solomon had nothing and they pushed him against the wall where they pointed a rifle at his face. Slowly, I got out my wallet, passport and placed them on the desk.

He gnawed at the mango stone, teeth tearing the flesh. 'And to think I complained when they posted me at this shitty road stop. I told them no one ever used this old road any more, and now look: a man like you comes along to make me rich.' I sensed from the nervous cackle of his men that they too were not sure if I was going to be freed or executed. They were awaiting their orders as I awaited my destiny. He flicked his knife at one of the men. They seized my arm and I grabbed Solomon as the guards bullied us out the door. They pushed me with a gun against my back towards the oil barrels, there was no need to raise the wooden pole for us, roughly shoving our heads under the barrier, and Solomon fell to the ground and picked himself up on the other side. We were across the border but guards had their guns trained at our backs as we began to walk. Solomon was in shock, his face like wax, unmoving, eyes searching the space before him as if tunnelling his body to the future. I took his hand and we walked slowly away. Solomon was trying to pull forward, to break into a run. Holding him back, I whispered as if singing a lullaby, 'Don't run, Solomon, walk with me, don't scare them, Solomon, just walk slowly, walk slowly, Solomon, walk slowly.'

I waited to be lifted forward by the smack of bullets against my back. I heard the man shout, 'Stop!' The guards ran over and held us in place as the main guard took his time walking towards us. He looked me up and down, relishing my fear, taking it in through his eyes and wide nostrils. 'I like your shoes, minister.'

I moved in the way you would before a wild animal; slowly, smoothly, I unlaced them, slipping them off. They looked odd there in the dim light of dawn, brown British things on a red dirt road. He admired them. 'They will look better on me.' I didn't nod, or smile, I knew silence and submission were all he wanted, humiliation was his goal, and he looked at my feet and said, 'Socks.' I took them off, rolled them in a ball, placed them by my shoes. Looking at my bare feet with a face full of disgust, he said, 'And your son's shoes.' Solomon took off his shoes and socks, gently placed them next to mine.

I took Solomon's hand and walked on. As we walked, my hearing became so sensitive that the world seemed to scream, shaking my skull, blurring my vision, crickets wailing as the metallic click and slide of rifles rang out, and we kept walking, walking away from the rising sun, our shadows stretching out before us, losing all feeling in my body except for the warm clutch of Solomon's hand in mine as we turned a bend, moving out of sight of the soldiers, chasing our shadows to safety.

Charlie

C*LICK!*
    'Hey, Willem, did you know leopards mark their favourite trees by scarring the bark?'

'Yes.'

'Oh. Well did you know that an elephant has a hundred thousand muscles in his trunk?'

'Now that I didn't know.'

'Pretty cool, eh? Where are you off to?'

'Golf course to play some holes.'

'Ah that's great. See you there. Mum, Dad and I watch the Big Day from the course.'

'Really?'

'Yah, really. Mum says we're not allowed to go to the stadium because we have to get everything ready in the hotel and every single year I beg her to let me go but she just says…'

'What sort of time do you go and where do you sit?'

'Whenever really, not sure. Sometimes we sit on the first tee, it's the best view looking down into the stadium. Are you super-excited? What do you think of the Big Day?'

'I think I'm ready for it.'

Click!

Hope

THE DOCTOR TOOK OUT his black bag: another myth. Supposedly filled with *sing'anga muti*. In fact it contained amphetamines, hot chemicals that Tafumo scorched his organs on. The doctor inserted the needle; fluid sank as Tafumo's head rose on its thin neck and a man appeared behind the cloudy gaze. Initially he loathed the lucidity, unwittingly pulled from his snug psychosis, but soon the concoction took hold, spreading like fire, his suit filling out as he whispered, 'Ngwazi.'

He admired himself in the mirror – examining his reflection as if reacquainting himself with an estranged relative – before we walked through the palace, led by Boma. Among the many faces, I spotted Essop. I smiled at him. He looked exhausted; his quick smile tight and formal. The staff lined the palace doors as we emerged into the crisp light. I searched the faces but failed to find Josef.

Tafumo nodded to everyone, walking and talking, smiling and full of power. He'd hibernated all year, preserving himself, not even wasting energy on clinging to reason, but letting himself drift into effortless insanity to prepare for the day he'd rise again. Miraculous to behold: the power of will. He waved to his staff. Following his line of sight, I saw that he was looking beyond them to his palace; waving away the thing he loved above all else. In the car the chemical rush slackened and he gazed irritably through the windows, watching his palace shrink. He used to walk the streets, talk to his people. With only one soldier to protect him, he'd visit the market and ask people their problems. Over time he went out less and less, more and more soldiers shadowing. Now he rose only once a year to check his kingdom, to show he was still the father of the nation.

Boma sat across from us and Essop sat next to me, silent, unmoving. The windows trapped our pensive reflections as Tafumo looked out on the plains of his country, its blank blue skies, its once green fields bullied to dust by drought. With tightly crossed arms Tafumo cradled himself in the corner as we politely ignored his panic. Part of me wanted to take the old man back to his bed.

A boy burst out of the bush, jogging alongside the car, screaming, 'Ta! Fu! Mo!' His fist, tight as a berry, beat the air with each syllable. 'Ta! Fu! Mo! Ta! Fu! Mo!'

The car slowed, the boy stopped and stared, captivated by the sight of God. Tafumo lowered his window and gave the child a fragile wave that ignited rapturous dancing. As we drove on Tafumo turned to watch the boy dissolve in the distance, then he whispered reverently, as though referring to some great man he had once loved, 'Tafumo.'

Sean

I CAUGHT A LIFT ON Des's pick-up truck with a horde of Viking backpackers. Standing up because it was too full to sit, pillared by smiling Bjorns and Stefanssons, we travelled down the road and, with the lake twinkling at me through the gaps in the bush, I thought, this is it: my last Big Day.

Even after an hour standing in a pick-up truck, I remained elated; sun gleaming like a new penny and me basking in my miraculous escape. Lady Luck was smiling down. We were waved through checkpoints, me hidden in a blond cloud of Scandinavians. Either the soldiers didn't have my name on their list or they just didn't see me. I was the luckiest bugger in Bwalo.

Town was spotless, everything ready, the stage set. As we drove along the main street I saw a policeman push a legless cripple on a skateboard down an alley. The cripple protested, waving his hands uselessly. Returning from the alley a moment later, the cop tossed a cigarette back at the beggar. The pick-up dropped off the grinning Vikings on the main street, then Des dropped me at my house and said, 'Have a great Big Day, Sean.'

When I got to my gate, I was so shocked I just stood for a moment taking it in. The lawn was mowed. The meandering vines of the bougainvillaea were clipped. Jacaranda pods no longer peppered the grass. And the shocks didn't stop in the garden. When I walked into the house, the kitchen gleamed like a scrubbed pot and the concrete floor was polished to its original cardinal-red. The cat sat in the hall looking as confused as me.

I grabbed him and sat on the sofa as questions vaulted over one another: Why had Stella tidied up? Was this a trick? What's the angle? Had she cleaned up in order to put the house on the market? Or did she have forgiveness in her heart? Was this her way of saying sorry? I heard a creak, and there at the bedroom door stood a sleepy Stella. She smiled. Good start. She came and sat with me. Still good. Better still she put her hand in mine. She smelt of sweat and sleep as she nestled into my neck. 'Sean, what are you…' She sounded unsure what to say and then finished with, 'You came back? Where were you sleeping last night?'

'Stella,' I said, kissing her forehead, tasting her sweet sourness. 'Trust me when I tell you that I've just had the wildest ride of my life but I've learned that I love you, my little chongololo, and no matter what happens we're going to make it, you and I. Now listen, I don't want you to freak out here but I think there is going to be a coup. So I just need to tell Stu and then we're off. You and I, riding into the sunset; well the sunrise, I suppose, but…' She looked at me like I was out of my mind and I asked, 'The soldiers at the bar? Did you give them my name? Did they interrogate you?'

'No, I ran too, we all ran, no one has been back to the Flamingo.'

'I know we have said some hurtful things but do you think we could start over?' As I waited for her reply, I wondered if I was dreaming; it had been so long since Stella and I had held a conversation of this length without violence breaking out. She kept nodding in a sleepy way, so I added, 'You cleaned the house.'

'Yes,' she said bashfully. 'Well I paid some people to do it.'

'Of course you did. I forgot we had nice floors under all that rubbish. Now, how about I make us a lovely cup of tea,' I said, getting up, causing the cat to leap to the floor.

And, as if the surprises would never cease, she stood, pulling me gently back down to the sofa, and said, 'I'll make a tea for you, my young man,' manoeuvring around me. I watched her go, then I got off the sofa, keen to begin packing.

I started in the study. But when I walked in I noticed Royal and all my books were already boxed up and the room was swept and tidy. Strange. I shouted, 'Hey, Stell, why's my study packed away?' gathering what few pages of my writing were worth keeping – a sad few – as well as tossing some books into a bag. On the way to the kitchen to quiz Stella, I passed the bedroom door and saw something move in the darkness. I let out a surprised yelp. Stella ran out of the kitchen down the corridor towards me but I held her back, whispering, 'Someone's in there, get back, I'll deal with this. Come out, you fucker, I'm armed and ready.'

The government had come for me; the soldiers or one of Josef's henchmen was standing there with a panga ready to cleave my skull in two. As I was about to step into the room, I wondered how many men they'd sent. I ignored Stella as she screamed for me not to go in.

And it wasn't until I burst into the bedroom, and saw through the open window this fella running across the lawn hoisting his trousers up, that I realised what an idiot I'd been. The way he limped I thought initially was due to holding up his trousers but, watching closely, I saw he had a bend in his back, causing him to lope across the lawn. When I came back out of the bedroom, Stella was standing in the corridor frozen, as if fixed to the floor.

'Are you fucking kidding me, Stell? Who was Quasimodo and why's everything packed up?'

All her sweetness turned so quickly to rage. 'You stupid fucking old man. Can't you see what is happening right before your nose? I didn't think you would be stupid enough to come back. I thought you were gone for good. I was just stalling you, so David would have time to leave before I told you everything was over...'

'Who the fuck's David?'

'David is the man I'm leaving you for. And he has already warned me that something is happening and David and I are running away together, with each other. We were waiting for the right time to run, which is early morning, and then we are off. Without you, you old man. You are finished to me.'

A sad sound escaped my mouth, 'Oh,' and Stella looked at me with such pity.

'And you're selling the house, that's why you cleared it up, packed up my stuff?'

'Your shit, my house, everything is being sold so that I can start a fresh life.'

I should have turned and left at that moment; should have simply gone peacefully. It was clear to me that Stella, to her credit, at least had the good grace not to try and pretend she wasn't shagging another man. I stood there stunned by just how foolish I'd been. Stella must have started cleaning up the house a day ago, before we had even clashed at the Flamingo; it had all been decided already. She'd cut me out of her life and all that had been between us was now behind us. So I should have accepted all of that and done the same. I should have nodded bravely and, with a certain stoical dignity, turned and said something like, 'It's been a wild ride, my dear, best of luck to you and your new beau.'

But of course I didn't, couldn't, I just couldn't. So instead, I screamed, 'I wish I'd never met you, you mad bitch.' And though it did bring a certain rush of satisfaction I knew, as soon as the words were out, that it was a bad move. It triggered Stella's temper and she was off: calling me every name under the sun, reaching such high pitches her voice kept cutting out, becoming so overpowered by rage that her English ran dry and in its place poured a shit-stream of the most violent, colourful Chichewa any Irishman ever heard.

Knowing it was only a matter of moments before she remembered her feet weren't glued to the ground, I jogged into the bedroom, grabbed clothes – which were already stuffed into removal boxes – and located my passport. In the meantime, Stella had rushed into the kitchen and was back in the doorway, now armed: a carving knife – which I noted was gleaming clean – in her right hand, her mouth wide open but no sound coming out. It was apparent that leaving me was now no longer enough; she wanted to kill me too. So I slowed down, held my hand out to show I was retreating, not advancing. I slung my bag over my shoulder and walked backwards towards the door, never moving my eyes from the blade. We stood either side of the corridor, so there was distance between us, at least ten feet of safety. When she found her voice it wasn't words that came but a long pained squeal, as I finally got to the front door and said, 'I hope I never see you again, you crazy fucking banshee.'

It was about the right tone for the ending of a miserable relationship. She raced at me, growing louder and larger, the blade flashing like a propeller. I jumped out of the house, slamming the door, locking it from the outside. Buying enough time to get on to my old bicycle and pedal like a bastard.

Still, she nearly caught me. Tumbling out the window and chasing after me, she almost swiped my rear tyre but the hill's incline and gravity's kind hand pushed me past her reach. As I picked up speed I glanced back to see her standing in the street, in her nightie like some tired child with a carving knife in her hand. After the screaming and chaos, I found myself pedalling through quiet streets, my bell clinking gently. Town was deserted, as the entire population congregated at the stadium. I rode hard towards the Mirage, flagpoles flicking past, road stripes blazing in the dawn light.

Charlie

EVERY YEAR I BEGGED Mum to let me go but every year she said, 'We always watch the Big Day from the first tee, it's tradition.' I replied, 'Dad said tradition's a dumb habit repeated to fool people into thinking it means something.' Mum raised her eyebrows. 'Well isn't your father just the fount of all knowledge.' The main road held a chugging line of hot shimmering cars. Dad let me use his binoculars and through them I could see down into the belly of the stadium where the great crowds churned. Up front, near the stage, dancers jiggled. Little boys were stuffed into miniature versions of the same suits as their dads and all the girls were wrapped in green and gold *chitenges*, topped off with bright swirling headscarves. A voice echoed out of the loudspeaker: 'Welcome, Bwalo, to the Glorious Day of Our Splendid Independence. To help celebrate this momentous day we have a superstar come all the way from the United States of America, greatly talented singer and incredible, marvellous artist!' People hollered and clapped and the announcer said, 'So put your hands together for Mr Truth.' With my binoculars still glued to my eyes I watched as Truth rose up on a platform right in the middle of the stage, singing as his dancers shimmied around him. They wore long African dresses and looked strange without their miniskirts. When Truth finished his song, he said, 'I'd like to thank His Excellency King Tafumo. I'd like to sing a song we call "Beautiful Africa".' The cheer of the crowd reached us in ever-louder waves.

I couldn't really hear what Truth was singing but I heard Mum saying, 'What's with Americans and their bloody razzmatazz.' Dad smiled, happy Mum was talking to him again. Instead of answering, he leaned over and gave Mum a kiss. I said, 'Ack, you guys, that's too gross.'

Sean

WHEN I GOT TO the Mirage, Beauty greeted me at reception. 'Happy Big Day, Mr Sean. The master, the missus and Charlie are all on the golf course watching our glorious day of...'

'Thanks, Beauty,' and I was off, past the pool, up the fairway to the first tee. As I ran, I wondered if Stella had already gone with her Quasimodo, breaking for the border, her house just an empty shell, nothing left but a stunned cat warming itself by a pyre of my burning books. I'd need to book in for an STD test as soon as I was clear of the country. Goodness me, straight out of Cork Airport and first stop the STD clinic where some sanctimonious GP would shove a stick down my cock's eye. What a fine mess you've made for yourself.

As I broke over the first hill, I caught a glimpse of the stadium looking like a boiled sweet smothered in ants. In miniature on the stage, young women were clapping along to Truth, the daft Yank, pogoing about in his baggy trousers. When you imagine a coup you think of tanks rolling through darkness. You don't envisage postcard skies, cartoon sunshine and some wee guy popping about on stage. I broke over the hill and spotted three stripy deckchairs: Stu in the middle smoking; Fiona beside him; Charlie on his feet, binoculars stuck to his eyes. I shouted to Stu but the ruckus from the stadium muffled my voice. Something darkened my periphery and I turned to see Willem moving towards me, golf club in hand. 'Willem, listen, all hell's about to break…' The noise of the stadium was cutting my words right out of the air. I started to yell and, with the woozy sense of a dream, he kept nodding and coming closer. 'Willem, all I can tell you is…' He was still nodding, his face in a forced expression as I noticed something strange about his golf club – this man, this drunken companion, this tourist, was carrying *a rifle* – he was so close now – and I knew more clearly than I knew my own name that he was the man sent to kill Tafumo – the mercenary – and the last I saw, in the second before blackout, was my vision filling with Willem's freckled fist.

Hope

W<small>E DROVE A CONVOLUTED</small> route. He believed it was in order to show the glory of his capital. Really it was designed to avoid the shantytown swelling like cancer to the east of this weary city. When we got to the stadium the car stopped and we walked through tunnels of soldiers. Deafening blasts of noise and ecstatic faces flickered through the gaps. Tafumo switched off his hearing aid, plunging himself into silence. Dancers pounded their feet; all these beautiful women with their shining faces raised to Tafumo like sunflowers. Their round bosoms, bums and bellies were adorned with his warped face, which kept swimming up from everywhere like a nightmare. It was twenty foot from the back to the front of the stage. Longest walk he took these days and every year it got longer, stretching away from him. At first he stood at the back like an old man come to see a show. Deep in his muted world the crowd must have sounded like a distant storm. Then he moved his feet and with each step they shouted louder, until he placed his hands on the podium. He stood for a long time, as if deciding if his people were still worthy, still loved him as much as he needed them to. Then he raised his hand and, one finger at a time, his fist bloomed as the crowd roared, 'My food, my tongue, my soul!' This delicate gesture conducted them to hysteria then, with elegant timing, he brought his fist down and they fell silent. The microphone sent out a screech and the nation was still. In that peaceful moment I saw beyond my natural vision, down the roads, past my waving tree, over the silver spine of the lake, as thousands crowded around radios in bars and huts listening to warm static seeping into the brief silence of a nation awaiting its king.

Charlie

A FTER ANOTHER LONG BORING wait, a voice finally came over the loudspeakers and said, 'Please rise for His Excellency the Life-King Tafumo.' For a split second everything was quiet. How could so many people all be quiet at once? Only the King could do that. A drumbeat started and everyone stood up to sing the national anthem, and just as they were getting to the chorus Tafumo appeared at the back of the stage. Through my binoculars I saw a nurse by his side. They looked like an old couple out for a stroll. At first he just stood there, like he didn't want to move. Then he walked to the podium as the old woman turned and vanished into the wings. I sang my heart out, my own voice drowned in a thousand others rising from the stadium. I felt as if Tafumo was looking straight at me in the way he looked out of all his portraits, staring at everyone every day, making sure we were all safe. They called him a god but to me he was always a superhero, watching over everyone, ensuring we were protected. The music ended and Tafumo raised his fist, then slowly, one by one, he pointed three fingers at the sky as the audience screamed, before bringing his fist down and silencing the whole world.

Hope

HE WAS MIDWAY THROUGH when it happened, when he started stuttering over his well-worn speech: 'For this reason we will not bow down to the guilt of old oppressors...We will not break alliances with our...We will not...it is time...there is...' Losing the thread, he was for a moment reduced to a doddering old man. 'We...the people...Tafumo?'

At first the crowd filled the awkwardness with their voice, giving Tafumo time. They sang and cheered but eventually their voice died and again they waited in silence. The speakers dotted around the stadium amplified Tafumo's breathing like remote lungs sucking in air to feed the dying man at the microphone. He was lost; his torn memory incapable of catching even fragments of speeches. Again the crowd began to sing, pounding the syllables over and over, 'Ta! Fu! Mo! Ta! Fu! Mo!' but below the noise – between the syllables – a silence was building. And as though stepping into cold water, I felt the moment when the drugs released Tafumo's frail organs back to him.

I didn't hear the gunshots but, like a bad spirit wreaking havoc, I saw their effect. The hanging portrait of Tafumo shivered, the rigging gave and the image fluttered and folded with peculiar grace to the stage. A soldier stationed near Tafumo flew back, his hands grappling at the bright mess of his opened stomach. A giant tail seemed to swish through the crowd, flicking swathes of people, stirring them into dark rips. A hand grabbed my shoulder but, without looking back, I tore free of it and ran towards Tafumo. Before I reached him a pink mist bloomed over his right shoulder and he moved like a vase toppling on its base, tipping back and forth before another shot pushed Tafumo forward over the podium.

I turned back to Boma and saw he was being dragged off-stage by a soldier. I realised that the hand that had torn at my dress was Boma's, grasping me as he fell. He was shot. The green of his trousers turned purple as blood soaked through. Soldiers pulled me by the arm, yanking me through the backstage and into the car. Tafumo was carried off the stage and placed on the floor at my feet. The crowd thickened and heaved around the car, which swayed as if at sea. I tried to staunch Tafumo's wounds. The noise of the crowd built like a violent wind reaching a terrible pitch then extinguishing itself, cutting itself mute, before rushing back in a monstrous roar. We drove fast. I heard bodies hit the car. Blood was pumping out of Tafumo's shoulder and someone was screaming, 'Faster, faster, faster.'

Charlie

As much as I loved the King there was always this really boring bit where he went on and on about freedom and stuff. So I walked over to the rough for a pee and saw a man lying flat on the fairway. I shouted over to Mum and Dad and when we all ran over we found Sean. He was drunk; he had a big egg swelling on his forehead and his tongue and eyes lolled around in a gross way. Mum held his wrist. 'Pulse is fine, must be pissed as a newt.' Dad hitched him up and they stumbled along like a three-legged race. Just as we got to the pool, Sean lifted his head a little and looked at Dad with one eye open and said, 'Stu, run, you buggers, run! The praying mantis is coming!' and then we heard popping as the cheering from the stadium turned into screaming. We looked down the golf course and Willem was running towards us and Dad was yelling, 'Run, Willem, run!' We collected Beauty as we dashed through the lobby into Horst's office and Willem stumbled in after us. We could hear people running past the hotel and soldiers shouting. Willem looked weird, sort of drunk, sweaty, as he lay on the floor and covered his head with his shaking hands. There was a knock on the door and Horst said, 'Open up, it's me. It's Eugene. Open this door.'

Dad unlocked it and Horst came in with Truth, Bel, some bodyguards and a few dancers. Truth and his bodyguard lay down in the corner and Bel crouched near them trying to get one of her hundred mobile phones to work. Everyone's eyes were popping out like frogs and everyone was yelling. Then Sean woke up and was pointing at Willem, screaming that something terrible was about to happen, but Dad told him he was too late, it was already happening.

I smelt burning, and Mum was rubbing my back saying, 'Stay down, Charlie, stay low, stay low.'

'Get Willem out of here,' Sean was saying. 'He's part of all this.'

Dad patted Sean's arm and said, 'You had a bad thump on the head, Sean, relax, just relax.'

But then Willem got to his feet, the only person standing in the room, towering over us all, and Horst stood and shouted, 'Willem! Did you do something stupid?'

'They offered me land, lots of it, and money,' said Willem, and Mr Horst screamed, 'Who paid you? Who! Who! Jesus, Willem, what have you done?'

Sean shouted, 'Just get him out of here, Horst, just get him out of here,' and it was the only time Horst ever agreed with Sean, when he said in a sad voice, 'Sorry, Willem, Sean's right. You're on your own. I want you out now, or you'll endanger everyone. I can't protect you this time.'

Dad jumped over all our bodies to the cupboard, where he got our emergency backpack, full of maps, food, torches, and gave it to Willem. 'Take this, take these keys for the white Peugeot in the car park and drive fast as you can.'

Mum kept trying to cover my eyes but I kept pushing her hand away. It was impossible to hear what everyone was shouting because of the noise outside but I saw Horst and Willem start to sort of hug each other then I saw that they were fighting. It wasn't like men fight in the films, it was more like hugging and falling. Mr Horst's shirt was torn and his belly came out of the gaps and Willem was bright red in the face. Sean and Dad tried to pull Willem off. Then there was a loud smash and Sean fell to the floor as the window broke into jagged pieces and Mr Horst's painting shattered.

Willem ran out the door and Horst followed. I spied out of the window but Sean jumped on top of me and there was disgusting blood pouring out from somewhere. I could hear Mum screaming, 'Get away from the window, Charlie,' and she shoved Sean away and wrapped her hand around my head so I couldn't see anything.

When the door was closed again, everyone silently looked at each other, as if no one, not a single adult, knew what to do next. Mum crawled over to Dad's desk and got out the first-aid kit and began to dress Sean's wound and gave him an injection, which made him look drunk again. The bandage soaked up the blood but it peeked through, like a red eye trying to see out of the material. Mum told Bel to hold the wound and she placed her hand on it.

Like a storm that was finally moving on, the noise from outside started to fade. The dull popping stopped and there was no more screaming. A soldier or a police officer was shouting through a megaphone somewhere in town, telling people they needed to go home, to stay off the streets. And we could hear people walking around outside, moving around the lobby. There was a knock on the door and Truth's bodyguards held their guns up and Dad held a golf club up and we heard, '*Bwana*, it's Ed. Are you being in there?'

Mum shouted, 'What's happening out there, Ed?'

'OK, madam, it's OK now, soldiers put everyone in their homes,' shouted Ed through the door.

Mum opened the door and she actually gave Ed a hug. 'And Alias and the staff?' asked Mum.

'Safe in the *kaya*, madam. Most of them, some of them have run home to their villages, some are hiding in town because the soldiers they are coming with their guns.'

Dad went out into the lobby first to check. Mum wouldn't let me go until Dad returned and told Mum it was safe. The lobby was a complete and total mess. Everything was ruined; even the streets were a mess, there was weird stuff everywhere, like shoes that people had left behind and lots of Bwalo flags trampled into the dirt. There were police and soldiers standing around. Bel was on her mobile shouting, 'No. No. You listen to me. Listen! We need to get Truth and everyone out of here now! Get the plane ready, we are coming as soon as we can, everything is fucked.'

Sean

I'M NO STRANGER TO blackouts. So I know the drill. When you come to, you have a fraught moment of pure discombobulation, then some small detail returns and the pieces start clicking into place. And it was my throbbing head which reminded me that Willem had punched me in the face, and when I spotted him in the room I hissed to Stu, 'Listen, I'm telling you, I don't know the ins and outs of it all, but Willem is part of all this and you need to get him out of here, get shot of him.' But before Stu responded, Horst and Willem started fighting. From down on the floor they both seemed like giants, these big men flailing around. Fiona was yelling, covering Charlie's eyes. Stu and I got up to prise the brothers apart, and when I heard gunshots the window shattered behind me and I felt like I was shattering too. Flung forward, I found myself rolling on top of people, hands racing all over me. I saw Willem run out of the room with Horst close behind. There was glass everywhere, someone somewhere was screaming. Fiona was yanking at my shirt and, in all the confusion, I noticed that Charlie was over at the window looking out. Blood was pouring out of someone but I felt strong as an ox as I pulled away from Fiona, lurched and fell towards Charlie in time to wrap my arms around his eyes and drag him down to the safety of the floor. Blood stained his blond hair as he struggled against me. Holding Charlie down, I craned my neck to see Willem in the car park with three soldiers pointing guns at him, and Horst running towards them waving his hands as the soldiers pumped holes into Willem who danced grotesquely. Thankfully Charlie hadn't seen any of it and Fiona took Charlie away from under me as I slumped back and darkness caved in.

Hope

TAFUMO WENT STRAIGHT TO the medical wing of the palace. After many hours in surgery, I helped Dr Todd remove his scrubs, as he said, 'The bullet to the shoulder wasn't the issue. But the bullet that travelled through his back and out his stomach. That's the bullet that will kill him.' He saw my surprise and said, 'Shot in the back by one of his own. Inevitable really. The nurses will need a break soon if you could please sit with him.'

When I returned to the recovery room, with my packed bag in hand, the nurses told me his vitals were stable, then they went to take a break. I sat down and watched him sliding in and out of consciousness.

Boma came to see Tafumo. The prodigy now the successor, Boma sat by the bed wincing at the pain in his leg. The bullet lay frozen in Boma's body, absorbed in a muscular embrace. Without looking at me or saying a word, Boma left Tafumo's side. He had to replace Tafumo's fading photographs with pictures of himself. He had to go and start telling the people of a new name: *Boma*.

Tafumo opened his eyes. Below the glaucoma gaze, his mind unburdened itself of the final vestiges of reason, allowing him to ascend to purest insanity. Slurring through memories that dissolved as they left his mouth, he fought the pressure pushing against his chest, making it harder to steal even a slither of air into his lungs. I could hear the noises of the palace around me.

Chaos. Neither Tafumo nor I were a priority. People running about with phones to their ears, soldiers stripping the place clean of anything of value, rooms full of people having meetings. They would find him soon. Tafumo was merely a guest now; a ghost who'd outstayed his welcome. What did that make me?

I looked out the window at the endless sky and for a moment I was scared, an old bird whose cage was opened, terrified of freedom. I switched on the radio by the bed: 'Please remain in your houses, Bwalo. Boma has taken over government and you will be safe, praise Boma, praise the great…Boma.'

Tafumo looked more withered than ever, the shrinking man, his prune-like skull lost in the clean sheets lapping around him. I cradled Tafumo's head. I lifted it, slipping the pillow out from under him. He grinned sleepily as I laid the pillow over his face. I placed my hands on the pillow, leaning forward with all my weight. His arms thrashed, searching for something to grasp onto; his left hand found my leg but it held it gently as one might hold a child's hand, before it opened and slid off. I returned the pillow under his head, checked his dead pulse, picked up my bag and left.

Charlie

AFTER WE CLEARED SOME of the mess, we sat around the pool as if nothing had happened. Crickets still screeched and birds still sang. Some things were different, I suppose. The blue sky was all scratched up by plane trails. The hotel was almost empty of guests. Mum, Dad, Sean and lots of the staff sat around talking. All the celebrities were calling home to get planes to pick them up. Bel had been pacing all day, shouting, 'No, *you* listen, we need it *ASAP*!' Truth sat near us and he looked scared like he had on safari; his favourite bodyguard didn't look too brave either.

Dr Todd came to the hotel. He said the King was 'gravely sick'. Dr Todd stitched up Sean's wound. Sean was convinced he'd been shot but Dr Todd said that in fact it was a piece of glass that had sliced a wedge out of his shoulder. He stitched it up in Dad's office and even though Dr Todd told Sean he needed to lie down, Sean still came out to the pool and demanded that Alias give him beer. Dr Todd shrugged and came and sat with Sean on a lounger and gave him drugs that made Sean start laughing even though there was nothing funny going on.

Dr Todd said, 'He needs to get back to civilisation, get looked at, lots of rest.'

Sean giggled. 'Well don't worry, doc, soon as I can raise the funds for a ticket, I know when I've outstayed my welcome.'

'We can lend you cash,' said Dad but Mum tutted as if that wasn't true.

Bel said, 'Listen, Sean, I'm getting Truth out of here later tonight in a small jet, come with us. I can get you to LA and you can get yourself to the UK from there, right.'

'Are you serious?' said Sean.

'Course,' said Bel. 'I can't let you die before you finish the next book.'

Sean looked at me and said, 'Hear that, Charlie, I'm off on a Learjet,' but then Truth shouted, 'Hold on a minute, I ain't having no freeloaders on my jet.'

Bel told Truth off with the same voice Mum tells me off with. 'Listen here, Clarence.' Truth flinched when she called him Clarence. 'That jet is not yours. Sean is not a freeloader, he is a human being who needs help. And the record company that owns the jet also owns you. So pipe down and do what I tell you until we're back home, when you can go about firing me. Sound like a good plan?' Truth sulked like a baby, muttering something to his favourite bodyguard, and Sean said, 'I need more morphine,' but Bel said, 'You're high enough.'

I sat at Sean's feet drinking Fanta. Mum and Dad were too busy to see that Alias was giving me as many Fantas as I wanted, which was so cool. Alias even plopped a spoon of ice cream into my Fanta, making it what we called a Fanta Float. With the electricity down, all the ice cream was melting so Alias said it was best to use it all up.

Dad asked about Stella and Sean shook his head slowly and said, 'Time to cut my losses.'

Mum touched Sean's hand and said, 'It's not so much that she'd had a bit of a rough past, the real problem with Stella was that she was a complete and utter maniac.'

'And you didn't think to tell me this before?' said Sean.

'I told you the first time you brought her to the hotel and I told you again at your engagement party right here at the pool in fact,' said Mum.

'Not listening is a talent of mine,' Sean said. 'My mother always warned me to be careful who I saved.'

When Mr Horst appeared at the bar everyone stopped talking. A lot of the staff got to their feet, as if to start working, but Horst waved his hand for them to relax.

'How are you, master?' asked Ed. 'Is Madam Horst safe?'

'Slept through the whole thing,' replied Mr Horst. 'I had to tell her what happened and she didn't believe me until I put the radio on.'

A few people smiled at this but Mr Horst looked like he was sleepwalking. He sat next to Mum, who gave his back a bit of a rub.

'Is Willem OK, Mr Horst?' I asked.

I thought maybe Mr Horst hadn't heard because he took ages before he replied, 'Yah, he's … fine. Just seen him off on the plane, back to Scotland. Fine and dandy.'

'That's good,' I said but Mr Horst didn't seem that happy, probably because he was going to miss having his brother around.

'Shoulder OK, Sean?' asked Mr Horst.

'Buggered,' said Sean. 'But the morphine's great. Sorry that your painting was collateral damage. Bullet holes and blood all over it.'

Mr Horst looked a bit mad then he just sighed. 'Ak, don't worry about it, it was a piece of crap anyway.' And Sean laughed really hard at this.

When Ed brought Mr Horst a beer he said, 'The electricity she is off, so the beer he is warm,' and Mr Horst just said quietly, 'Fine, Ed, fine, get yourself one. Everyone get a beer, eh. This one's on me.'

When it got dark we lit candles around the pool. Most of the food had been stolen in the riot but the buffalo biltong was still left. So for dinner we drank warm Fanta with melted ice cream and chewed on jerky. It was the best dinner ever.

Mum said, 'Well, I'll book the tickets to the UK, shall I?'

When Dad didn't reply, Mr Horst said, 'I take it that was your way of resigning?'

'Sorry, Eugene, but we're done,' Mum said.

Mr Horst nodded as he spoke. 'So much for the Big Day putting my hotel on the map? Looks like I'll be hosting nothing but cockroaches for the next few years. No tourism here for a long time.'

There was an odd silence, as if everyone was waiting to speak, like tipping on the pool edge about to topple in, until finally Mr Horst said, 'Probably time I shut her down. I'll sell her to the next Big Man, Boma. I'm getting old, time for me to retire and focus on my hunting, go after the big six. Listen, Stu, Fiona, let me buy your tickets back? My treat.'

Mum actually hugged Mr Horst. I'd never seen anyone hug Mr Horst, he wasn't very huggable. Even stranger still, Mr Horst hugged her back, arms tight around her like he never wanted to let go. Mum kept furiously rubbing his back then there was a funny popping sound and the electricity returned, the dark hotel burst into light and the radio on the bar shouted loudly.

It was tuned to the BBC and there we were again, twice in one week, on the BBC. The BBC said there had been a failed assassination; that Tafumo was in a critical condition. They said local reporters were suggesting a white supremacist had tried to kill the King. When I asked what a white supremacist was, Sean said it was someone who likes wearing sheets on their head.

But then when Dad flicked over to Bwalo FM, DJ Cheeseandtoast told us there was a new king, a king called Boma. It was all pretty confusing stuff. Clearly the BBC hadn't spoken to Bwalo Radio about what was going on.

Everyone was quiet for so long it felt like no one would ever talk again, so I said, 'Hey, Dad, does this mean I don't have to go to school? Until we go to the UK?'

'Well no, you may have to go back for a time until we have everything sorted out. But at least you finally have something exciting to write about in your school project.'

'Really,' I said. 'Can I really write about all of this cool stuff that's happened?'

Dad ruffled my hair. 'No, probably not, son, probably not.'

Looking around the pool at everyone, I felt sad about leaving Bwalo, leaving all my friends, Aaron, Solomon, Ed, Innocence, Beauty, Alias, and leaving the Mirage. I felt scared about going to this place called the UK with all its bad weather and punks. And the thought of the King in his palace injured made my sadness turn to tears and Mum sat by me and gave me a hug, saying, 'It's fine, Charlie, it's been a big day but everything will work out, we're safe now.'

I wiped my tears and muttered, 'Why would anyone want to hurt the King?'

Dad looked as if he was going to say it was complicated but Mum spoke first. 'It's fine to cry, Charlie, because as bright as you are, sweetheart, there'll always be things in life that just don't make any sense.'

Hope

THE PALACE HAD BEEN turned inside out. Boma's soldiers had gone through every room. Official papers seized, paintings taken, even silver cutlery, the whole place gutted. Soldiers even ransacked servants' quarters, taking the money that most of us kept under our beds. Many palace staff ran, some straight from the stadium, in their best shoes all the way back to their villages.

I went to the kitchen to say goodbye to Chef. I knew Essop wouldn't be there; I'd glimpsed him running from meeting to meeting, sticking close to Boma. I sat down with Chef who poured warm beer into a plastic cup. 'The crystal glasses are stolen so we are using plastic, and the beer is warm too, but this is how things are for now.'

We touched cups, took a sip, and I asked, 'What now, Chef?'

'Boma has a belly like Tafumo. I'll keep cooking.'

The kitchen door swung open and both Chef and I jumped to our feet. Essop was at the door raising his hand and saying, 'It's just me, don't worry, don't worry.'

Chef still looked anxious as he poured Essop some beer. Essop took a drink and was shaking slightly as he said, 'Pandemonium! These soldiers are like animals. I am sorry to both of you for the state of the palace. Have you lost many possessions?'

'It's not your fault, Essop,' I said. 'We knew this was coming.' Essop wiped his hand over his bald head; sweat was streaming down his face. I said, 'The worst of it is over now.'

Essop shook his head as if that were not true. 'I…it is a violent day, more violent than I expected.'

'Breathe, Essop, breathe, please,' I said. He took a few breaths as his mobile beeped in his pocket but he didn't pick it up and I said, 'What are you going to do?'

'Boma speaks as many languages as I do, so my time is up. I'm going to try and stop the soldiers running riot, help Boma build a government then I'll disappear. I'm too small for such big events. Too old a dog for new tricks. What will you do, Hope? Boma's health isn't good…'

'I'm done caring for Big Men,' I said and handed Essop a piece of paper. He glanced at the address, his forehead bunched into furrows. 'It's a small place near the lake,' I explained. 'I bought it long ago and I'm going to live there.'

Essop's phone rang again and a soldier came to the door and shouted, 'Boma wants you now.' Essop looked flustered and nodded at the soldier, then said to me with a sad voice, 'Well, Hope, I pray that you are happy there. You deserve happiness.'

'But I was thinking,' I said. 'Maybe you could come and see me sometime.'

His forehead smoothed. 'I'd like that, Hope. Yes. Very much. Yes, I would like it, yes. I would. I will come, yes. I will.'

'Well then I would like it too.'

The soldier made a grunting noise. Essop folded the paper, placed it carefully in his pocket and said, 'See you soon, Hope.'

Then he put his hand over mine and when he took it off I felt the warmth linger long after he left the room.

Chef smiled and handed me a paper bag. 'They didn't steal everything, those bastards. Your favourite, Hope: guava.'

I took it, shook hands with Chef and left.

I walked out the gate and down the road into the maize field and up to my tree. When I got there I touched the scarred bark, reached into the hole, deep up to my shoulder, pulling out all the bags, taking from each my rings, pearls, jewellery and earrings. It was enough for an old woman; I would sell it when the dust settled. Months back, when I had sensed that trouble was coming, I'd started my nest egg, my little bank in the mango tree. I knew if we had a coup that magpie-soldiers would ransack our rooms for anything shiny. And also that all the money I had in the bank would, in the collapse that follows a coup, become valueless, inflated to worthlessness, people carrying sacks of cash just to buy bread in another African nation of starving millionaires. My hand felt something else in the hole. A folder, manila, and sello-taped to it was an ochre-red bus. I opened the file and the first photograph made me cry. Levi. The handwriting scribbled wildly over every space was Josef's: a confession, explanation, the history of deceit that led to where we were now. I'd long suspected that Tafumo and Josef were bound by unbreakable twine but I never dreamed they were friends, that they were two barefooted boys who sculpted a legend from village clay. The more I read the heavier my heart grew. If you carved away all of Josef's lies there would be no man left behind. I put the folder into my bag and made my way down the hill into the deserted town. Only the occasional policeman or soldier was there and one said to me, 'Go home, mama. It's not safe.'

I walked to the hotel, its brass letters looping like syrup: *Hotel Mirage*. When I pushed the bell, the door opened and a child poked his head out. 'Welcome to…' A man appeared behind him, shouting, 'Charlie, get back from the door,' but when the man saw me, he said, 'Quickly, quickly, in you come.'

Charlie

'WELCOME TO THE MIRAGE, and can I just say what an honour it is to have you stay with us.' The lady politely waited for Dad to finish and because it was the first time anyone had let him finish in a long time, he looked pleased, saying, 'I'm Stuart, hotel manager, and this is my son, Charlie, he's the hotel mascot.'

She smiled down at me.

Dad got out the registration book but then said, 'Actually, let's not bother with all of this palaver, it's on the house. Let's put you in the splendid Tafumo Suite.' Then he whispered, 'Though I'm not sure how much longer it will be called that. I'll leave you in the capable hands of Charlie.'

I lifted the lady's bag, which was small but really heavy.

'I think we can manage together,' she said. 'And I wonder if you could post this for me.' She handed Dad a folder. He flicked it open and it was like a spell: he froze – like he had so many questions boiling in his head that he didn't know where to start – then he snapped it shut and said, 'Yes, I can take care of this for you.'

Sean

*L*IKE THE BUFFALO TRYING to outrun its agony, I wanted to be far from my shrieking nerves. My pain was intricate. Not the monotonous throb of a crushed thumb or slammed toe. Mercifully, Dr Todd wasn't stingy with the morphine and in a matter of seconds I was seriously considering a full-time career as a junkie. The smack was sublime. Complications unfolded and resolved as everything that once was impossible now seemed effortless. My wound, an excruciating laceration, was reduced to little more than an academic consideration. Some distant, uninteresting detail. For there was no longer pain, fear or neurosis, just joy racing around me like excited children. In the fresh opium blush, I decided I was capable of writing another book. All I needed was the spark of an idea and of course enough opium to last the years it would take to complete it. On second thought, the smack might get in the way of my drinking. The opium made me realise that – even though my life was a mess – I couldn't care less. I was released from caring. Then, rather splendidly, reality reflected my inner bliss when Bel offered me an escape from Bwalo, hitching the most glamorous ride of my life on a Learjet no less. After thanking her a million times, I sat back and watched my final Bwalo sunset. It should have made me sad but it didn't. Possibly due to the opium but also because I'd exhausted myself of this place and it was exhausted of me. The sun released a last pink scream and splayed on the lounger, in a warm morphine hug, I drowned in gallons of warm colour. Planes passed overhead, their contrails unzipping the sky. The world was leaving and I wouldn't be far behind. I closed my eyes and listened to rusty crickets grind down the sun as the ancient machinery of another day juddered to a stop. Jesus, this was good stuff.

Stu's face floated by, sunset fizzing through his beard. I was distracted by details. Weaved into the blackness of his beard were puffs of dandelion-white and stalks of saffron-red. I was saying something about this when I realised he was handing me a folder and whispering, 'Sean, hide it, get it through customs, should be fine in all the chaos and you on a private jet, then write that book you've been pissing around with all these years.'

Smiling like a gom, nodding at everything, it wasn't until I saw what he'd given me that I sat up. The faces of men and women, all of whom had stood up to Tafumo, stared out at me. Alongside each were descriptions of where their bones lay, names of killers, and the name that authorised all the killings, scrawled in oddly familiar writing. Shock cleared the opium fug, as I heard myself say, 'Jesus Christ.'

Even from a brief glance, I knew the author was Josef. That this was Josef's life I was reading. How had this found its way to me? I was sure Josef would be displeased at this strange turn of events but I had a sense that he was no longer with us, that these wild scribblings were not the sort of thing a man like him would do unless he knew his time was up, that this was a final testament.

'Hide it,' Stu hissed.

I slid it below my bloody sling and whispered, 'Jesus, this is incredible.'

I checked the file was secreted. Below the bandage the manila folder, faint as a mustard stain, was just visible but it would soon be hidden by the slow spread of my blood.

'If that doesn't unblock you nothing will,' said Stu and I replied, 'Nothing like a small coup to unblock a useless bugger like me.'

I reached over and patted Stu's arm. 'Look, Stu, yes, I know I'm high as a kite...' Stu joked, 'Makes a change from being drunk as a skunk,' but I talked over him. 'Let me speak, man! I know you're a stoic Scot who'll wither under the praise but there aren't many men like you, Stu, who've helped people, some who might have vanished if it weren't for your secret room. You're a dying breed, Stu. A beautiful human who does more for others than you do for yourself. So thank you. Thank you for taking care of me all these years.'

He looked down and muttered, 'That morphine must be good shit.'

I was glad I'd said it. I somehow knew that Stu and I wouldn't sit like this again. Maybe, if we were lucky, we'd meet once or twice more, in some cold pub in England for a reunion where we would reminisce about old times. But I knew our friendship was so closely woven into this dysfunctional and beautiful country that this was the last time we'd ever be this close. Stu was nodding slightly; he knew this was the end of something. We both sat silently watching the sunset. From where I lay the sun seemed to drop into the pool and I half expected the water to boil as the sun sank into the deep end.

When I said, 'I'll miss that Bwalo sun,' Stu replied, 'It's all the same sun, Sean,' and I snapped, 'Only a fool thinks that.'

He laughed then said, 'Can you believe Willem was a mercenary?'

'I had my suspicions,' I replied and Stu joked, 'But being the modest sort, you kept them to yourself?'

'You're right,' I admitted. 'I really liked the guy. Who'd have thought? OIA.'

'We search in the wrong place for the thing that'll destroy us.'

'Scots saying?'

'Stu saying.'

'Won't be when I steal it.'

'Just dedicate the bloody book to me.'

Hope

ENTERING THE MIRAGE LOBBY was like stepping into a memory. A vandalised memory. Cracked mirrors, broken chairs, the parquet floor peppered with bullet holes, but aside from the damage, it was unchanged from when we had honeymooned here. Strange to realise that as a young woman I'd believed this place, this tatty hotel, to be the very height of sophistication. With older eyes I now see that it's a rather gaudy hotel, with its zebra-skin carpets and elephant-foot ashtrays, preserving something long dead, a museum more than a hotel, an antiquated Africa as seen through the eyes of sad old men.

Muttering about stolen computers, the manager, Stuart, took out an ancient register book. If I leafed through it I knew I'd find Josef's signature, small evidence of a past life. But before I could look, Stuart said, 'Actually, let's not bother with all of this palaver,' and the heavy ledger gave a muffled clap as he heaved it shut. He handed me a key dangling off an elephant. 'It's on the house. Let's put you in the splendid Tafumo Suite. Though I'm not sure how much longer it will be called that.'

In a fast decision, I dug out the folder, and said, 'I wonder if you could post this for me?'

He searched for an address. Then flipped it open and looked like he was going to be sick. Immediately he knew its power. Unable to talk in front of his watchful son, we stared at one another, before he closed it. 'Yes, I can take care of this for you.'

He took the folder away and I followed the little boy, who guided me up the stairs and opened the door saying, 'This is the Tafumo Suite: best room in the house.'

Just as it had always been: tranquil and spacious with the four-poster bed and a mosquito net quivering in the breeze. Charlie chatted away about the mini-bar, playing the perfect hotel porter. He knew what he was doing, this little one. He opened a door and with a little embarrassment said, 'And that's the bathroom.' Then he came and stood next to me at the window. The riot was over, broken glass everywhere, here and there fires flickered as smoke-threads sewed the earth to the sky. Heavy fatigue overcame me, so I sat on the bed, saying, 'It's still a lovely room.'

'Dad says we need to rename it because of . . . what's happened.'

'You sound upset.'

'The Ngwazi is great. Who'd hurt the King? Sometimes nothing makes sense.'

'Well, what would you call the room if you had to change the name?'

'We could name it after my dad. The Stuart Room. We're leaving soon, though, so everyone would ask: Who's Stuart?'

He sat next to me, close, as if we were old friends, feet swinging back and forth, forgetting his role as hotel porter. Resisting an impulse to touch him, I said, 'Why don't we call it after you? The Charlie Room.'

'Sounds cool. But I'm leaving too, so that's not right. What about your name?'

Before I replied, an explosion rattled the windows and we fell to the floor. I placed my arm over Charlie who cradled in to me. The second blast hit with such force that when it rumbled back to nothing it left a vacuum, silence: no birdsong, no crickets. Just a tight suspended hush. Then into the stillness rushed the long-forgotten song of rain. We went to the window and he stood so close his head touched my hip as he whispered, 'It's raining.' And what a storm. It was as if the lake was scooped up and cast back to earth hollowing out potholes, blasting soil, washing away paint, churning mud so it boiled and flowed and turned roads into rivers.

Acknowledgements

Special thanks to my generous in-laws, George and Carol, for letting the family live in Opoutere, where I started writing this book in their cool caravan. To my intrepid parents, Jimmy and Eileen, not only for showing me so much of the world, but also for going off to volunteer in Africa and letting us live in their cottage in Brittany, where I finished this book in their garden shed. To my lovely readers who gave me so much advice: my ever-insightful wife, Jemma; the great Steve Kane; the wise Charmaine Guest; and my friends and book soulmates, Jane and Nick Moore. Special thanks to Stan, as always. And to my lovely editor, Helen, and all the smart people at Bloomsbury who helped bring this book to life.

ALSO AVAILABLE BY ROBERT GLANCY

TERMS & CONDITIONS

'Every book seems to have "funny and life-affirming" written on it but this one actually is'
MATT HAIG, AUTHOR OF REASONS TO STAY ALIVE

Frank has been in a car accident*. The doctor tells him he lost his spleen, but Frank believes he has lost more. He is missing memories – of the people around him, of the history they share and of how he came to be in the crash. All he remembers is that he is a lawyer who specialises in small print. But when Oscar, his brother, takes the family company into business with an inventively cruel corporation** and Alice, his wife, starts to seem oddly unlike the woman he remembers, Frank's world starts to unspool and the terms and conditions that he has lived his life by*** begin to change.

'Original, very funny and very poignant. Read it!'
PAUL TORDAY, AUTHOR OF SALMON FISHING IN THE YEMEN

'Entertaining … Insights into the predatory aspects of human nature are spot on'
NEW YORK TIMES

'Hilarious'
SUN

*apparently quite a serious one
**we can't tell you what it's called for legal reasons, but believe us, it's evil
***and which are rarely in his favour

ORDER YOUR COPY:

BY PHONE: +44 (0) 1256 302 699; BY **EMAIL:** DIRECT@MACMILLAN.CO.UK

DELIVERY IS USUALLY 3–5 WORKING DAYS. FREE POSTAGE AND PACKAGING FOR ORDERS OVER £20.

ONLINE: WWW.BLOOMSBURY.COM/BOOKSHOP

PRICES AND AVAILABILITY SUBJECT TO CHANGE WITHOUT NOTICE.

BLOOMSBURY.COM/AUTHOR/ROBERT-GLANCY

BLOOMSBURY